FREEING MY SISTERS

WILMA HAYES

In the Sticks Publishing

Ludlow, Shropshire

First published in 2011

© Wilma Hayes

This edition published in 2013

ISBN 978-0-9576179-0-2

Cover Photo by M Watkins

Author Photo by R D (Bob) Hayes

Freeing My Sisters is published by In the Sticks Publishing, Woodgate Cottage, Bleathwood, Ludlow, Shropshire, SY8 4LX

e-mail: Inthesticksbooks@aol.com

website: wilmahayes.co.uk

facebook: Wilma Hayes – Author

twitter: @BooksWilma

FREEING MY SISTERS

With Best Wishes

Thelma Hayes

For Cameron

who would have been a wonderful engineer

Wilma Hayes is a native of western Canada but fled to England in 1985 to avoid snow and harsh winters.

She is a Professional Home Economist, educated at the University of Saskatchewan (Saskatoon) and had a career the profession in Canada for several years. In England she worked in state and public school administration as Bursar until she finally escaped to the countryside in 1996. So far they don't seem to have missed her.

Since moving to north Herefordshire, she has taken a keen interest in local history, and has become an accomplished advocate for, and trained user of lime putty.

Her passion for writing is occasionally interrupted by the needs of four cats, a dozen chickens, a cottage garden and of course her husband.

This is Wilma's first novel.

Also by Wilma Hayes

Tenbury and the Teme Valley, People and Places

I Wouldn't Have Missed It (written with William Hayes)

Acknowledgements

I am grateful to Ann Levitt, Chartered Architect for her advice on technical matters. Also for reading the manuscript when it was still at the 'bad writing' stage and for remaining my friend in spite of it.

Thanks also to Andrew Rattle at Frank H Dale Ltd for information about structural steel fabrication.

And to Kate Jones who taught me everything.

Bullying Doesn't End in Death ... usually.

Teachers tyrannise pupils;

Managers terrorise staff;

Even ghosts persecute into the present.

Some of us will fight back and lose everything;

Some discover more than we wanted to know;

Some die.

1

Somebody always comes to the door when you're in the shower. Tim wrapped a big pink towel around his hips and put on his glasses. *It's probably in the small print of the contract when you buy a house, but …*

Opening the bathroom door into the extension to tell whoever was shouting through his back door that he didn't want religion or double-glazing, he felt his foot skid on the floor tiles and condemn the rest of his body to follow.

When the slide across the terra cotta finished, his feet were folded under him and his cheek was pressed against a tin bucket. A mop handle wavered above him in the early evening gloom. Through little patches on his glasses clear of steam, he looked up over the shoes and long colourful skirt of a small, plump, 40-something woman to her fluffy light brown hair and face; eyes wide with horror. His back hurt and his breath had disappeared down his throat. He wrenched the towel tighter around his waist and struggled to sit up on the cold tiles. The mop handle and bucket clattered over beside him.

An emotional voice that must have been hers mumbled past him. '… you all right?' She knelt beside him and grabbed his arm. Her fingers were like ice.

'My back,' he croaked gulping for breath. He clutched the towel, hoping he was still decent and with mutual incompetence they got him into a sitting position on the slippery tiles. She looked at his back. 'I'm sure it's OK. Just a scrape.' She disappeared and returned with a cold wet flannel that she pressed onto his back. The shock shot air back into his lungs.

'Thanks,' he gasped. 'It doesn't feel too …'

'It doesn't look too bad,' she interrupted and turned the flannel over. 'The skin's grazed but I think the towel must have... Look, I'm really sorry about this. I can't believe – I mean – oh hell.'

Something began to seem very funny. 'I suppose introductions would help here. I'm Tim Spencer.'

'What?'

'Tim Spencer.' He offered a moist hand over his shoulder.

1

She shook it while holding the flannel with the other. 'Mary Mitchell. I really am so sorry.' She rushed on, embarrassment obvious. 'I live in the cottage next to you – down the lane - and I just came over to say hello and ask if you could help me move my new piano. I feel really bad about this – really ...'

'No harm done.' Tim pulled the towel tighter over his knees. 'As a rule, I don't introduce myself to my neighbours in quite such spectacular fashion.' He had to admit that as a chat-up line, hers was one of the best and he felt a bubble of laughter rising in his throat, but she got there first and then they were both laughing with relief and the silly joke. 'Let me get some trousers on,' he gasped and they started all over again. Then, wiping his eyes, he choked, '... I'll help you with your piano.'

'What in heaven's name have you got in these,' Tim grunted, pushing a stack of packing boxes across Mary's sitting room carpet, 'the Elgin Marbles?' He felt sweat prickle on his temples.

'They wouldn't fit in the car. These are either books or the remains of Brinks Matt – I can't see the label from here.'

The small crack in the wall plaster was unremarkable; benign but malevolent, it waited.

Together, they slid the boxes into the middle of the room. 'Tim, this isn't fair. I moved into this cottage two months ago...' She grabbed the top box to steady it, '... and I'm still in a state of chaos. You moved into yours when? Last week? I bet you're completely straight.'

'Not a chance.' He pushed the last box into the centre of the room and tore the plastic wrapping off the front of the piano. 'Anyway, it's nice to meet the neighbours.'

'Introductions aren't supposed to kill you.'

'I fall down steps all the time. Come on, push.' They bumped the piano over the carpet.

The old oak boards underneath woke grumpily and groaned in sleepy protest. The crack curved upwards in the evening darkness.

One of the piano's casters jerked over a ruck in the carpet pile and the heavy instrument gently thumped the wall. A fist-sized piece of plaster fell into the thin back of the piano with a tiny hollow ting.

The crack crawled higher and widened into a silent black gash.

Tim pulled another sheet of bubble wrap off the piano and handed it to her. 'Lovely instrument, Mary.' He ran an index finger over the keyboard cover. 'Played long?'

She bundled the plastic into a squeaky mound. 'Oh, I've never played, but now I've a little time on my hands, I thought I might learn.'

'Why've you more time on your hands?'

She lifted one eyebrow at the direct question. 'Call it a mid-life crisis if you like, but I've just extricated myself from a couple of difficult positions - a teaching job and...' She seemed to regret her words, but then carried on. '... so my life style's changed quite a bit.' She tossed the plastic beside the mound of boxes with more force than was necessary. It bounced off into the darkness.

He regretted the question. It was intrusive. He cleared his throat, ran his fingers through his curly dark hair and turned to straighten the piano against the wall. 'Damn – plastic's still stuck on the back.' They inched it forward again.

With a sudden crack like a rifle shot, a large slab of plaster split and dropped off the wall, smashing onto the piano. It shattered into hundreds of dusty pieces all rebounding into the air. Then another large piece broke, cracks slicing to the ceiling. Jagged plaster and ancient cobwebs crashed onto the carpet, bounced across the room. Stale air sucked down from above, drove dust, dirt, bits of plaster, paint, toward them both. Into the darkness of the room. Up to the black beams of the cottage ceiling. Past the wall timbers. Through the little pine door. Into the room beyond.

'Christ.' Tim grabbed Mary's arm and wrenched her backwards. They ducked and ran, stumbling as they blundered into the kitchen. Mary slammed the door behind them.

With wide eyes, each stared at the other. 'What was that?' Mary's voice shook. There was emphatic silence behind the door.

Tim reached for the door handle and with exaggerated caution, opened a crack. They looked through the slit. Dirt swirled through the slanting light of a table lamp and was absorbed in the gloom beyond. In the corner, a dark lumpy stone wall loomed above the piano and on top of it, a pile of slowly sagging debris. He rubbed the dust from his glasses with his sleeve.

Swiping a small torch from the counter, Mary pushed past Tim and opened the door, aiming the beam into the grimy murk. As if there was an absurd need for silence, they tiptoed in and stared at the wall. The dark surface yawned six feet across, from the floor almost to the ceiling. Dust rolled in slow billows through the room. Clods of plaster and small pieces of splintered lath slid off the piano and onto the floor.

'Good God.' Tim whispered picking up a piece of thick plaster from the carpet. 'Plaster doesn't do that. Break off, yes, but fly half way across the room?'

Mary looked at the wall. 'Is it safe?' Her voice was clipped and tense. 'The rest of the wall isn't going to come down?' Tim pushed on what little plaster remained on the wall. 'That's loose but the stonework's sound.' He brushed several large pieces of plaster off the top of the piano to look behind and stopped in surprise. 'Look. There's a hole here.' Almost hidden by the piano, it was about four inches square and went deep into the wall. Mary shone the torch into the dark cavity. Dust sparkled in the beam of light. Small chunks of plaster dangled from ragged pieces of the narrow lath still pinned to a rough timber frame. Cobwebs covered with thick black dust swung in a downdraught of air.

They bent to look inside.

A smell of mould, stale air and history settled with the last tiny noises of sliding plaster. A fly flew in a stunned spiral from somewhere nearby and in staggering stages disappeared into the darkness of the room behind them.

'Why is there a hole in my sitting room wall?'

'It's got a timber frame, so it's not just a gap in the stones. Is there anything inside?' Tim whispered again, as if reverence was required.

Mary brushed the cobwebs aside, pulled the remaining pieces of lath off the timber and dropped them on the pile on the floor. In the dark hole, Tim felt through the dirt and broken plaster.

'Yes,' he grunted, '... there's something ...' He pulled out a small lump with square corners and tipped the dirt off it onto the pile. It was about 3 inches square and made of heavy paper or card folded into a flat parcel. Grey and crisp, it smelled like very old dust.

Tim carried it as if it was a bottle of something chemically unstable to the dining room table. Mary pushed the clutter aside and switched on the overhead lights. Tim sat down and turned the little package over looking for a way in.

4

'Will it open up?' whispered Mary over his shoulder.

He hooked his thumbs in the folded ends. 'I'm afraid it'll crack.' Although the stiffness resisted, he pressed open two end flaps and then the side folds. 'It's empty.'

Mary bent closer. 'Can you open it more or flatten it out?' she asked and he pressed down the edges with thumbs and forefingers. 'Hold it there a minute.' She rushed off and returned wearing a pair of large dark-rimmed reading glasses.

He grinned at her. 'They make you look like an owl.'

She looked over the dark rim, '…or the dragon of the English department.' They both peered at the stiff page. Tim turned it around and tilted his head to look at it from different angles. 'There's something there, I think I…' They leaned closer. 'It's very faint but I think I can make out slanting lines and pointy things'. He blew on the page and a fine powder of dust scattered across the table. 'It's writing. There are fine lines, faded. Handwriting? I'd guess it's very old.'

Mary snatched a sheet of paper from a book on the chair beside her and with the aid of the torch, they identified or made guesses at what they saw. When they reached the end, Mary had written: 'Jo__ ___ _____ fro_ harm _ y__ld _____su_____ nor ___ condemn _____ ___ I _____ fear _____ seduc _____dev _____ enchant none ____ are_____ Chris___an_ Pr_____ I will love _____ alway_ . M___'

They looked at each other in amazement. 'What does it mean?' whispered Mary. 'It's – it's, well, there seems to be so much pain…' She hugged herself as if she felt cold.

'I think it's quite romantic. I mean, two lovers in trouble and one of them condemned for something. Wow.' Tim brushed the sweat from his forehead onto his shoulder. 'Can I let go of this now? My fingers are getting cramped.'

They watched the paper refold itself: a lumpy little package embracing again, the mystery of at least two people's lives. 'It sounds so sad.' Mary wiped her glasses on the hem of her skirt and folded them up. 'Who was being harmed? And why? Who is condemning and seducing whom? Who are they?' The people arising from the tiny scrap of heavy paper had moved into the present. They were becoming real.

'We need to find out what it says.' Tim wiggled his fingers. 'There's got to be more writing – things we can't see. Do you know anyone that can help?'

'There's a little museum in town. They might be able to read it, or know about old documents. I'll call them in the morning.' Mary put her feet up on the chair and pulled her skirt hem over her toes. 'But who, when, how long ago? And what was it doing in my wall?'

'The wall!' Tim dashed to the sitting room. 'The mess. If you give me a bin bag, I'll clear it up. The wall's safe enough, but I'd feel better if the ceiling timbers were shored up a bit just to be sure – until you can get someone to look at it. Don't want the whole thing coming down on you during the night.' She followed him into the sitting room. Dust had now settled on the deep stone windowsills, the two dainty settees in front of the open fire and the stupid frilly curtains. 'Look there's room at my place if you want.'

'No, I'm sure you're right and it's safe. Thanks for the offer. That's kind, but I'll be OK and don't worry about the mess. I only dust when I can use a shovel. I'll clear it up in the morning.'

'I'm not leaving until I've braced it up. You might not mind, but I'd like to sleep without thinking of you buried under a collapsed cottage.'

In half an hour, there was a frame of ladders, odd timbers, boxes, a new piano and a large pile of broken plaster against the wall - a visual if not practical bastion against imminent or imagined collapse.

Tim walked up the lane behind the beam of Mary's little torch. It cut a tiny line through the heavy darkness. Apart from its feeble efforts, only starlight showed the contrast between roadway and grass verge. He stopped and looked at the wonder above him. *City life with its hot tarmac, and rushing, rushing people has a lot to answer for. How many people there ever see this kind of thing?* The night sky was filled with silver sparks. Long forgotten constellations and mythological names unfolded in Tim's mind where they had not been for years. He breathed them in, and held them in the bottom of his chest. *It's easy to understand the power of all this. The ancients were closer to reality than we will ever be.* He could see the blaze from prehistoric fires and hear the muted songs of the storytellers. He turned off the torch to listen.

The air was still, but far from quiet. Tiny creatures rustled in the grass and a solitary owl hooted in the valley below. By holding his breath and concentrating, he could just hear the slapping of the little river at the bottom, in its eternal course through the Marches. When he drew breath again, he smelled new grass, early spring flowers with no names and fresh, fresh air. He knew that what he felt was peace.

It's been a long time since I was out in darkness this deep, he thought. The sudden memory of another dark night and a dark haired young woman dissolved the softness. Pain and guilt ran like an avalanche over his mind. The crunch of the gravel of his drive under his feet dented the spell and with a struggle, he pushed it back into his past. He marvelled instead on the little package from Mary's wall. Their discovery was a tangible and direct link to antiquity. Someone in the past had reached through the hole and offered them a way into history. It was intriguing, exciting and frightening all at the same time. Was it a love story with a happy ending or – or what?

Mary stuck the scrap of an envelope on which she had written Tim's phone number, into the frame of the kitchen pin board, and saw the little package on the dining room table. It deserved better than to be left on the table among the dishes, clutter and wine bottles. She carried it to her old desk, cleared a space among the dust and papers and laid it down with sensitive care. *There's life there. Two lives at least. What are they saying?*

She sat down in the desk's dusty chair and pushed the heels of her hands into her eyes. Sudden sadness and hurt rolled up from her emotional bottom drawer. It flooded into her heart and she pushed hard on her forehead so that she wouldn't cry. Everything she had wanted to leave behind was still blunt, hard and painful. She took a deep shaky breath and held it until her thoughts cleared. With an effort, she turned away from her own mind and went toward the dark stairs and the warm safety of her bed.

2

Loose gravel skittered under the front bumper of Tim's car as it slid to a stop in front of a triangular portico propped on a steel pole. He knocked the car out of gear and rammed on the handbrake with one motion then grabbed his brief case.

For Christ's sake, get a grip on yourself. It's Saturday. He leaned back in the seat, forced a long breath through his nose and gave himself permission to be late. He got out and closed the driver's door with deliberate calmness. The 'C' in 'Conmac Steel Ltd, Hereford' on the main glass doors had lost most of its gilding and the mosaic front of the building defined its 1970's heritage. Tim opened the door and stared into the broad face of the security guard.

'Morning, Mr Spencer.' The big man – his security badge said 'Clive' - turned the daybook around and pushed it across the counter. 'I didn't expect to see you in today.'

'Thought I might catch up on a few things.' Tim signed beside the man's pudgy finger. 'Anyone else in?'

'Nope, just you and me – and transport. They'll be here 'til 12 and Mr Racine usually comes in about 10:30 for an hour or two.' Clive took back the signing in book.

Tim felt his stomach tighten, but took the stairs two at a time to his little screened space. He liked his 'office' on the crowded design floor among the sales desks, purchasing and fabrication clerks, structural technicians and estimators. Another manager and the managing director occupied corner offices and the quotations manager's sprawling empire of estimators lapped along the wall in between. Tim's drawing board looked out on the side yard where three huge flat-deck lorries waited to be loaded with steel at the bays behind the building. He had been offered a proper enclosed office, but declined preferring to be where there was noise. Taking an old triangular ruler and steel pencil with flaking paint out of his case, he aligned them together on his desk and poked the computer switch. As it began to hum, he lifted his teetering in-tray out of the bottom drawer and caught the top bundle as it slid onto the desk.

Finish this and sign it off– that should take half an hour - then the rest. He unfolded the huge paper, stuck it onto his drawing board with magnets. Plan and elevation of steel frames of accommodation units for a motorway service centre blended on the paper and the three-dimensional structure rotated in his mind. He pulled his concentration back to the drawings. *Four years designing off shore oil platforms should make this easy. It'll show them I know something at least. For God's sake, I sound like*

8

some wheeze in a school play. He opened up the calculations software and turned the screen to block the sun.

'Morning.' Tim jumped and spun his stool around. A little man smiled at him over a fine silk tie. 'It's nice to see you on a Saturday morning.'

James Racine, the managing director was short and slim with a small dark moustache that looked as if it had been trimmed with a spirit level. If the trousers, shirt and tie were his idea of 'dressing down' on a Saturday, all that was missing was the jacket. *Probably has a crease pressed in his pyjama bottoms too.* Tim smiled at the thought and then directed it at James. 'I thought I'd use the quiet to finish a few things.'

'Good for you.' James' voice was patronizing. Tim felt obliged to continue.

'I'm looking at the plans you gave me yesterday.' Tim stretched his back. It felt stiff. 'The calculations seem OK but I'll check them anyway. I'm not really happy with the grade of steel, so I think I'll send it back to the designers before I sign it off. Then I want to visit some sites.'

James Racine nodded, as if he knew something Tim didn't and turned to his office. 'Send me a list when you have it ready.'

Tim opened the finance section of the company on his computer and searched for completed projects done in the last few years. He selected several for possible visits. On the invoices he saw Royston Construction. His grandfather had a brother Royston and as Tim had been fond of his grandfather, he included it as a sentimental gesture. He left a note for Susan to organize site visits and send the list to James and then turned to other projects and other calculations.

Morning sunlight at Rosemary Cottage highlighted two realities. The wall was still there, but so was the broken plaster. Dust covered everything like thin grey snow – all except the little folded package on Mary's desk.

Mary pulled a sweatshirt on over her head, turned her back on the wreckage and went to the kitchen. The plastic lid popped off the coffee tin and she breathed in the civilized smell, then prepared a little pot for the Rayburn. While it burbled a tune to itself, she unfolded the old message again. In the daylight she was able to add a few more letters to the crib they made last night but it still made little sense.

She thought about Tim and wondered how tall he was. As she went back to the kitchen, she tried to calculate how much space there had been between his head and the beams in the cottage. It wasn't much. But it was nice to know she now had a neighbour; it was nice to feel less lonely. The fresh coffee, black and strong, swirled around the bottom and sides of a pretty china mug with cats on it. Yes lonely. She glared through the living room door at the destruction.

The air outside was clear and fresh, with just a little wind to make the last few daffodils nod in the tall grass. Mary tipped the wheelbarrow upside down with a crash on the heap of plaster now dumped behind the garage and rubbed the dirt from her hands onto her thighs. She heaved up the uncertain metal door of the garage, wrenched out her bicycle and pedalled with effort a short distance down her little lane and onto a long narrow track to Brick Cottage Farm.

The farmer, blue overalls stuck into green Wellington boots, swung a metal pail as he walked up the short path to his little house. A colourful group of kittens sparkled behind him. 'Hello,' he called. He was stocky with thinning dark hair and red cheeks on a round face.

Mary clanked her bicycle to a stop and looked over the fence as he poured milk into a row of saucers by the cottage door. 'Learn the sound of a milk pail quick don't they?' The little animals pushed each other, stood in the dishes, soaked their whiskers and noses. Mary felt herself smile. 'You want one?' asked the farmer.

Mary surprised herself, 'Yes – in fact may I have two?'

'Y' can have yer pick when the time comes.'

'You're Harry Dobbs, aren't you?' Mary wiped her sweaty palm on her jeans and held out her hand, 'I'm Mary Mitchell. I moved into Rosemary Cottage a couple of months ago, but we've not actually met.'

Harry's huge brows clutched each other but then he shook her hand - his smile crooked like his fingers. 'Nice cottage that - bin there a long time it has. Settlin' in all right?'

'Well yes, more or less. Some plaster came off my living room wall last night and I need someone to re-plaster it. Can you recommend a builder?'

His face relaxed. 'Come in, I'll see if I c'n find George's number for y'.' He led her into his warm bachelor kitchen, with piles of newspapers and farming magazines on the floor and a sink piled high with milking equipment and odd pieces of crockery. He emptied a square basket onto his tin top table and spread an assortment of business cards, paper clips, drawing pins, coins, screws, bits of straw and envelopes across it. 'Here we are,' he tore the bottom edge off a newspaper and looked through the bits for a stubby pencil. 'George here – he'll be your best bet. Lived around here forever and won't charge y' a fortune. Does good work 'n all. My number...' He scribbled. 'It's there jus' in case y' needs it like.'

She thanked him, tucked the paper into her jeans pocket and spent a minute watching the kittens before cycling back towards the lane. Dog violets were in bloom at the end of the track and the hedge was becoming thick and solid with fine new leaves. For the first time in over a year, she felt her heart rise with a tiny flutter of joy.

Then she thought about the wall, and that made her think about Tim again. She recalled fragments of their mealtime conversation last night. What brought a young and attractive professional engineer – structural wasn't it - from a busy and exciting life in London to this quiet part of the country? How old was he – 35 maybe – so younger than she. Did something dispirit him? He seemed to be keen about his new job. But it was less than a month since he started and she sensed there were already tensions there. He didn't mention any friends or a wife and he lived alone now – or so it seemed. The nightmare vision of him, just out of the bath, clutching a towel, sliding across the tiles in the back extension of his house choked her with horror again. *I thought I'd killed him.*

While the coffee pot made more slurping noises on the Rayburn, Mary sat on a kitchen stool and called the number on Harry's scrap of paper. George was out on a site somewhere, but Mrs George was at home.

'Oh yes, I know Rosemary Cottage. You've just moved in haven't you?'

'Well, a couple of months ago.'

Mrs George laughed, 'That's "just moved in". Things don't move very fast in this part of the country. I'll call George and ask him to stop in on his way home. That'll be about 2:30 if that's OK. He works half day on Saturday.'

Mary thanked her and then spread the telephone directory across her knees. The message at the town museum advised, in the embarrassed voice of a volunteer pressed into making the recording, that it was open only on Wednesday morning. Summer hours would resume after May Bank Holiday. Mary poured the coffee and toasted a bagel for lunch. Of course the museum wouldn't be open all week in the winter months. With her lunch plate in the sink she went into the garden sun with a big book and spent all afternoon identifying plants. The ones that were meant to be there would, she hoped, tell her where the edges of the derelict borders might be.

The bruise on Tim's back was beginning to very stiff by the time he'd finished with the calculations and he stretched it on the way to the staff room. With a plastic cup of plastic tea from the antiquated machine, he thought about Mary, seeing her again for that fleeting second, short, plump, middle aged with fluffy hair and then an upside down view of a long patterned skirt. Back at his desk, he searched his pockets for the piece of paper with her number on it. He was on the point of going out to search the car when he found it jammed into the back of his briefcase.

Tim leaned back in his chair as Mary's telephone rang. He liked her. He felt comfortable with her – even when dressed only in a fluffy towel. He smiled again in spite of himself – as introductions went, it was more unique that most. With one hand he dragged another stack of drawings out of his in-tray, and waited for an answer but there was none. There was something in Mary that was very raw and sensitive. As a teacher, she was used to having children, especially teenagers around her, but here she was, alone in a cottage in the country with its walls falling down.

He realised, as he put the phone back, that this put some obligation on him. But an obligation to do what? No looking after was required; she was quite capable – she left him in no doubt about that. Nor was it an obligation to put her house back together; she'd be arranging that already. The obligation was to be a neighbour – a friend. That wasn't such a heavy burden and it felt good to have someone living nearby that he could call a friend. But he wondered about the life crises that had driven her here. Were they anything like his?

At about 2:45 a small dark man in jeans and a t-shirt that might have been white once, came through the gate of Rosemary Cottage. He was George he announced - he'd come to look at Mary's plaster or lack of it.

He looked at the bracing and the dust that Mary hadn't yet shovelled up, sucked on the side of his mouth and pushed on the stones. Then he rapped the remaining plaster with his knuckle, listening like a surgeon tapping a patient's chest. He looked inside the hole and sniffed. Then he broke off a piece of loose plaster and went into the kitchen to examine it in the light. His eyebrows narrowed and he frowned.

'Y'see this here...' He pointed at the edge of the plaster. 'It's lime and it's got hair in it – means it's old, not new plaster. Now, I can give y' a new coat of hard plaster on it if y'want, but I'll tell y' it'll give y' trouble with the damp. Y'see, the stones is sound, but new hard plaster won't breathe like this stuff and so y'd be better off havin' the lime.'

'Can you do this – this lime?' Mary swallowed a laugh and bit the inside of her lower lip.

He looked at the piece in his hand and considered before he answered. 'I dunno.' Another pause. 'Oh, I can do lime all right, but there's summat about that hole... '

'Do you mean it's too big to fill or something?'

Another pause. 'Nay, it's just... well, there's summat bad in there. I can tell y'see.'

The tickle of laughter vanished and Mary felt a little bubble of alarm in her throat. 'What do you mean, bad?' This man couldn't be serious.

He handed her the plaster. 'If I were you, I'd find out a lot more about that hole before I filled him in. There's summat' else going on here.'

Tim put his elbow on his keyboard and watched little 'm's scamper across the screen. He hit the 'undo' button with the mouse and re-read the summary of the specifications he'd reviewed, then pulled his mobile out of his briefcase and tried Mary's number again.

'Hello?' Her voice surprised him.

'It's Tim. Just wanted to see if you were all right and that the ceiling hasn't collapsed on you during the night.' He strung one thought on top of another and began closing down his computer. 'And to say thanks for supper last night.'

She laughed, 'Hello Tim. Yes I'm all right and yes, so is the ceiling, and supper was the least I could do. But are you still at work? I just heard a beep.' This time he laughed.

'Yes as matter of fact I am just shutting things down now.' He looked at his watch. 'It's almost 4, I'd no idea I'd been here so long.' He clipped a memo to Susan, onto the plan. James seemed to have gone some time ago. 'Did you manage to find a builder who can do the plastering for you?'

Her voice dropped a little, 'Well, yes and no, but it was quite peculiar. Why don't you come over tonight and I'll tell you all about it.'

'I'd love to, but why don't we go for a drink or something – there must be a pub somewhere...'

'Well, there is a pretty place, just on the Atherton Road, the other side of Croftbury. I've heard it's nice.'

'Perfect, I'll pick you up about 8 if that's OK.' It was and he rang off. He dropped the in-tray back in his bottom drawer and knocked it shut with his foot. Then he put the old ruler into the front of the briefcase, the old steel pencil back into its special clip in the lid and snapped the case closed with a click and a smile.

Tim drove into Mary's at exactly 8:00 pm. Her voice through an open upstairs window told him to come in.

'Can I look at the wall?' he called at the kitchen ceiling.

A muffled voice answered in the affirmative and in a few minutes she appeared. Her fluffy brown hair was pulled back and held in place with a big gold clip.

'How is it?' She was wearing a long blue skirt and a soft blue blouse with a big cream sweater over her shoulders. The sleeves were knotted in front. Brushed and made up, she looked confident and relaxed. He was surprised at how pleased he was to see her.

'Seems perfectly stable to me. There's no more sign of movement or cracks to make me worry, and the ceiling beams are sound.'

She smiled up at him. 'That is a relief. But as for going out for drinks - heavens, I hardly know you. Ah ha! This is so you can hear about the builder and the package.'

'Madam, I had no idea I was so transparent. Shall we...?' He held open the door and she walked out under his arm.

3

The Rock public house was clutched in a fist of hillside; a garden pleating into whatever cracks or plateaus as could be found. The old privy, now painted white to match the rest, wore a string of coloured lights along its gutter. The pub was popular and crowded. Inside it was warm, with a smell of wood smoke from a large ash-spilled fireplace.

Tim levelled the wobbling table with a folded beer mat while Mary held the drinks. 'All right...' he said around the edge of the table. '... what did the museum tell you and this mysterious builder? What did he have to say?' She put the glasses on a selection of beer mats.

'The museum's not open until Wednesday, so that'll have to wait. But the builder - he was strange. He looked in the hole, then at the plaster and he just sort of stopped.'

Tim picked up his glass and stopped too. 'Stopped?'

'Yes, he went quiet – he'd been muttering away to himself and then nothing.' Tim saw that the sky was dark in the window behind her. A wind was beginning to whip the trees.

Tim laughed but it sounded like a scoff when she told him what George said. 'Oh for heaven's sake. How would he know if the hole was bad or not?'

'I don't know - just said he could tell. Said there was something going on and I needed to find out about it before he'd fix it.' She brushed something unseen from the knotted sleeves of her jumper.

'Weird. Do you suppose he has sixth sense or something?'

'Tim. You're a hard-nosed engineer – you don't believe in that sort of stuff, do you?'

Tim drew a deep breath. 'Wow.' He sorted eight peanuts in order of size, lined them up, and looked up at her. 'No I don't, but what happened next? Did he see the package?' Mary took another sip of wine and shook her head.

'So he couldn't have concluded anything except from the damage to the wall. Amazing. Do you believe him?'

Mary seemed to think for a moment. 'Yes, I do. I think there's a lot more I need to find out and I've got to start with that package.' Darkness obliterated everything outside the window now. 'You don't believe me, do you?' A smile lifted one side of her mouth.

He shifted on his chair. 'I'm a bricks and steel sort. I don't know what to think about it.'

Mary put her drink down. 'But it's your turn. What about this company you work for. Just what does it do?'

'It does a variety of things. It has a section that does structural surveying for buyers or insurance claims and it also does design and calculations from plans sent in by architects who are submitting them for building regulations. Then it has a design and build section, and that's my job. We design, then project manage things from start to finish.' He leaned back and the chair creaked. 'The company also does renovation works; you know where some sensitive structural work is needed to stabilize a building or bridge and that's what James is in charge of. He knows the conservation and listed buildings issues. The company found that the design and build side of the business was growing and James couldn't handle it all.' He wiped the bottom of his beer glass on another mat. 'So I was hired to carry on with the new-build stuff.'

Mary emptied a bag of peanuts onto a napkin and pushed them towards him. 'So how do you do that?'

'I've been looking at the contracts in progress, to see how it's being done now. Also some completed projects - I've got several to visit - until I've got a good idea of the range of stuff Conmac has done in the past. At the same time keeping up with the new stuff that comes in.' He smiled. 'But that's pretty boring stuff.' He could see her attention fading. 'What made you move to Herefordshire, Mary?' he asked. She seemed to choke on her drink as if surprised by the question.

'Sorry, I was following what you were saying.' She cleared her throat. 'I got fed up teaching in Birmingham and when my marriage ended at the same time, well it seemed like a good time to make a few dramatic changes.'

Tim saw her colour change. Even in the low light of the pub, he knew there was more to it than that. 'Must be tough – to have a relationship end – like that I mean.' Something caught in his throat, and it was his turn to cough.

'Oh it was sudden all right. The bastard arrived home on the same day I'd had an almighty row with my Head, to give me the news. Sorry I don't swear – I just make an exception in his case.'

'Maybe he deserved it.'

'Perhaps. I just know how it looks from my side and to be told in ten words or less that it's all over, well, it rather knocked the stuffing out of me.'

Tim's hand felt clammy on the cold glass and he wiped it on his jeans. 'Yes, well... but...' He needed safer ground. 'I've always thought that teaching must be satisfying.'

'Don't believe everything you hear.'

'I sense some bitterness here.' He could feel his smile was crooked. Depending on how she reacted, he hoped his face showed both sympathy and irony.

She smiled at him. 'And you'd be right. Teaching isn't a shortcut to sanctity and many teachers do more harm than good.'

Tim's eyebrows disappeared under the curls over his forehead. She rushed on. 'And to listen to them – anyone would think they all have hell for lives.' She put the wine glass on the mat sitting it precisely within the green lines of the border. 'I can't think of any profession where there isn't pressure and paperwork – teaching is no exception. It's just something that we have to get on with. And there is no other profession that I know that has 12 weeks off every year to 'recharge' or holiday, catch up or plan ahead.'

'But why the row with your Head?' He felt the need to divert the sermon before it became emotional.

'Some day when I know you better, I'll tell you all the gory details, but in short, it was all about what was happening to some of our gifted students and how one of my colleagues in particular was treating them. I did the professionally unthinkable.'

'And what was that?'

Mary's colour had returned. 'You're very sweet, but you've had quite enough of my dark history for one evening. Tell me instead, how is the bruise is on your back? You have no idea how terrified I was.' She relaxed in the chair. 'I thought I'd killed you.'

Tim pushed his glasses up his nose and smiled. 'All I could do was swear at myself for unpacking only the pink towels, while trying to keep somewhat decent.' A chuckle begin somewhere in his lower chest. 'I still have no idea where my bathrobe is and I intend to put a curse on whoever built a bathroom in the rear extension.'

'And how is your back?'

'A bit stiff where it hit the tiles, but otherwise no harm done thanks to your first aid.'

The stiffness in his back woke him in the morning. It seemed that daylight must be several hours old and he drifted in and out of sleep a few times before he realized where he was. Pushing a pile of clean socks off the bedside table, he located his glasses and focussed on the red display on his clock radio. He sat up with a shock. It was almost 10:00. He hadn't slept in like this since he was18 and hung over. He was neither of those; just relaxed for the first time in... well, a very long time.

He swung a leg out on top of the duvet and one by one gathered his wits about him. It was Sunday – no need to rush anywhere – he could decide what he wanted to do even before he got out of bed. What a delicious thought. But so was a cup of tea and for that he had to get up. He pulled on cold denim jeans, a t-shirt and slid his bare feet into last night's loafers. Today he would find his bathrobe if he did nothing else.

As the water boiled, he thought about Mary. Something had drawn her back from telling him everything. Was it that painful? Or just embarrassing? He wanted to think that she could confide in him, but was that just him being nosy? It was none of his business.

He squeezed the tea bag on the side of his mug, dropped the soggy mass into the bin and picked up Saturday's post from the little kitchen table. Opening the back door he stepped out into wonderful sunshine. From the step he looked over the fields and back to his hedge that must have been neat and trim once. Inside it now was a shaggy garden and weed-strewn drive.

He sorted the post: one to send on to the previous owners; several for the rubbish; an electricity statement asking him to confirm the meter reading. Then a real letter – a personal one. As he slit it open, his house telephone rang.

'Tim?' His mother sounded as if she wasn't sure she'd dialled the right number.

'Mum?' asked Tim, imitating the tone of her question.

She laughed. 'Stop that. I know it's been a week since we spoke. How soon you do forget. But tell me, are you settled in now?'

'Well, there are still boxes everywhere. I am struggling to find the hours to get them unpacked, but,' he rushed on lest she feel the need to come and help, 'I expect I can get most of it finished this week.'

'Good, because I doubt that I can find the time to come and help you.' *And Herefordshire is the other side of the universe,* he thought. 'Jennifer seems to have developed an aversion to school and Peter is trying to cope. Ann's had to go to her mother's and so I'm trying to help out and be a sympathetic ear for Jennifer if she needs it.'

Poor kid. 'Poor old Peter.' He tried to put some synthetic sympathy into his voice. 'He finds it hard to cope with two teenagers even when Ann is around to keep things together. Haydn will stop him thinking he's got things under control.'

'That's what younger brothers are supposed to do – or have you forgotten that you are one. For some reason, Jennifer seems to have taken a sudden dislike to most of her teachers and has decided that GCSEs are a complete waste of time. She's refusing to finish her assignments or to do any revision. Examinations start soon and Peter and Ann are getting worried. She's done so well, so far.'

'Boy trouble?' Tim pulled a stool from under the edge of the kitchen counter with his foot and sat down.

'I don't think so – her friends seem to be the same three or four girls. But goodness knows what they get up to when they aren't under Peter's roof. It's a real worry, I can tell you. I'm glad both you boys grew up when you did.'

'That doesn't seem like Jennifer, but she's clever, I'm sure she'll be all right.' Something was knocking at the back of Tim's skull – something that Mary had said or almost said, but his mother went on, interrupting his search for whatever it was.

'I suppose so, but what about you? How is the job? And what is the cottage like? Your father and I will come up to see it as soon as we can.'

'Well – it's Victorian, red brick with a little garden of some sort out the front – a front path through the middle of it and a side path that leads to the rear extension.' He had a vivid picture of Mary standing at his back door wide-eyed with shock. 'There's some more garden at the back, but don't ask me what's in it because I have no idea – just green things as far as I can tell. There's some lawn because I know what grass looks like and I think there are – or were – some daffodils.'

'How will you manage to keep up a garden? You don't know one plant from another.'

'I'll get someone in to fix it up for me and then maybe I'll be able to learn a bit so I can do some of it myself.'

'Can a neighbour recommend someone? You do have neighbours don't you?'

'Yes, but...' He didn't want to talk about Mary – not just yet – why? But his mother interrupted him again.

'What's it like inside? Will there be much decorating to do? You know your father will come and help if you need it.'

Tim cringed, 'It doesn't need much, thanks just the same. It's not in bad condition.' *Well, it will be once I get these old carpets out of here and the walls painted and those old tiles taken off and...* 'The two rooms at the front are dining room and living room; there's a kitchen at the back and an extension. Then there are two little bedrooms upstairs and a bathroom and loo in the extension.' *That needs sorting out too – it's inconvenient and bloody freezing.*

'Well, I can't wait to see it. We'll arrange something soon. But there is something else I wanted to tell you.' Tim pulled open the envelope he was holding. There was a card inside – something funny about moving into a new house.

'Oh yes, what's that?'

'Well, I had a telephone call yesterday from .... ' Tim opened the card and read the signature at the bottom. '.... Macie.' He turned the envelope over. It was her writing – he hadn't noticed. That meant she had his address. Shit.

'Macie?' he stammered. A pain ran through his chest, but he deflected it. He was getting better at it.

'Yes. I promised I'd talk to you. She's taking this very hard. Can't you speak to her? Try to sort it out.'

'Mum.' His voice hardened, or at least he wanted it to. 'There's nothing to sort out. It's over.'

'But Tim, she's so upset – I'm worried she might do something.'

'Mum,' Tim pleaded, 'you know as well as I do – she gets hysterical whenever she likes.'

'Tim, that's not fair.'

'It's true. She won't do anything she can't recover from and if it looks like it's going to affect her mascara, it won't happen. Believe me.'

'Would you just talk to her?'

He felt trapped – claustrophobic – again. 'I'll try.' Then trying to break out again, he added, '...but I won't change my mind.'

'Thanks dear. Your father's just come in so I'd better see to his coffee. I'll call you next week and I promise to bring him and all his paint brushes up to see you soon.'

'OK Mum. Bye.' He tore the card and its envelope in half and slammed them into the kitchen bin.

Then he ripped open the first packing box he could get his hands on and found a place for every single item in it; then the next box and the next. He worked as if possessed and by evening he'd cleared every room in the cottage. In the gathering darkness, he lit a fire in a barrel he found against the hedge and, tearing the boxes into little pieces he burned every scrap.

It rained on Wednesday – a deep drizzle. The museum on Market Street was a single room in the old Victorian workhouse; it was stacked with memorabilia from a thousand years of quiet rural history. Walls that reached to a high open roof were hung with horse collars, regimental flags, bombe glass with sepia photographs of long forgotten local notaries and paintings of historic battles. Glass cases displayed Iron Age artefacts and shrapnel from the last war; clay pipes and arrowheads; printing plates and ribboned medals. Static displays told how cider was made, corn harvested and hops grown; how ore was mined and smelted on the hills and the routes of long lost canals and railways. It was a good museum – and the cold inside was perishing.

The volunteer curator smiled with delight and put out her hand to greet Mary. She was tiny, grey and old. 'Please do come in. I'm Alice Mattlock.' Singing to herself she led Mary into a little office at the back of the large silent room where a small electric fire tried to make gains in the temperature. 'How can I help you?' Mrs Mattlock gestured to a wooden chair, flipped on an old fashioned conical lamp on a spring coiled arm that looked as if it belonged in the other part of the museum and unwrapped Mary's little package with exaggerated care.

'My, my.' She looked up. 'It's very hard to read isn't it?' She adjusted her very old spectacles on her very old nose and squinted at the faint writing. 'I'm sorry I am unable to help you, my dear,' she admitted at last. 'It's too faded for me to see the detail. But there is someone else who might be able to help you.' She straightened her bent back with an effort. 'Richard Fletcher is the local Vicar. As you might expect he has some experience with old documents.' She smiled at her own joke and looked at an ancient clock above the desk. 'He'll be at the vicarage about now. If you want to go over – it's across from the church – I'll telephone him to say you are on your way.'

Mary thanked the old lady and found her way via a tiny back lane to the vicarage where the Reverend Fletcher was waiting for her. He was an elderly round red-faced man and she was grateful his hand was warm.

'Come in my dear. My sister called to say you were on your way over. Come into the study and let's see what you have.' There he eased his short bulk into a squeaky swivel chair on tiny old casters.

He too unfolded the package with great care and looked at the fine writing for a long time before he released the edges. The document refolded itself. He leaned back in his chair and let out a long slow breath. 'Mrs Mitchell.' He spoke as if beginning a counselling session. 'I have to confess that I don't know what this message means – and I'm not able to add very much to what you have discovered, I'm afraid.' He smiled at her. 'It – well – this just leaves me uneasy. I don't know what it means and I wish that I could advise you to leave it, but…' He tried to laugh and the chair squeaked.

'Leave it?'

He seemed to be embarrassed and his laugh also squeaked. 'I'm sorry; I should have been more thoughtful before I spoke.' He shook back his rounded shoulders and stood up. 'I am sorry that I can't help you to understand it.' He pressed her toward the door.

4

The ring of the phone gave her such a surprise that Mary splashed coffee in a wide arc over the newspaper on her knees and up the front of her sweatshirt. Flicking drops off her fingers she grabbed the little phone. 'Sandy!' She wiped her wet hand on her jeans. 'Good to hear from you. But what are you doing calling at this hour – classes can't be finished yet?'

'I finish at 2 on Wednesday, now I'm part time again. But how'n'hell are you anyway?'

Sandy's bluntness made Mary laugh even when she didn't want to. 'Well, today, it's gloomy and dark. The clouds are just missing the roof and it has been raining all week – so I am feeling gloomy with it.'

'Then I'm here to cheer you up – tell me about this wonderful cottage. Have you located the rosemary – I bet it grows like a weed all around the place.'

Mary looked out of the library window; after the morning drizzle, the rain slashed down in blown waves. 'None anywhere. However I'll make it my business to plant some. And the cottage, well – it's lovely – in spite of the fact that I'm taking my time unpacking and you know what kind of a housekeeper I am.'

Sandy spluttered. 'Oh, yeah – you had to pay your cleaners double time whenever someone visited. But come on how about the guided tour?'

Mary walked through the little door out of the library and into the sitting room. 'If you insist. This is the sitting room: a huge fireplace overflowing with ash, piles of wood and logs in a broken basket; two flowered settees on little stubby feet in front of it, numerous pretty tables, a TV and stereo and assorted bits of my mother's old furniture – none of which suits the place. The whole lot is covered with unpacked junk that I haven't found a place for yet. Then there's a new piano, covered with dust because a section of plaster has come off one of the walls and I am waiting for a builder to give me an estimate of the cost to re-plaster it. Got the picture? Need I go on?'

By now Sandy was snorting with laughter. 'What happened to the wall? Are you sure this living alone in an old cottage is a good idea?'

In spite of Sandy's infectious glee, Mary became serious. 'It's the best idea I've had in my life. I don't know what made the plaster fall off, but once it's repaired and I get straight, it'll be great. I promise.'

Sandy's guffaw said she wasn't convinced that Mary had made the right decision about an old cottage. 'And what do you do with all this time – you lucky devil - I'd give anything ...'

'To be honest, I don't know what I'll do with the rest of my life. I've promised myself six months before I decide on anything and in the meantime I sit in my little library and read until I am cross-eyed and – you'll like this – I've tried making bread and ... Stop laughing.'

'And, truth now, was it any good?'

'OK, well no, it wasn't. The first lot burned while I was showing a builder around. Smells don't get out of the Rayburn and I forgot to set the timer and well, it wasn't until he left that I remembered it.'

'So has there been a second batch?'

'Well, yes and no. But it didn't rise, so...'

'So?'

'Bird food with the first lot and slug food with the second? But come on, gossip time. What juicy bits have you got?'

'Not much. Don continues to shout and sneer his way through all his classes. You're right Mary; the man's a psychopath. And Harold continues to amuse with total incompetence. How that man ever made Head is the miracle of the decade.' Her voice became serious. 'You made the right decision, Mary even though you paid an enormous price for it.'

'Just wish the cabal in the staff room had seen fit to see it.'

'Well, none of us has any guts – you know the mantra: do the professional thing – think of the poor man's pension. But look this wasn't a call to drag all that up in front of you again old friend. I wanted to know how you were and be sure you're happy and settled at last. It's been a hell of a year for you and you deserve this one to be better.'

'Thanks, I hope so too.'

She couldn't tell Sandy the rest – the mysterious package with scratchy writing on it that she didn't understand; the builder who looked at her wall and gone away with the colly wobbles; her new neighbour whose back she'd all but broken and all the hurt and anger that she was still trying bury.

But she smiled as she hung up. Sandy was the one colleague who kept in touch. The others treated her like some pariah or assumed that she'd moved to dark regions on the remote side of the planet.

Mary showed a small red-faced man out of the back door as Tim arrived. The little man's overhanging stomach cantilevered on a large belt and his shirt and trousers disappeared somewhere underneath. Tim turned sideways to let him pass and she saw that the sky was bright in the west.

'Another builder.' Mary realised she still wore the large sweatshirt that ended just above her knees with the coffee stains on the front and its sleeves rolled up above her elbows. She felt like a penguin – a tired, grubby and crabby penguin.

'Any luck?'

'Not yet. I get different advice from each one of them. He, for instance, wants to take the rest of the plaster off and put up plaster board.'

'And the others?' He took the wine bottle and corkscrew she handed him.

She led him into the sitting room, and in imitation of a Welsh accent, 'Mr Griffiths wants to put up hard plaster, none of this lime stuff – just nice hard stuff.' She changed to full country vowels. 'Then there's Mr Hughes, who's so busy he can't do anything for weeks because of that big job he's got for a very important client with lots of money, and...' imitating the last man's shortness of breath, she puffed, 'then there's always Mr Moran who wants to plasterboard the lot.'

Tim pulled the cork and laughed. 'Let me guess, you taught drama as well as English.' He poured into the glasses she held.

'Off and on.' She moved a pile of magazines and flopped onto her stiff settee – *these are terrible. Whatever made me think they were in the least comfortable?* 'I didn't think this would be difficult – it's only a hole in a wall and a bit of plaster for heaven's sake.'

Tim pushed some newspaper into a pile and stretched his long legs out in front of him. 'Cheers.' He lifted his glass. He was wearing a dark shirt with tie of the same colour, light coloured trousers that had lost some of their crease and brown brogues. His curly hair looked like it had sustained a day's wear. Mary saw his dark eyes and cheerful cheekbones. *Why hasn't some young woman snatched him up yet?*

'It's becoming obvious that I need to do some more research. I don't know what's best and I don't know a thing about plaster.'

'I might have some books on historic construction methods somewhere. I'll dig them out.' He leaned back on the settee. 'But I stopped by to see if you found out anything at the museum. Today wasn't it?'

Mary pulled her feet up onto the settee. 'It was an interesting morning. The old dear at the museum would have made a good exhibit herself. She was about a hundred. But alas, she couldn't read it – whether due to poor light, poor eyesight or the state of the document, I don't know. But she did send me over to see her brother, the Vicar.'

'Aha, I can see you moving in high social circles of our little town already.'

'You'd think so wouldn't you? But he was very uncomfortable with it.'

Tim looked over his glass, and lifted his eyebrows in surprise. 'Really?'

'Yes. He started to say that he had some strange vibes from it, then recovered himself and said he just spoke without thinking. But that there was nothing he could do. It was all very odd. But as he pushed me out the door, he said that I should try the Records Office.'

'Good idea. It's amazing what they have there.'

'There might be someone there experienced at old script. So I'll give them a try.' She finished her glass. 'Will you stay for tea?'

'No, thanks. I've got a meeting in the morning to prepare for and I'm determined to get the last of my stuff in the extension put away tonight. The house is beginning to feel like home at last.'

'Well, you inspire me. I've made a start myself.' She nodded her wine glass at six empty boxes and three bulging bin bags.

Tim started fresh coffee in the machine in the little meeting room. He was setting out cups, when Susan opened the door with her bottom and put two plastic carrier bags on the table. Her enthusiasm even at this hour of the morning made Tim smile. Sweet and cute, with short blond hair, it was obvious that she was in love with her first real job and everyone involved with it. She started at Conmac just before Tim so he inherited her with the rest of his team. Who was the more terrified, was anyone's guess but Susan worked very hard to get it right.

'Croissants and sticky buns as requested.' She unpacked the bags. 'A breakfast meeting's a great idea, except for getting up half an hour earlier. That coffee smells fantastic.' She set the buns on a large paper plate.

Bryn Jenkins arrived looking as if he had found his clothes in heaps on the floor and didn't have a clue what he was wearing. But then with red hair, he may just have given up trying. Today he wore light trousers with no observable crease, a patterned shirt whose predominant colour could not be defined and a tie of a discordant pattern, badly knotted. His socks didn't match. 'Mornin' darling.' Susan ignored him. 'Great idea boss, we should do this every morning.'

The short, balding quotations manager Derek Thompson followed him in and stretching himself as tall as he could, leaned over Bryn's shoulder and inhaled. 'Why does it always smell better when it's fresh?' He helped himself to a cup and balanced a sticky bun on a plate. 'Where's Howard?'

'I don't know.' Tim straightened his papers. 'He knows we're meeting and said he'd be here.'

'Probably can't get away from the house. His missus will have him hoovering the drive before he leaves.' Bryn grinned and bit into a sticky bun at the same time.

'Here he is.' Tim looked at the stairs, "Shall we get started so we aren't too late getting to work.'

Tim looked around at the little group. They were new to him and he was new to them. Derek dropped his jacket on the back of his chair and drew himself up as tall as he could, trying to make up for his lack of height. *One quotations manager.*

Bryn put a second spoonful of sugar into his coffee. *A young, enthusiastic if inexperienced cad/cam technician whose confidence could look like arrogance.*

Howard arranged his papers in a severe tidy stack. *One very experienced but very flappable and trained but unqualified engineer with a severe shortage of confidence.*

Susan twisted her pencil through her fingers making little dots on the notepaper in front of her. *One very young and bright-eyed secretary or whatever they're called these days – desperate to make a good impression.*

In twenty-five minutes, they'd accomplished what Tim had set out for the meeting and he sent them back to work. They all drained their coffee cups and Bryn helped himself to another sticky bun as they exited. Tim and Susan cleared up and as he opened the door for her to carry out the tray of dirty crockery he came face to face with James Racine. 'Can I have a quick word?' He turned and walked toward his office. Tim and Susan exchanged glances; she raised her eyebrows in mute question.

Tim shut the door to James's office but before he could deliver a greeting, James glowered at him. 'What was that all about?' he demanded, face reddening.

'Do you mean the meeting?'

'Of course I mean the meeting and why didn't I know anything about it?'

'I didn't imagine that it would interest you. Just my staff and I ...'

James interrupted and his voice rose. 'I <u>know</u> who it was. What made you decide that I wouldn't be interested?'

Tim's mouth went dry with shock. 'We were just getting to know each other and that was for my benefit – and for Susan's – she hasn't been here very long either.' Every word felt like an excuse.

'Are you planning any more of these cosy get-togethers? Did you stop to think how the other staff will take to you all having chummy chats? A bit conspiratorial don't you think?' James' mouth contorted to control his breathing; his neck was red.

Tim felt anger rising in his own chest. Surely he was able to have a meeting with his staff without having to explain it to James. 'Yes, we are planning to meet again next week and you will have noticed that we met before the normal work day so that we wouldn't interrupt the others or expect them to cover for us and we met in plain view – it can hardly be considered conspiratorial.'

'I want to know what happens.'

'Susan took notes.' Tim dropped the ball back on James' side of the net. 'Do you want a copy?'

James nodded. The interview was over.

In a small measure of defiance, Tim whistled as he returned to his desk, but he shook inside.

Students and researchers of all ages, leaned over ancient documents and huge maps held down with little bags of sand on large tables. The Records Office was lined with shelves of local history books and shallow drawer file cabinets – in an open one Mary could see thousands of microfiche slides. A small dark alcove contained a dozen or more microfiche readers where people were staring at negative images of ancient registers. A young woman looked up from polishing the counter and smiled. 'May I help you?'

A moment later Mary met Duncan Frazer, a County Archivist, who seated her at a large table in his office. He leaned forward from his chair. 'What have you brought?' His voice betrayed newly qualified eagerness. Mr Frazer was a history graduate according to the degree framed on the wall and it wasn't that long ago. He looked just old enough to be allowed out alone after dark.

Mary unwrapped the little package. He adjusted his lamp and his glasses and studied it with a huge magnifying glass, while she described how she had found it and what she had found out already. She did not mention the worries of George or the Vicar.

Duncan looked up. 'We don't see this sort of thing very often.' There was another pause. 'I think we can identify some more of the writing and give you a rough idea of the age of the document from the manner of the calligraphy - that sort of thing. Now, may I keep this for a few days? I'd like our document expert to have a look at it. I promise you that it'll be well cared for.'

In the gathering gloom of early evening Mary sat in her tiny library – a small fire burning in its huge grate. *I love this room.* The book lined walls made her feel hugged. Books were precious and she was most comfortable when they surrounded her. Her suburban house had no nooks into which to put a book corner, so they lined the walls of the sitting room and looked uncomfortable in their plastic-wood shelf units. Now she was sure they were contented. They leaned into each other with affection and gave off a calm whiff of history, intrigue, lust and love. There were exotic places in her books with exotic people doing extra-ordinary things; there were peaceful places, and fields of war. Some of them chanted the charm of poets, ancient and modern; others described the horror that mankind has dealt to itself since the beginning of time.

The dark settle built into the wall under the window was made for a book lover. She stuffed it with pillows and put the current reading stack on the floor within reach. Putting a glass of sherry on the little table beside her, she switched on the lamp and reached for the book on the top – a novel, an escape, why not?

As always happened when she read she lost all contact with time or place and surfaced from the fast moving story only because a sound pricked the darkness. Lowering the book and sliding her glasses down her nose, she listened and wondered if it were there at all.

Silence clicked in hollows of the room, then a delicate noise like paper rustling untangled itself from a pile of magazines beside the big arm chair. She laid the book on the table as silently as she could and put her glasses on top. The rustling grew in volume and power but retained an alluring and delicate quality – like tender waves on a pebble beach. It filled the room but with no focus to it. She could not identify its source. The sound was not alarming or threatening, sharp or dissonant. It was soft and elegant. As Mary concentrated, it developed highs and lows with pauses. She could not understand what it was and when she tried to speak in reply, it ceased without echo or resonance.

The silence that flowed back into the room was heavy and dark. Mary's heart wanted the beautiful sound. Her ears remembered it, repeated it and wanted it back. Emptiness replaced desire, and sadness filled the hole it left. She leaned back on the pillows of the settle and tried to recover it. But it had gone. She was alone with no understanding of what she had heard.

5

In the morning Mary felt empty, but whether from loss or exhaustion, she didn't know. The sounds in her library couldn't be confirmed by any real evidence or even in the crevices of her memory. Stress? Imagination? Sadness? Whatever it was, her body felt thick, heavy; her brain slow and clumsy. She knew she had to retrieve herself before the demands of depression began again. With the shreds of muscular strength that remained, she went outside. To her great relief the sun was shining. It warmed her skin and she forced one foot in front of the other until she was in the garden. With physical effort she began to bring her brain back to reality.

Through the soup of her mind, she focussed on the rockery. It needed attention, but she wasn't able to summon the mental strength to start on it. Soggy leaves of once cheerful spring bulbs and tall couch grass ran in organic rivulets over the rocks. She looked at the trowel and garden fork for a long time. The heat of the sun warmed her back and she picked up the big fork. After a time its weight became purpose. As her body strengthened, she became angry at the state of her mind, and rammed the tool in again and again until her muscles and her brain woke. She went on and on until there was a large pile of dug grass and roots. It was then that she came across a plant that made her stop. Friend or foe? Dig it out or not? Her thoughts were generous enough now for her to know she needed her book of garden plants and a cup of coffee.

As she straightened up, the postman's van stopped and he leaned over the gate with a clutch of post.

'Hope it stays like this for the long weekend,' he called nodding in the general direction of the sky.

'Let's hope so,' replied Mary taking the stack. *Long weekend? One loses track of time here.*

'Things'll be growin' now'.

Mary forced a smile, 'They already are.'

She committed the circulars to the recycling bin without opening them. The rest she took, with her coffee into the library. There was a belated card from a former colleague, welcoming her to her new house, but without a single word to wish her well. The last was from her solicitor saying that her husband's legal advisor was giving notice that the regular payment to Mary would be delayed next month and that it was Robert's intention to re-negotiate the settlement in view of reduced company receipts.

Mary sat up in her chair, anger rising through her chest. *How dare he? What reduced company receipts? The settlement's been negotiated and agreed – he agreed – I agreed. The total value was known and agreed. The contract is only 6 months old. He can't do this. He can't. What's he up to?*

She threw the letter onto her desk and grabbed the telephone, shaking with anger. Cold hard rage alone prevented her brains from losing control of her mind.

On Saturday morning, Tim stopped at the little iron gate at the end of his front path. The big side gates open on the drive were lost in weeds and tall grass, but the little one was just moveable. It needed some oil and a coat of paint but it would keep for another time. Then he heard the bird again. A warm watery warbling song rose and rose in waves and then trilled and stopped before it began again. The song was melodic and tender. He thought of some lovelorn cock bird singing his heart out without knowing that it was a female he was looking for.

The tarmac of the lane was warm under his feet; the grass still glistened with the dew. A day or two of sunshine and plants had begun to grow at an amazing rate. There were dandelions in bloom and he recognized some cowslips hidden in the tall grass. A pretty stem with several pale pink blossoms caught his eye. He picked one and thought he had seen it before, but didn't know its name. Mary would have a book about wild flowers in her library. Nettles he recognized and something that might become a bluebell. Fine red stems with branching leaves and small red flowers crowded near the hedge and tall plants with plates of tiny white buds seemed to be appearing everywhere. The enthusiastic bird continued its determined song in the valley bottom.

Broken cardboard boxes, torn and crunched packing paper, and black bin bags spilling a miscellany of contents onto the gravel were scattered outside Mary's back door. Tim reached for the bell and lurched as another box tumbled past his shoulder. Then he saw her inside; a baggy shirt over dirty jeans and a look on her face that said death before surrender. She relaxed when she saw him.

'Am I interrupting a purge or something?' he asked, one hand up to deflect the next attack.

'Oh Tim, I'm sorry. I don't intend to kill you, although it seems I keep trying.' She kicked a box blocking the doorway to clear the entry. 'Come in. I'm - well, it's a kind of therapy. Coffee? Or tea?'

'Coffee thanks.' His voice sounded timid even to him as he stepped over the torn ends of a cardboard box. 'Can I assume you're unpacking…?'

'Contrary to what I feel like, I am making myself unpack.' She moved the kettle onto the Rayburn hot plate.

'OK, what's wrong?'

Mary let out a long ragged breath and ran a hand through her tangled hair. 'I had a notice from my husband's solicitor yesterday.'

'And?' Tim knew he was prying.

Mary spooned coffee into a cafetiere. He saw her fighting to put her emotions under control. 'He's decided that he wants to renegotiate our financial agreement and I am afraid if he does, I won't have any income.'

'Can he do that?'

'Robert can do more or less whatever he wants. He's that sort.' She lifted the kettle from the Rayburn, and held it as the boiling subsided. 'Lets sit outside and I'll tell you all the gory details.'

He removed the bin bags from the chairs and she put a tray on the table. 'I was married to Robert for 24 years and we built up a company that sold office furniture and equipment. It was successful and when we separated, I was able to make a case for half of the value of the company. I supported him and it with my salary in the early days and until I became head of English, I did all the accounts.' She sat down and rolled her sleeves up over her elbows. 'We agreed that he would create a fund equal to half of the value of the company when we separated and pay it to me as an annuity until I collect my superannuation. I am also entitled some of the future value of the company – a bit like a shareholder - and I can call out anything remaining in annuity fund at any time. So, I get by, but without it I have nothing. It's just like him to do this just before a long weekend.'

'So why does he want to renegotiate?' Tim felt a large lump of anger on her behalf. He hated the guy already.

'Well, he claims that the borrowing he had to do to create the fund for the annuity is too much of a hardship for him and the company and wants to – well, I guess, to have some of it back. I spoke to my solicitor yesterday and she is investigating, but to be honest, I don't trust him. The future fund is insured so that's safe – well I think it is.'

She banged the cups down on the wooden table and pushed the plunger down on the cafetiere. 'You see, he's a very sharp business man – always has been. He was never afraid to take risks – God knows I lost enough sleep over the years every time he re-mortgaged the house for another scheme.' She poured the coffee. 'But he always pulled through and made it work somehow. The company was worth quite a bit when it was valued and my share of the house – thankfully not totally re-mortgaged at the time - bought me this cottage. That's all I have to go on.'

'But no details yet?' He offered her the milk, but she shook her head.

'No, only enough to make me capable of murder if he showed up right now.' Her knuckles were white on the cup handle.

'Which explains the energy expended on unpacking ... '

Mary nodded; tears heavy on her lashes.

'Look, this is none of my business, but it seems to me that there's not a lot you can do – except worry of course – until you have more information. So my role here is to take your mind off things. Shall we go somewhere and clear our heads?'

'You too?'

'Let's throw a few things into the car and get to know this part of the world we live in. Then I'll tell you mine since you were kind enough to tell me yours.'

Corvedale is gentle on the eye. On a hillside they found a place that overlooked its soft slope and ate a picnic of bread, cheese and fruit with a bottle of wine. The customary wind today trickled around them into the valley. They watched farm tractors till precise, dark furrows in the soft soil. For early May, the weather was warm. Lambs and their mothers hovered over pasture grass in benign groups and a church tower shivered with the distance.

Mary stretched out on the blanket and propped herself on one elbow. 'Thanks for listening to my tale of woe earlier; I feel a whole lot better now.'

'What are friends for?'

Yes, friends. 'But you promised to tell me yours.'

'My what?'

'Woes, I guess.'

For a minute, he seemed to consider whether to share his concerns. When he spoke the words were timid. 'I'm probably just tired, but something happened at work on Thursday that I don't understand.' He filled up his glass. 'I've been working all the hours

I can this week – on site after site all over the place. Monday I was in Kent all day, Tuesday I think it was Cumbria, yesterday, Surrey and I can't remember where I was Wednesday, but on Thursday I had a staff meeting – a breakfast meeting. Anyway it was just to make a team out of my staff. They all worked for other people in the past and I've been imposed on them.'

He draped his elbows over his knees. 'We were just wrapping up when James called me into his office and demanded to know what was going on. He was sarcastic and really over the top. I just don't understand what he's so upset about.'

Mary lifted her chin to the sun. 'It reminds me of a Head I had once. Had to have control over everything. It was as if delegating something meant losing it. Is James anything like that?'

'He's very experienced at managing people – I think everyone is terrified of him. But you're right; he seems to need to be in control of every detail.'

'Is it that he has to have control, or is it because you're new and he's unsure about you?' She pulled the back off one earring, pulled out the stud and rubbed her ear lobe.

He shrugged one shoulder. 'I'm sure it's assumed more importance in my head than it deserves. Maybe I just need to keep him informed, just to show that I'm not hiding anything.'

Mary raked her earlobe with the stud and pushed it back in. 'It wouldn't hurt and it might just keep him calm. If it were me, I'd give him every trivial bit of information I could think of until he was so sick of getting reports, he'd beg me to stop.'

Tim's laugh relaxed his face and it stayed that way.

On the way home he put back the sunroof on his big black car and let the wind and sun stream in around them. They both felt better.

The stack of flattened boxes in Mary's garage complicated her insecurity on Tuesday. She didn't feel quite ready to get rid of them. She threw the last box in and slammed the door.

The morning sun was warm and Mary pulled on a new pair of gardening gloves. Why oh why were they always so big? She picked up the big garden fork with determination and made a fierce start on the small square of bare ground in the middle of the back lawn. Mary assumed that it was once a vegetable plot and the idea of fresh salad greens and new potatoes gave her enthusiasm. In three-quarters of an hour, her back was stinging with strain, but a large tub was heaped with weeds. There was still half of the plot to finish.

In spite of the pain, she purged some of the heat and annoyance she was building up against Robert, her solicitor and just how long it took to get anything done. What was he up to? She recited some choice adjectives. Her solicitor was not to blame – Joanne was just the messenger.

By lunchtime she finished the plot, but could no longer see the tub for weeds piled on it. She raked the crumb-like soil and put some seed packages from a drawer in order of planting. The notes on the backs said to plant in May when all danger of frost had passed. It was May, but when was the danger of frost passed? She took a chance and spent a happy afternoon making small drills around the tub of weeds. By four o'clock there were neat, tamped rows of lettuces, radish, cress and some root vegetables. She sat on the garden bench looking over the orchard, aching but satisfied. The cherry blossoms were full now and the showy blooms covered the trees with little, frothy white wigs. Whether real or imaginary, Mary was sure there was a light perfume on the air. A cuckoo sang an enthusiastic cadence nearby. There was magic here and life as it should be. She was meant to be here – she knew it.

Mary was almost asleep in the late spring sunshine and it took a few rings for her to realise what it was. By the time she got her phone out, her solicitor was about to ring off.

'Mary, I thought you'd gone out.' Joanne sounded disappointed. That meant that her news was not good. 'I'm afraid Robert's solicitor wants to re-open the negotiations on your agreement. I think it might be a good idea to set up a meeting.'

'But I thought we had an agreement – that everything was already negotiated. What is there to discuss?' Mary felt like she was shouting.

'By the sounds coming from Stewart and Anderson, it looks like Robert is finding the funding of the agreement harder than he thought. It might be wise at least to discuss it with them. If there is no money to pay it, the agreement falls apart in real terms. All you can do is sue for breach of contract and that could have the effect of forcing bankruptcy in the worst case.'

'Joanne, I understand what you're saying, but I know what the accountant said about the business – that its value was sound and Robert could afford to support the payments to me with only minimal borrowing. He's got some other reason – I can't believe it's just the vagaries of the business.'

'Do you want me to get some financial details from them first?'

'Yes. I'd rather not make a trip to Solihull just to hear what Robert wants to tell me – I can suspect that from here. Then, maybe, we can meet if we think it's necessary.'

'I think I'll talk to the accountant who did the valuation. He seemed to have his head screwed on.' Mary heard papers being shuffled in the background. 'What was his name again.....'

Mary's hands were shaking as she put down the phone. There was a sour taste in her mouth and a dull ache in her back. She ran a hot tub and poured a large glass of brandy. Damn him. All she wanted was to be rid of him and what's her name.

Mary woke in the morning while it was still dark, unable to move. Her back muscles were so stiff that she could get only up by rolling onto her stomach and pushing herself up on her knees and elbows. Why on earth hadn't she stopped yesterday when it had begun to hurt? *Some people are slow learners.*

A hot shower at 6 a.m., a large cup of coffee and a hot water bottle strapped to her back with a belt from her dressing gown made her feel better and she was able to get dressed and sit at the garden table.

Phil's rusty car dragged itself into her gate and settled on the drive, as if in need of a rest. He hoisted himself out of the relic and pulled up his sagging jeans.

'Morning,' he called and waved. ''Nother lovely day.' He went straight to the lawn mower and soon was making happy concentric patterns on the grass. Phil's card had been tacked on a board in the small green grocers on Croftbury high street. The boy behind the counter said that everyone knew Phil and he'd fit in a few hours for her – no problem. He was there within days. Tall, with greying wavy hair, and with no particular body shape, his clothes always seemed in danger of falling off. He arrived every Wednesday, gave her good work for half a day and didn't charge a fortune. He lived somewhere close by, seemed to have been in the area always but more than that Mary was not able to find out.

At mid morning Mary held out a cup of strong tea. It was a ritual they established from his first visit and it was a signal for a chat.

'Missed seeing you last week.' His wide smile widened. 'So I just got on with that hedge since it was too wet to mow.'

'I was at the museum and it seems that Wednesday morning is the only time it was open.'

'Have you got some grand old antique that you can't identify then? Or were you just lookin' as they say?' He gave her his most charming smile and swept back his hair with thick fingers.

'I was trying to get a document deciphered. Believe it or not I found it in the cottage and it was so old that I couldn't read the writing, so I was hoping the museum might be able to help.'

He wanted to know all about the document, where it had come from and together they mused on how it had come to be plastered up in Mary's wall. He was fascinated. Then putting down his cup, he gathered his clothes around him and said, 'Right then, what else for today?'

She winced from the pain in her back and after hearing her confession of horticultural enthusiasm; Phil insisted she lift nothing heavier than secateurs. So she cut bunches of fruit blossom and filled all the vases she owned with them. They flooded the house with light and scent – they made a white space in a black week and their gentle aroma floated throughout the house like gauze angels.

6

Tim enjoyed every minute of his site visits. In the last weeks he'd seen so many, they were beginning to blur in his mind. But the work on all the sites was progressing well and the contractors were pleased that he had taken the time to see their projects. He discussed the designs and the work with them and then checked that they were getting the steel when they needed it and that the specifications were being met.

There were some sites where he seemed to be less welcomed. In spite of Susan having told them he was coming and making arrangements for him to meet the site manager, he was barely let into the site office. He found the contractor less than enthusiastic, but could not identify if it was a problem of Conmac's making or if it was just a difficult set of circumstances out of his ability to affect. Although he loved the work, the noise and the buildings rising from the foundations, his visits were short and he left feeling that he had achieved nothing.

Mary's back felt better by Friday, but most of the blossoms were now on the carpet and she bumped the vacuum cleaner down the stairs to tidy up. As she shut the machine off and bent to unplug it, the telephone rang.

'Records Office here.' A crisp voice stabbed her ear. 'We have a translation of the document you left with us. Do you want to collect it or shall we post it to you?'

'Oh no, don't post it. I'll collect it this afternoon.'

At the Records Office a young woman in sombre grey skirt that went to her ankles, a plain blouse and with a stud in her nose met her at the front desk and took her to one of the long tables. 'Thank you for letting us see this.' Her voice was nasal. 'It's very interesting. Here's what we think it says.' She pushed a single sheet of paper to her and Mary read:

'*John. Keep thyself from harm. I yieldeth not in suspicion nor be condemned though I be sick with fear. We not be seduced by the devil and enchant none but are true Christians. Pray for us. My love cometh to you always. Mary*'

Mary read it through twice. The sadness and desperation that she felt before pattered in her heart again.

'It's hard to tell without destructive chemical analysis, but we don't think the ink is an aniline dye. Probably carbon based in animal glue. The paper is a poor quality, thick parchment rather than proper paper and the language and script are similar to documents we have here from the 17th and early 18th centuries.' The young woman leaned forward and frowned. 'Sounds a bit creepy doesn't it?'

Mary read the translation again. 'It certainly does. But can you tell me with any more certainty when it was written. I know you said 17th or 18th century but that's quite a long space of time.'

'Not with complete accuracy. It might help if you could determine more about when the document came from...' She looked at the parchment again. 'Where did you say you found it?'

'In a wall in my cottage.'

Mary looked puzzled and the young woman went on, 'For example, how long has it been there; is the house very old – I mean, has it been there 100 years or 300 – that sort of thing.'

'Do you mean I should try to find out how old my house is?'

'Well that would give us the earliest date that the document is likely to be assuming it's not been moved.' She slid the translation into a brown envelope and handed it to Mary. 'Do you live in this county?' Mary nodded. 'Then we might have information here about it.' She got up and led Mary to a large drawer cabinet full of microfiche cards. 'For example, from the census records here, you can find out if it existed and who lived in it, back to 1841.'

'Why 1841?'

'That's the first census which lists the names of people and their ages and things like that. But for the periods before that you can look at the Parish Records of births, deaths and marriages if you have a family name. They go back to 1509 in some parishes although that may not give you the place of residence. If your cottage was part of a larger estate – and you might be able to determine that from the enclosure acts of the area – there may be estate records like rent books and such like.'

'I had no idea that so much information existed.'

'Sometimes you can be very lucky and find all kinds of things. Other times there's nothing at all, but it's always interesting to look.'

Mary looked at the large clock over the reception desk. 'It's a bit late to begin today, but I'll come in next week.'

'When you come, bring some identification and some passport type photographs, so we can issue you with a reader's card. Then you will be able to look at the original

40

documents if you need to. In the meantime, do you want us to keep your document here for safe keeping or would you like to have it back?' She led Mary back to the desk.

'This may sound silly, but I think I would like to have it with me. At least until I've looked into things a bit more.'

The girl folded the document in soft tissue and handed to Mary. 'Good luck.'

Mary drove into Tim's just before 6:00 p.m. to find him in the shower. He called for her to go into the living room and make herself comfortable. He'd be out in a minute and no, he had no intention of sliding across the floor again.

The extension led into Tim's gleaming new kitchen. Everything was tidy and the worktops clear. For a tiny space it gave the feeling of being very modern and grown up. The living room beyond was the same. There were two large, soft squishy settees and a matching chair facing a small opening in which a little log burner was installed. A large gleaming flat screen television fully occupied one corner. The walls needed painting, and the curtains would benefit from ironing, but everything was in its place, neat and casual. Mary bounced up and down on the big chair and oozed back into it.

But before she could fall asleep, Tim appeared in jeans, a t-shirt with a lager logo across the front and damp curls over his forehead. He was wiping his glasses on a tea towel.

'I promise not to make a habit of interrupting your ablutions every time I come.'

'Glad to hear it – the human body can only take so much.' He grinned and disappeared into the kitchen, returning with a bottle of red wine and two glasses. 'This is nice – you visiting me I mean.' He pulled the cork.

'And this. . .' She held up her wine glass for him to fill, '... is as well.' She put it down on the coffee table. 'I came by to show you this.' She pulled the translation out of the envelope.

'Well, well.' Tim read it and then he read it again. 'There is something going on here. But what?'

'The archivists seemed to think that the writing and style were 17th or 18th century but to find out when the cottage was built.' Tim's brows lifted in mute question so she explained. 'Well, that is likely to be the earliest the document will be. They have quite a lot of information from censuses, births, deaths, estates and that sort of thing, so I might be able to find out something about the age of the cottage and so ...'

41

'What did the estate agent say when you bought it – or the surveyor. Or the deeds?'

'Well, the stuff from the estate agent just says about 18th century and I never saw the deeds. They went straight to the solicitor I guess. The Home Information thingy didn't say much and I didn't have a survey done, because I've no mortgage ...'

Tim tutted through his teeth. 'No survey? Shame on you.'

'Well, I was not really in control of all my faculties and I figured that if it has stood for 200 years it would last long enough for me to get myself together.'

He filled up her wine glass. 'All right, I'll let you off this time. Look it's my turn to cook ...'

'But will I be safe from a man whose culinary talents, by his own admission leave something to be desired?'

'You will be amazed.'

Tim steered her to a kitchen stool at the gleaming black counter and turned the kettle on. Mary hoisted herself onto the stool and laughed. 'Can I help with anything?'

'No, just don't take notes – I'll be nervous enough cooking for you.'

'For heaven's sake, why?'

'Well after what you put in front of me ...' He poured boiling water over the contents of a package of quick cook saffron rice and put it in the hot oven.

'That was just pasta.'

'Yeah, like the Mona Lisa is just a painting.' Then he filled a huge pot with more hot water and put it on the electric hob to boil.

'This kitchen is lovely.' She twisted around on the stool. 'But it's new. Did you have it done or is this what sold you the place?'

'The one here was so bad, I hired some local lads to rip it out and repaint it. Then I called up a kitchen place, picked what I wanted from a catalogue and let them go to it. Shame I didn't have the time to do the same with the rest of the house. Here since you are just sitting there, slice these carrots up into little stick things will you?'

'I think you mean julienne.'

'Show off.' He rinsed a large bag of bean shoots in the sink and opened a bag of washed snow peas.

Mary chopped as instructed and he heated up a large frying pan and tipped a bag of vegetables, the peas and Mary's julienne carrots into it with a flourish. 'Establishing the age of your cottage fascinates me. I think it would be a good idea to have another look at that little hole. We know it has a frame round it so it wasn't just an accidental hole but we should see if it was cut out and framed after the wall was built or at the same time.'

'How will we be able to tell that?'

'If the stones have been hacked away, then the hole could have been made anytime and that's not much help. But if they are laid and the hole built with the wall then it's the same date as the house and you might be able to find out what that is. Pour the last of that wine will you? I don't know if red goes with chinese-out-of-a-package, but then I am a food heathen remember.'

He poured a large jar of sauce over the vegetables, threw the shoots into the boiling water and slammed on a lid. In three minutes exactly, he strained the shoots with a tennis racquet jammed over the edge of the pan - 'I can't find the strainer and it's OK, I washed it.' – and tipped them into the frying pan on top of the others.

He struggled with the cork in the next bottle. 'Damn. Why are some so easy and the others give you a pulled muscle?'

'I'm surprised you have to use a cork screw, I'd have thought a large sword would be more your style.' He raised his eyebrows. 'Well, anyone who uses a tennis racquet...'

'Ah, it gets worse.' He snatched back the bottle as he was about to pour. 'Promise you won't laugh...' She tried without success to batten down a fit of giggles. 'But I used to use a machete in the kitchen.' She hooted. 'It was great – did just about everything you ever needed doing and impressed the hell out of dinner guests. I've even fried an egg on it – it did taste a bit metallic come to think of it, but ...' Unable to speak behind the giggles she wiggled her wine glass and he filled it up at last. 'Then someone told me it should be registered as a lethal weapon or something, so I got rid of it.'

Mary's eyes were streaming with laughter. 'I can just see you with a tennis racquet in one hand and a machete in the other inviting people in...'

'A fencing mask would have been better, the holes are smaller, but they're hard to come by.' He put down the wine bottle. 'In my own defence, I used to wear an old army helmet in the kitchen.'

Mary snorted. 'Whatever for?'

'The girl I lived with at the time used to leave the cupboard doors open. They didn't bother her, she was short enough, but I smashed my head on them so many times, that I took to wearing the helmet. It made her remember to shut the doors and if she didn't then at least I didn't have to sit through dinner with a concussion or blood running down my face.'

'The vision just gets worse.' Mary wiped her eyes. 'Imagine being greeted at the door by a man wearing fencing mask, army helmet and wielding a machete.'

'Come to think if it we didn't have many people over for meals. I wonder if that had something to do with it.'

He took the rice from the oven, picked up the frying pan – 'Pretend it's a wok.' And they carried it all into the dining room. 'I said you'd be amazed.'

By the end of the second bottle, he would not let her drive home. She would not let him walk with her and, borrowing his torch this time, she arrived home very late indeed.

As she closed the gate, she looked at her pretty black and white cottage. 'What secrets have you got and what are you prepared to tell me?'

7

Tim did something on Sunday morning that he hated. He got up late – again. The bottom of his mouth felt like it had been marched over and his head hurt from too much sleep. In dressing gown and bare feet, he collected the Sunday paper from the post box. Then taking the biggest mug of tea he could find he sat outside on his one garden chair and leaned back in the sunshine.

On the point of falling asleep again, he felt himself sitting in the early morning sun on the narrow balcony of his London flat. The roar of distant traffic drifted over him, but he felt acutely conscious of every noise he made – he didn't want to wake her. All he wanted was his own space and time. The paper began to slide off his knees and he grabbed for it, surprised to find himself in the Herefordshire sunshine. He realised he had been on the verge of sneaking away to find his own space; like golf which he hated, running, which he hated more and working, which made him so tired he began to hate even the job.

Why on earth did I stick it out? Why wasn't I just honest with her? The answer was plain. He didn't know what he wanted - or didn't want - until it was too late and she'd set up the style and custom of their relationship. She managed everything, even to the metal rack in his kitchen that the tools hung on – the one that he hit his head on time and time again. Back to the helmet. How like her. How like him. What a coward. Running off to another job, another house, a plot in the country, but hard to find. There was no honour in the way he'd ended it.

He unfolded the paper and pushed his glasses up on his nose. When he finished the front section, personal finance and a piece of toast, he re-folded the paper and put his mug on top, sat back in the chair and closed his eyes in the sun. The warmth felt near perfection.

Then his mobile rang. *Mother, please don't talk too long today – I just want to be on my own.*

A small voice asked, 'Uncle Tim?'

'Jennifer?' *What's she doing telephoning on Sunday morning?*

She sounded close to tears. 'Uncle Tim. Can you collect me please? I'm at Ludlow station. I've left home.'

Yet more books; Mary tipped them out of the packing box onto the library floor. As she tried to find places for them on her shelves, she thought about the age of the

45

cottage. Would it be possible to find out when that package had been plastered into the wall? On the way through the living room with the empty box, she looked again at the hole. Did the message of pain and panic, owe its survival to the woman who wrote it, or the man who received it? The hole gave no answers. The ragged edges of timber reminded her that she'd made no decision yet about repairs.

Mary went again to her bookshelves. There was no information about old houses to be found amongst the novels, literature or fine bindings. She pulled a road atlas off the shelf and found that Hay on Wye was less than an hour's drive away.

On the drive home from the station Tim got little information out of Jennifer. Silent most of the way, she brightened when they stopped in the drive. While she rushed over the house in excitement, he put her bag down in the kitchen and plugged the kettle in for tea. *The universal antidote for a crisis.*

Tim started with the small talk. 'It seems to me that the last time I saw you was around Christmas when you were looking quite grown up – although I'll never understand how you can walk on shoes like those. They made you almost as tall as me.'

'I'm nowhere near 6 foot...,' she flapped her hand, '... whatever you are.'

'Three, Jennifer, 6 foot 3.'

'Well, Granddad still says you should have been a guardsman.'

Tim swatted the comment into the back of his mind. 'I have to say you don't look quite so glamorous today. Either you've been pulled through a hedge or slept all night on a park bench. Which was it?' He filled the teapot.

'I stayed at Heather's last night and caught the train this morning. And if you'd been around for more than just a few hours at Christmas, you'd know I've been out of little girl dresses for years.' She clutched a chunk of her long cream coloured hair in her fist and threw it down her back. It looked as tired as she did. He could just about imagine what a night with a girl friend was like and reckoned that sleep didn't enter into it much. Her jeans flapped around her ankles and her big jumper, its sleeves hanging over the ends of her fingers, made her look small and lost.

'Well, you know how Macie liked to organise things.'

'Mainly you.'

46

Had it been obvious to everyone but him? He handed her the tea. He needed to divert this conversation and tried to make his voice sound conversational. 'Lucky I was home – I mean, what would you have done if there'd been no answer here?'

She looked at him with confidence borne of adolescent planning. 'I used your mobile number.' That was the answer to life, the universe and everything. It never occurred to her that he would be anywhere else.

He bit off his next comment since there was little point in frightening her and he was relieved she was safe. 'Look, I am flattered that you thought to come to me when you – well found yourself in ...' he was about to say 'trouble', but realized the emphasis was wrong – lord God he hoped so, '... well in need of help. But you've got to realise that you can't stay here and your parents will be frantic by now.'

'I'm not going home.'

Should have seen that coming. It's going to take a bit of time to get to the bottom of this. 'Whatever your problem is, it can be worked out, believe me.' *Can I start again? This was not the way to conduct a discussion with a distraught teenager.*

'No it can't. I've left home and I don't want to go back - ever!'

Well that was to be expected. I'm not very good at this. 'If I'm going to be able to help, I need to know what's wrong.' He began again.

'Nothing. I just need some space - to sort my head out.'

What on earth did that mean? He needed a firmer tack. Trying not to sound patronising, he began again. 'Look Jennifer, I'm happy for you to stay here for a few days if it'll help. But only on the condition that you let your parents know where you are. If you don't telephone them, I will and it would be a lot better coming from you.'

She was sullen and silent for a moment. Whatever. But you phone them. And...,' she emphasised the word, 'I'm not going back.'

Ann answered when Tim rang. 'Hello Tim.' *She's too damn cheerful. She doesn't know Jennifer is missing,* he thought with a chill. *The stupid girl could have been killed and dumped in a ditch and no one ...* 'It's nice to hear from you. How is the new house?'

'Fine thanks, but ...'

She interrupted before he could say more. 'Your mother told me you were having trouble with the decorating. Peter'll be glad to come and give you a hand if you want. It must be such a chore, an old house like that and in the middle of the country too. Can you get to a shop if you need to?'

Tim was exasperated – his sympathy for Jennifer deepened. 'Look Ann,' he tried again. 'I called to let you know that Jennifer is here.'

There was a shriek that he was sure Jennifer could hear in the other room. He had to raise his voice and cut in over the string of panic. 'She is fine, but says she wants to stay here for a few days ... No, I don't know what's wrong, but ... Hold on I'll ask.' He turned to Jennifer. 'Your mother would like a word.'

Jennifer was in the doorway, making sweeping no-no motions with her hands. 'Since when has she ever been able to say just one! No I don't want to talk to her.'

He turned again to the telephone. 'I'm afraid she doesn't want ... no ... no ... well ... I'll call you later and ... Ann, it will be all right ... no she doesn't want to talk to you now ... no I don't know yet... We'll call later.' Eventually he hung up.

'See what I mean?' Jennifer leaned over the bread bin. 'Got anything to eat, I'm starving. You know I'm vegetarian don't you?'

Jennifer was still in bed when Tim left for work in the morning. He managed to find out that it wasn't boy trouble so he hoped that ruled out teenage pregnancy, but little else was forthcoming. He called Ann and Peter again and managed a few words with his brother before the telephone was yanked away and he was forced to have another fractured conversation with Ann.

What in God's name was he to do with a 15-year-old niece? And he was late for work. A message on his desk in James' handwriting asking for a few minutes as soon as possible was all he needed. Tim threw his jacket on the back of his chair, took a deep breath, nodded at a puzzled Susan and rolled up his sleeves on his way to James' office. 'Morning chief.' He sounded more cheerful than he meant to.

James looked at his watch and Tim ignored him volunteering no explanation. He worked weekends when required, be damned if he was going to explain why he was 10 minutes late on Monday morning.

'I'd like a list of the companies you still plan to visit.' James' vowels were sharp. Tim blinked. 'If you want...'

'Look Tim, I'm prepared to support enthusiasm when it's appropriate, but I want you to be damn sure that what you're investigating is going to produce what we need.'

'I won't know that until I've seen them and looked at...'

'I don't want egg on my face and neither do you.' He gave Tim a hard look. He was clearly dismissed.

Tim felt shaken and sat down heavily when he got back to his desk. What on earth was that all about? Susan brought him a cup of coffee. 'Are you all right?'

Tim managed a smile – or hoped it was one. 'Yes thanks. What have I got in my diary this week?' But it was hard to concentrate.

Tim had a local site visit and by noon, he took the chance that Jennifer would be up and rang. There was no reply and he realised that she wouldn't answer in case it was her mother. He spoke to the answering service, asking her to call back. Then he began to worry that she'd gone off again. Maybe Mary would pop up and see if she was all right. He rang Mary's number but there was no reply. Where the hell was everybody?

He didn't manage his afternoon inspection very well and got back to the office about 3. He realised that he had achieved nothing all day. He tried both numbers again with no reply. He yanked his jacket off the back of his chair. 'Susan, will you close down for me. I've got to go home.' Any other work on his project list was not going to happen until he sorted out his niece.

He felt James watching him go.

Hay on Wye was unique and Mary felt its warmth surround her. The village of grey stone stumbled down a steep Welsh border hill on which an ancient castle silently crumbled. Narrow bent streets glistened grey from an early morning rain and a clock announced the quarter hours from a tower in a misshapen square. Residents went about their regular duties and visitors lingered in doorways and shop windows, plastic carrier bags rustling.

Narrow, crooked, low ceilinged houses, large rambling shops and even an old cinema were now devoted to books: thousands and thousands of books – used, new, almost new – specialists from marine engineering to antique horticulture; children's books to poetry; from newspapers and magazines to cookery and Russian language literature.

The first to attract Mary was a warm little house with rooms, upstairs and down that drew her on and on. Books were piled on shelves, stools, benches, stairs and the floor. Convenient chairs encouraged her to sit down to read, meditate or just rest. She spent two hours there and when she emerged at last blinking in the murky sunshine there were already five novels in a carrier bag.

It wasn't possible to look at every title in every shop Mary decided. She must narrow her search to what she was looking for, then browse in joy if there was time left in the day – or in a lifetime. The next shop had a tall, glass double front and dark interior

49

with deep wood panelled walls and a high dark ceiling that stretched into a gloomy infinity. A directory handwritten on a large piece of card, hung by wires from huge roof beams and a crooked arrow pointed to wide wooden stairs and promised architecture and DIY on the first floor.

Sections of narrow shelves went on and on and rose to a height that she could see only if she used a portable stool some kind person put there for short browsers. Some unknown time later, having just taken a quick look at the literature section, where she found an early edition of American poetry and a slim leather bound volume of war poems, she located what she'd come for – renovation.

Later at a sidewalk table, she ate whole grain bread and a creamed parsnip soup, both pushed to one side, while the book on renovation took up the rest of her place. A grey-haired gentleman took a chair opposite and by mute agreement, neither spoke, but retreated into the treasures they'd found.

The author of a 1980's book presented a firm case in his introduction, for respectful repair rather than renovation. His sympathetic understanding of heritage and the practical rationale for appropriate techniques and materials made a lot of sense. Mary decided that her wall had to be repaired properly.

She narrowed her research in the afternoon, to books on lime plaster and methodology. By the end of the afternoon, she felt confident enough to fix the damn wall herself. Her feet hurt, her back ached and sinking into the stiff upholstery of the car seemed like therapy. The back seat rustled with plastic bags full of books. She felt good all over in spite of how much it hurt.

Jennifer was wearing a tiny top, even tinier shorts and a great deal of makeup. *Good God*, Tim thought, *how on earth do they stay safe?* 'You're home early,' she observed from the blanket in the tall back garden grass. 'It can't be 5 o'clock yet'.

He sat down on a corner. 'I tried to call and got worried when you didn't answer.'

'Well, I was afraid it might be Mum.'

'I thought so.' He took a deep breath. 'Look Jennifer; I do need to know what's going on. You have a life, your parents have a life and I have a life.' He put up a hand. 'Yes, I know it's hard to believe that anyone over 20 does, but there you are.'

She smiled a little. 'I just got fed up with it all.' She pushed her sunglasses up on her head. 'I needed some space.'

'Let me see if I can translate. 'All' means either school or boys or lack of them. And 'space' means time. How am I doing so far?'

'OK'

'School?'

'Yeah, OK, so what?'

'It's GCSEs this year isn't it?' Silence – or at least no contradiction. 'Exams are coming up and you're not ready.'

'I don't care. They're useless.'

Tim bit off the usual sermon about grades being the passport to the rest of her life. Then remembering what his mother had said, 'If I remember, you're pretty good at school.' Maybe a little flattery?

'Yeah, well it's the teachers – they're all crap and I'm sick of them. They're horrible.' The last word was said as if it contained the complete definition of her life.

'Trouble with a teacher? Serious?'

'They're all crap.'

What was it Mary said in one their conversations? Something about gifted children and control. It was becoming clearer.

'OK, I think I understand – a little,' he added hastily before she could tell him that it was impossible for anyone of his advance age to understand anything - at all - ever.

'Come on. I'll tell your mother that you are going to stay for a few days to sort yourself out. Now do you want to make the tea or wash the car? I'd suggest the tea, 'cause what's stuck on the car can only be found in the countryside.'

'Thanks, Tim.' He noted that she dropped the 'uncle'. Good sign or bad?

8

The cold morning air bounced around Mary's lungs as she went out to the car. She put her notepads and bag in the car then went back for another jumper. When she came out again, she could hear the banging bass beat of music coming from the direction of Tim's cottage. It was almost a quarter of a mile away – what on earth was going on? Could it be Tim? It was not likely to be burglars trying out the equipment – that had to be a quieter occupation. Back inside she dialed Tim's work number. If he wasn't there, she'd assume it was his noise, but if he was ...

'Mary.' Tim sounded surprised when her call was put through.

'Tim, I'm really sorry to interrupt you, but I wanted a bit of advice.'

'Yeah?'

'Well, I'm not sure what to do. I can hear loud music coming from your cottage and well, I thought it odd. I ...'

Tim's voice relaxed. 'Don't worry. The noise is my 15 year old niece who surprised me on Sunday by using me as a bolt hole from home and school.'

Mary laughed, 'I'm glad I didn't rush up there demanding to know what was going on.'

'She's OK on her own and there's not much chance of her getting into trouble while she's there, but I am worried about just why she doesn't want to go home. I think it's school trouble. I could use your opinion.'

'As it happens, I am on my way into Hereford to start some research at the Records Office. Shall we have lunch or coffee or something ...'

'Great. There is a small bistro in the little lane behind the cathedral – 1 o'clock?'

With a map of the area around Rosemary Cottage, Mary followed the route the census taker walked in 1911. She was surprised to find that these were the most recent records available.

At her cottage, she found that in 1911 Edward and Mary Evans lived there and in 1901 they were also there, this time with their daughter Mary, who was 17. In 1891 there were two children – George who was 10 and Mary who was 7 at the time. How regal she thought. In 1881 Edward and Mary were already there, but George was then a few weeks old. Ten years before that, Charles and Alice Clifton and their daughter Mary were there.

Mary followed Rosemary Cottage back to 1861 when she realised that it was time to meet Tim. She returned the fiche films to the nice lady at the desk and said she'd be back after lunch. The archivist reserved a microfiche machine for her and wished her 'bon appétit'.

The bistro was packed when she got there and Tim was outside. They bought some filled baguettes and sat on a bench in the cathedral yard under a chestnut tree that looked as if it had been full grown when King John was on the throne.

'You look shattered.' She unfolded the wrapping on the bread. 'Is a visit from a teenager that exhausting?'

He managed a tired smile that returned his face for a second to one she knew. 'It's been a bit harrowing and I'm out of touch with teenagers. I'm not sure I got anything of any significance out of Jennifer, so I'm guessing.' He poured some still water into a plastic cup and handed it to her. 'I think that she might be having trouble with some of her teachers. I don't know how to approach it. It's been 20 years since I was in school and to be honest, I don't remember much.'

'Has she ever shown any reluctance about school before?'

He handed her a napkin. 'Not that I know of. She's always been very good at school - her brother Haydn is too. Haydn is in trouble all the time, but he's a clown and always trying to find ways to beat the system as it were. Jennifer was the quiet one.'

Mary tucked the napkin onto her lap. 'What makes you think it might be a teacher conflict?'

'Just that she kept referring to them as crap and horrible. Nothing else much I'm afraid. Examinations don't seem to be worrying her, but she doesn't want to go back.'

She folded up the paper around the baguette. 'Do you think it would help if I talked to her? I don't think she'll talk to me because, well I'm a teacher for one thing and for another she doesn't know me from Adam, but she might listen – for a few minutes anyway.'

Tim's face resumed some colour. 'Would you? I don't want to relinquish my responsibilities in all this, but I don't know what to do – the chances are that whatever I do will be wrong.'

Mary smiled. 'What are friends for? Maybe if I came over tonight for a few minutes, just so we can meet and then tomorrow I'll try to talk to her?'

Mary stared into census microfiche films until her eyes hurt and she began to feel queasy and gave up. At home, she laid a large sheet of paper on the kitchen table and wrote the dates of the censuses across the top, then the names of the people living there at the time. From their ages, she was able to calculate the years in which they were born. Some of them lived in the cottage for some years then vanished. But it seemed that husband and wife always disappeared in the same 10-year period.

She made a cup of coffee and looked at the results. It was interesting that there was a woman named Mary living in the cottage almost throughout the period from 1841 onwards. Many of the girl children were also named Mary. She had another look and noted that when the family names changed, the elder woman bore the same birth date as the child from earlier censuses. Could it be the same person? The same family? Was the cottage being handed from mother to daughter?

Tim wasn't sure how Jennifer would react to Mary, but when he told her she just shrugged, and returned to the television. Tim went back to the kitchen and leaned his head on the cupboard door; *I'm counting on you Mary. I won't be any good at this for much longer.*

He was relieved when he heard her knock on the back door. He lifted his eyes to the ceiling as he greeted her. She nodded and looked in the direction of the living room. 'Not going well?' she whispered. He shook his head but put his arm across her shoulders as he introduced her at the living room door.

Jennifer looked at them both with a look of disgust. Mary took an involuntary step away from Tim. 'Hello Jennifer, your uncle Tim has told me that you are visiting for a few days.'

'Yes, I wanted to see Tim's new house,' Jennifer replied. Mary noticed the omission of 'Uncle'.

Mary slid Tim a conspiratorial smile that said; this too is normal. They managed polite conversation for an hour and by the time she left Tim had invited Mary to have lunch with Jennifer with no opportunity for the girl to decline.

In the morning, Mary considered how to approach Jennifer. Then something Jennifer had said gave her an idea. It had to do with living history. Instead of waiting for lunch, she collected Jennifer earlier than agreed and they drove through the spring weather, up the A49 and into the Welsh Marshes. The broad fast road wandered through lumpy hills north of Ludlow over a narrow flood plain and bumpy railway crossing. A hillside of wild bluebells made them gasp from the depth of the colour and the leaves filled the hedges with new bright green. Past Craven Arms, they turned right towards the Acton Scott Historic Working Farm. Jennifer had overcome twenty minutes of initial shyness and now seemed relaxed and talkative. Mary relaxed a bit as well, but felt as if she were about to betray the trust she was only just forming with the girl.

A farm worker in 19th century costume led a huge shire horse towards them as they walked to the entrance from the car park. Feathers of silky hair plumed around its feet and its ears flicked to hear the farm sounds around them. The huge animal tossed its head and tiny bells on its harness jingled. The man said something to it and it nuzzled his shoulder. They stopped in front of Jennifer and he spoke again to the animal, which turned its huge head to her. She put up her hand and stroked the animal's face and ears. 'This here's Captain, an' he likes you I think.' The man brushed the big horse's neck. ''Cause you knows how to pet him.' Jennifer looked puzzled. 'You see, to a horse a pat is like a blow, but a stroke is like his mother's tongue.'

'He's so beautiful.' Jennifer was captivated.

'We're just going out to do some drillin' and you can see us in that field there in about half an hour if you wants to.' They did and watched as man and animal worked together with the practice of hundreds of years, pulling a high-wheeled drill that put rows of tiny seeds into the fine tilth.

In the small barnyard they walked around the aromatic mound of straw and manure and laughed at the small flock of chickens and two ducks that chattered and scratched in the pile. The stalls where Captain and his mate Pat were housed at night had their names in plaques hanging from the rafters and were clean and spread with fresh straw. Nearby, a deep grunting and banging caught their attention. Jennifer looked over the low wall and jumped in alarm just as a huge russet coloured snout and head with enormous ears appeared over the top. They both laughed to cover up their shock.

'That gave me a fright.' Mary's laugh was ragged. 'But what a wonderful creature. The guide says they're Tamworth pigs.'

Jennifer looked over the wall of the next pen with some trepidation, but then shouted in delight. 'Oh do come and look at this.' There was another Tamworth lying in the straw with eight wiggling piglets pushing and grunting to be fed.

Behind them a blacksmith hammered a shoe and fitted it with smoke and steam to another shire horse who they assumed must be Pat. In a small shed a wheelwright was shaving wooden spokes for a wagon wheel. Leaving the yard to look for the cattle, they were overtaken by a group of children in Victorian dress who rushed past. Somewhere behind came a class teacher, also in costume calling them to stay together. The giggling group disappeared and Mary and Jennifer watched butter making, bread making and leaned on a wooden fence to see the vegetable garden being planted.

A woman was taking sturdy little plants out of a wooden frame on top of huge mound. 'This is a hot frame,' she explained to Jennifer. 'The lid is made out of sash windows and it's heated by the decomposition of the manure underneath. Everything has its uses.' She lifted out another tray. 'We use it to start these early plants. Now they're hardened off and are being transplanted to the garden.'

'What are they?' Jennifer pointed to the feathery plants.

'Tomato plants. Everything that we produce here goes to the café.'

'Really?' Mary and Jennifer looked at each other.

The café was in the old school house and its fresh bread with farm-made butter and homemade soup was, Jennifer confessed, the best ever, ever, ever.

'I sense, then,' Mary passed the butter back to Jennifer, 'that you are feeling a bit better than you did yesterday.'

'Yeah well, I thought it was going to be very boring at Uncle Tim's, but this is a great place.' It did not escape Mary's notice that the word 'uncle' had slid back into place.

'I haven't been here before either and I have to admit that it is incredible. Can you imagine how much hard work farming was a hundred and more years ago?'

'Yes, but those beautiful animals. Did you see those geese travelling around in a tidy little group like that? And the pigs! They were wonderful.' Jennifer was sparkling.

Mary did not have the heart to remind Jennifer that the purpose of all those wonderful animals was to provide fodder for the plates of the owners and workers. But Jennifer surprised her.

'I'm a vegetarian you know. I couldn't bear to eat them, but I know that they aren't here – well maybe these are, but most aren't – just for decoration, and if people didn't eat meat, they wouldn't be here at all.'

'That's a very shrewd observation, Jennifer. Your uncle Tim said you are a bright girl.' She had to make a start somewhere, so she added, 'Do you do well at school?'

Jennifer's face clouded. 'I hate school.' She twirled her spoon in her soup. 'I didn't always, but I do now.'

'Can you talk about it?' There was no reply, so Mary rushed on, willing Jennifer not to shut her out for a few more seconds. 'I used to be a teacher, you see.' Jennifer's face blackened with betrayal, but Mary hurried on. 'I left teaching because I didn't like what some teachers were doing to bright young people like you.'

9

Jennifer's face was frozen in hostility and Mary knew she had found the source of the problem. 'I saw they weren't being fair. Instead of helping pupils to do well, they seemed determined to stop them excelling, by embarrassing them in front of their friends, by not encouraging them. It was wrong.'

Jennifer put down her spoon and straightened it beside her bowl. She spoke in a whisper. 'Is that why you left?'

'That was the cause, but not the reason. I was forced to leave because I did the unthinkable: I complained to the Headmaster about the colleague I saw bullying bright pupils.' Her voice close to collapsing; she clenched her hands together in her lap. 'You see, all teachers have to realise that many times in our careers, we will have to teach pupils who are brighter than we are. That doesn't mean pupils who know more than we do, but who can pick up and learn faster than we realize. My colleague hadn't grasped that fact and he was turning these wonderful young people off learning, maybe forever. Some of them will never enter a place of learning again. And that is a teacher's greatest failing.' Mary dug in her pocket for a tissue. 'But because of the way schools work I was forced to leave.'

'But that's not fair.' Jennifer looked like one large mark of indignation.

'No it wasn't fair, but things get in the way of what is right.'

'But – if he was wrong....'

Mary wiped her nose. 'My other colleagues didn't think I should accuse someone of being a bad teacher, even though everybody knew he was. They felt they owed him their loyalty I guess. I felt that the young people he was turning off school and learning were more important. But there are things like a man's livelihood and pension to consider, and not upsetting the other staff or causing a rift in the staff room that come into it.'

'What happened to him?'

'Well he's still there as far as I know and I'm not.'

'But that's wrong!'

'Yes, it is.' Mary felt as if she faced an important corner; one with forgiveness on the other side. 'But what's important now, is what I might be able to do for you. Am I right? You've had a problem like this haven't you?'

Jennifer sighed as if a huge confession was about to be released at last. 'It's my history teacher. I love history, but he's such a horrible git that I hate it. Today, I realise that I really do love it. Now I don't know what to do. I can't go back to his classes.'

'What sort of things does he do?'

Jennifer's indignity returned. 'Well, if I make a mistake he makes a big deal about it. So I don't offer any answers, but then he asks me in front of everyone. If I get it right, he makes a big deal about that – like I've never had a right answer before.' She stirred her tea, banging the sides of the cup with the spoon. 'He reads my assignments out loud to everyone else and makes fun of them. He always marks me down even when the work is good. I just don't want to try anymore and so I told him just how horrible I thought he was on Friday. He said he would have me excluded.'

'What a horrible man. Have you talked to your parents about it?'

'Oh yeah. They went to see him once. He said I was just wasting time and needed to try harder. And then he just got worse.'

Mary let Jennifer talk. This was not the time to offer solutions and by the time they got home Jennifer had let it all out. Tim opened the door, but before he could say hello, she bubbled with details about the farm. Tim looked at her in amazement.

Mary declined to stay for supper but thanked Jennifer for a lovely day and suggested that she come to Rosemary Cottage some time tomorrow. Tim looked like he was desperate to know what had happened. So she smiled and tried to nod to reassure him as she said good night.

In the morning, Mary grabbed the bedroom curtains and threw them open like she was taking a bow from a huge stage. The view from her window hadn't been rolled up like a roller blind during the night; it was still wondrous, the horizon hill floated above a scythe of low clouds. In the garden, Phil's concentric circles still showed on the grass and the herb bed looked fresh from the weeding he'd started.

As she dressed, a list of things to do today began to form: check that Phil hasn't pulled out the herbs and left the weeds, check the oil tank to see if the delivery had come and maybe chop some more wood – it could still get cold, check the grocery situation, and on and on.

Downstairs, she put a pair of sheets and some pillowcases into the washing machine and while it thrashed away in its simplistic cycle, she heaped jam from Acton Scott shop on a piece of toast. She made an attempt to tidy the kitchen with a little left over enthusiasm and when the washing machine had stopped, jumbled the laundry into a basket and took it to the washing line. The rain would hold off for a few hours.

As she was hanging up the last pillowcase, she heard a tractor stop at her front gate and looked up to see Harry dismounting from the dirty cab. 'Hello,' she called.

His grin preceded him over the gravel. 'Just thought I'd let you know that them kittens will be ready next week, if you still wants 'em.'

'Oh yes I do want them. Shall I come over and collect them?'

'If you wants to.' He looked as if he wanted something else, but was too uncomfortable to ask. There was a short silence but he seemed reluctant to leave.

'Would you like some coffee?' Perhaps it would loosen his shyness.

Harry hesitated a moment. 'Nay, thanks – got sheep to move.'

What a strange man. Are they all like that around here?

After lunch, Mary settled herself into a soft library chair with a copy of Mansfield Park and lost herself in the plot somewhere about page 4. She was startled when at page 121, there was a knock at the back door. It was Jennifer, who called as she came in, 'It's starting to rain. Do you want to bring your laundry in?'

'Oh heck.' They pulled everything into a large basket, pegs and all and got it into the kitchen without either of them getting very wet.

'Thank you Jennifer. When I have my head in a book, I lose all track of time. In fact...' She looked at the clock. 'No wonder I'm gasping. Can I make you some tea or coffee?'

'Oh yes, tea please. I just came by to say thank you for taking me to the farm yesterday. I really enjoyed it.'

'Weren't those horses wonderful?' Mary still knew how to get straight to the heart.

Jennifer softened. 'Wonderful.' Her sigh sounded sad and there was a silence. It trailed on for another minute and was broken by the kettle boiling.

'Can you hand me that tea pot behind you – the blue one on the shelf – and a cup for yourself?' *Take the initiative Mary.* 'Have you been thinking about your problem teacher?'

'Yeah.'

'And?' She filled the teapot and made some instant coffee for herself.

'I know what my teacher is trying to do – it's all about power isn't it?' Jennifer slumped back in the chair. 'But I don't know what to do about it. I won't go back if I have to go to his classes.'

'Well, I've been thinking about your problem and I have a suggestion.' Mary looked into the bread bin. 'It's very unprofessional of me, but since I've given up on the lot of them, maybe there's no harm.' She cut two slices of fruitcake on a board and put it on the table. 'But you'll need to talk it over with your parents.'

Jennifer took a piece of cake and looked alarmed. Mary sat down. 'Because you're under 16, you can only make these kinds of decisions with the approval of your parents. But here it is: if you are unhappy with your history teacher, and it's evident you are, I doubt you will get the GCSE grade you're capable of. However, I presume you have been entered for the exam and your coursework sent off?' Jennifer nodded. 'So...' She poured the tea and pushed the cup to Jennifer. 'You could suggest that you'd be willing to finish the course – perhaps even put in some extra work or take some outside tutoring, to get a good grade...' Jennifer looked horrified. '... *If* you could be excused from going to his classes again. The alternative as I see it is that you are ready to refuse to go back to school at all or take any of the examinations.' Jennifer stared at her.

'Do you mean that I could go back to school as normal, but just not do any more history with Mr Hinks, and still take the exam?'

'It should be possible, but you and your parents would need to negotiate that with your headmaster. He'll probably insist that you continue to attend history, but – and this is just between you and me - if you refused to attend school at all, the potential for good grades in all your other subjects – and I suspect that you are in line for some As and A*s - would be lost to your headmaster and he would see his total results reduced. It'd make a good bargaining position I think. And if you have had some grades on your coursework that you are unhappy with, you can have them re-marked by another examiner if you felt they deserved better. You could insist on that too as part of the bargain.'

'Wow!'

'I can't help you very much with your parents, but perhaps Tim can.' She did not call him 'uncle' either. 'But if they would like to talk to me, I'll be glad to do what I can.'

She refilled Jennifer's cup and cut some more cake. 'But look, enough of that. Come and see what Tim and I found in my wall.' Jennifer was mesmerised. The stars were back in her eyes. Mary hadn't seen that kind of keenness in a young person for a long time – in school or out of it.

The crooked post box hung on the gate. Mary said goodbye to Jennifer and lifted its rickety flap. The local paper, a leaflet from the local dairy offering huge boxes of broken biscuits at reduced prices, the oil bill, a flyer from a septic tank emptying company and a letter from her solicitor.

She braced herself for the fact that Robert was indeed going to re-negotiate their agreement. What court in the land would force him to maintain an agreement he could not afford?

She slit open the letter. There were no surprises. Robert's case was that he had not been able to secure funds to cover 50% of the company and had been paying from the operating funds. He proposed to pay half the annuity for the present while he continued to find a way to borrow what was required. Joanne suggested that Mary think about the offer and discuss it at a suitable time, etc. etc. Mary took off her reading glasses and leaned against the washing machine. Anger was again threatening to throw her out of control. She gripped the machine. Bitterness stung the back of her eyes. Her mind became grey; with sparks of anger so intense they hurt her eyelids.

The bastard would find a way to run her life until the end of his days. He'd done so every day since she met him.

She screwed up Joanne's letter in her fist, one finger at a time. Then she screwed her courage into a ball, one point at a time. She did not want to see him or speak to him – this was a problem for him to sort out, not for her. She did not have to agree to the first thing he put in front of her. Robert thought he could write the script as he always did. How dare he? He owed her this much at the very least. He rejected her and now he wanted to deny her even what they had agreed upon. Her small mound of courage was swamped by a huge wave of anger. The bastard! He was not going to win this time. There had to be a way to get what was hers by right. In fact, if there was a way to get more than her share from now on, she'd damn well have it and not apologise or suffer one tiny morsel of guilt.

She threw the screwed up letter at the recycling box.

10

Jennifer was unusually quiet when Tim got home. He prepared their tea while she set the table. As they sat down, he could stand it no longer.

'Everything all right?

There was a minute of silence as she dipped a chip into her red sauce. 'I've been thinking.' He knew better than to interrupt so he waited.

'I don't want to go back to classes with Mr Hinks – ever.' Tim breathed in to speak, but she rushed on. 'I'll take the exam and all the others, but I won't go back to his lessons.'

'Can you do that?'

'Mary says I can – if I get Mum and Dad to agree and because we're so near the end of the course, it shouldn't be a problem. She even suggested that I could get my assignments re-marked because he has been such a bastard in not giving me the grades I should have had.'

Tim did not respond to the swearing. 'Will your Mum and Dad agree?'

'They don't have a choice – either they help me to get old man Francis – he's the head teacher – to agree or I'll refuse to go back at all or sit any of the exams. Simple.'

'But what happens once you've finished with old – er – Mr Francis? Don't you need him for a reference to college or something?'

'Oh sure, but I'm in line for several A's and A*s in my other subjects and if he wants to have those on his "league table", then he'll just have to be nice to me won't he? So,' she continued, 'I've just got to get Mum and Dad to visit Mr Francis and get me a bit of tutoring in history for a few days. I've got to ace history if I'm going to take it at A level.'

'Looks like you've got it all sorted out then,' Tim felt genuine admiration and relief. Good old Mary.

'Except for Mum and Dad. Tim...' She turned on the charm, 'Could you have a word with them first – just to soften them up a bit. You know what Mum's like and well, I know I've got to be firm, but with her it's not that easy.'

'Of course I will.'

'What's this?' whispered Jennifer. The archivist laid the Parish Register on a foam book form and with great care pushed it in front of Jennifer and Mary.

'It is the register of marriages for the parish that Rosemary Cottage is in. I've traced the families living in the Cottage between 1841 and 1911 and I have a theory that they were in fact one family.'

'Why?'

'Well, see here – these are the notes I took from the census records the last time I was here. In 1841 George Clifton and his wife Mary lived there with their son Charles who was born about 1825. Then in 1851, the same family people but 10 years older; 1861 Charles Clifton and his wife Alice lived there and had a daughter Mary who was 6 years old; same family in 1871, but by 1881 a Mary Evans and her husband Edward lived there with their baby. They were still there in 1891...'

'So what's so ...'

Mary interrupted, 'Well I think that Mary Evans is Mary, daughter of Charles and Alice Clifton. If we can find a record of her marriage we can prove the name change. That might indicate that the cottage was being passed down the family - but it was handed down to eldest daughter instead of eldest son.'

Jennifer crackled with excitement. 'So if it is the same Mary and she was born when...?'

Mary looked at her notes, 'About 1855.'

'That means she would have been married about 1875.' She turned the thick pages of the heavy book to 1875 and they began to search. They did not find Mary Clifton's marriage until 1880, but there she was 'daughter of Charles and Alice, married Edward Evans on January 2, 1880'. Jennifer bounced on her chair with the discovery. 'Can we find out more about them, from earlier registers? I mean the family might be quite old and maybe they lived there for a long time.'

'You may be right.'

For several hours they went back in time, following the births, deaths and marriages of a succession of family names. They were surprised to find that the eldest daughter always named Mary, that the families were small – two or three children at most. They were more surprised to find that Charles Clifton's mother Mary had been recorded as a bastard child at the time of her baptism in 1790. And that he had two sisters named Mary and Jane who had both died as very young children. That, they decided could be the reason why the cottage passed to him and not to a daughter named Mary. The records drew them further and further back in time.

On the way home, Jennifer was still bouncing with excitement. 'I wish we knew what they were like – I mean what they looked like, and wouldn't it be great to see what they wore? Did they wear underwear in those days?'

Mary laughed. 'We can find that out too. There will be historical records of dress and fashion in the public library I'm sure. But I doubt that we can ever find out what they looked like, unless we could find a direct descendent perhaps.'

'Do you think that there are any still living here? Why did the last owners leave Rosemary Cottage? Were they part of the family too?'

'I don't know. Since we don't have access to the census records after 1911, it's hard to tell. The birth records are kept nationally since 1837 or so and you need to know who you are looking for to trace them according to the archivist.' Mary turned off the main road towards Tim's cottage and Rosemary Cottage.

'But what about the package you found in your wall? We're no nearer finding out about who they were, are we?' She took out the notes she had made. 'Mary!' she screamed.

Tim felt tired when he got home and was reading Jennifer's note on the kitchen table when her heard Mary's car on the drive. Jennifer was still excited and bounded out of the car eager to tell him what they found. Mary smiled at the display of enthusiasm but excused herself from staying.

Jennifer continued to bubble while Tim started supper. 'We found that there had always been a woman named Mary living at Rosemary Cottage, except for around 1860 or 70, but the man who lived there had had a sister named Mary – and one named Jane, but they had both died in 1830. So we decided to look back down the family and see if we could follow the Marys. Sure enough there was always a Mary in the family – always the eldest girl.'

Tim tried to keep up as he turned some vegetable burgers over under the grill.

'We couldn't tell if they all lived in Rosemary Cottage because it didn't always say where they lived, but here and there it did and it was always Rosemary Cottage. Isn't that fantastic? We got back to a birth of a Mary in 1679.'

Tim stirred the chips from the oven and put them back for a few minutes. He handed Jennifer the plates and without being able to interrupt the flow, indicated with hand signals for her to set places on the little kitchen table.

'Then on the way home, we made the most amazing discovery. I found that this Mary's father, William Fletcher - we don't know where he lived - had two older sisters and you'll never guess what they were named.' She paused for dramatic effect, but not long enough for him to make even an uneducated guess. 'They were baptised in the same year, so maybe they were twins. They were called Mary and Rose. What do you think of that?'

This time there was enough time for him to reply. 'That is pretty impressive stuff. Do you think that that could be the origin of the name for the cottage?'

'I'd say it was incontravutable evidence!'

Tim didn't have the heart to correct her. 'What year were they baptised?' He drained the peas and put them onto a mat on the table.

'1650,' she declared without referring to her notes. 'Interestingly, their parents, another William Fletcher and Joan were married only a few months before the girls were born or baptised at least.'

'I suppose it happened. What happened to the girls?'

This time she did have to look at the sheet. 'Well, they died. I copied it from the registers because it sounded funny. They both died in 1670 but it was added on the side of the register only with the year – like they'd forgotten it or something. All the others deaths in the registers, say that the person was buried, but Rose and Mary are different, it says that they were 'interred'. Do you know what that means?'

'You're the historian. I am afraid I have no idea. What did the people at the Records Office say about it?' He put burgers and fries on their plates.

'It was closing time by then and we had to pack up. Mary will have to ask when she goes back.'

Tim did not miss the phrasing of the reply. 'Does this mean that you won't be going with her?'

Mary was not prepared for what met her when she got home.

Things were innocent enough in the kitchen as she dropped her papers and bag on the kitchen dresser and took off her shoes. A fly looped erratically around the mugs on her open shelves bouncing suicidally off the pretty china. She opened the door again and it made its random way out, followed by another that appeared from somewhere.

In the living room there were several more, but when she opened the library, foaming mounds of them swirled around the little room. The air inside was dark and the sound of them in their thousands made her heart stop. In a single gasp, she slammed and latched the door in the face of the advancing horde and braced it with her back. With her eyes and mouth shut tight she slapped at her hair with her hands. The low humming droned on behind her. Her skin crawled and she pulled her shirt out of her waistband, shaking the fabric in panic. She opened her eyes to slits. A few escaped flies bounced stupidly against the window glass.

Mary backed into the living room expecting to see insects flowing out underneath the library door like smoke but there was only a dark humming and a dull smack as insects struck the wood. Where on earth does one find fly killer at 6 p.m. on a Friday night? Tim, who would rescue her from the jaws of death if she asked wouldn't know what fly killer was. As far a she knew they didn't have flies in London. It had to be Harry. The slip of paper with his number was still on her desk.

Harry arrived in minutes with assorted aerosol cans of insect killer. He opened the library door enough to get his arm through the crack and waved the spray into the room. Then followed the few escaping into the living room, with several short blasts.

He and Mary fled outside to wait for the poison to do its worst. 'What on earth are they? Where did they come from?' Mary coughed as the spray caught in the back of her throat.

'Dunno,' he drawled. 'I'll have a look at 'em when 'er dead.'

Mary coughed again.

When they listened at the library door again the humming behind was subdued. Harry opened it and put on the light. They looked around in amazement. A few flies were drunkenly crashing into the windowpanes and walls, but the floor and furniture was littered with thousands of still or spinning insect carcasses. Mary with a tissue jammed over her mouth and nose, mumbled through it, 'There must be millions of them. How did they get here?'

Harry brushed a path with his boot and picked up a body from the little table. 'Looks like what we calls a cluster fly.'

'A what?' Mary's muffled voice asked behind him. He dropped the little body back onto the floor.

'Cluster flies. They overwinters in lofts and such. Then they all comes out at once and summat' makes 'em all move together. Y' can see 'em in bunches on the side of building's like.'

He shuffled a path to the fireplace and looked up the chimney. 'Most like they came down the chimney from the attic or summat.' He shook the aerosol can and looked up the stairs. 'Wan' me t' check the res' of the house?'

Mary nodded and coughed again. She could hear him making his way from room to room, opening doors and making brief spraying blasts, then down the stairs and again in the library before he shut the door once more. 'Jus' a few up there, but I giv'em a blast just t' be sure.'

He lingered a moment or two. 'Thanks so much.' Mary sneezed. 'I don't own an insect spray.'

'Well, y' needs a few around a farm, like. D'y' want me t' stay an' be sure?'

Mary was touched. 'No, thanks all the same Harry. I'll just give that stuff a few more minutes to work and then I'll hoover up the carnage.'

'Right y'are.' He nodded with a flat smile as he headed for the door. 'Leave y' a can shall I?'

Late on Sunday afternoon, Tim found Mary swinging in a striped hammock strung between two large fruit trees - a newspaper across her knees and big glasses on her nose, toes in the grass. The May sunshine was strong and hot where it was direct. Bees and flies hummed hysterically in the few flowers that were now open. Tiny white star-like flowers, vivid dandelions, majestic white plates and vivid red-stemmed things he'd seen before bloomed at the hedge. There was a small table beside her on which stood a tall jug, an open book upside down and a large straw hat with a huge fabric flower on it. She was wearing a loose flowered skirt and short sleeved top. It looked like the cover of Country Living.

Mary looked over her glasses and the newspaper. 'Bring a glass for yourself from the kitchen and have some lemonade,' she called in greeting.

He also dragged a folded lawn chair out with him and set it up beside the little table. 'Now this *is* civilised.' He filled the glasses. He was wearing a dark t-shirt and khaki shorts, with bare feet in brown loafers. *He'd look good in a paper bag,* thought Mary.

He stretched out his long legs and leaned back in the chair. 'I am being very brave showing you my white legs,' he confessed. 'I'm hoping a few early rays might just do some good.'

'Then you should be out in the sun and not here in the shade from all these trees.'

'Well...' He turned his face to the vivid sky and scalding sun, '... maybe a bit at a time then.'

She laughed into her lemonade. 'Have you spoken to Jennifer since she got back? It was good of her to stop in yesterday before she left.'

'I called this morning. Ann seems to be a bit shaken by it all and I can just about imagine the furore when Jennifer got home. But Ann promised to listen and Peter promised to make her listen. So Jennifer will have her say. It's a bit too early to know if they will agree, but, it looks like Jennifer has it all figured out – thanks to you.'

'Well, I hope for her sake it all works out. She is a very clever girl and she deserves better. It's amazing how many teachers never accept that they might have to teach someone who's brighter than they are.'

'I've never thought of that.'

'A lot of teachers haven't either.'

Tim looked down into his glass. 'Jennifer told me why you left teaching.' It was quiet for a few seconds between them. 'I'm sorry.'

Mary could feel her nose filling up with tension – she willed herself not to cry. 'It's still a very sore wound. But...' She plunged on, 'Harold, my headmaster wouldn't listen when I tried to make an informal complaint about Don Johnson, the teacher who was bullying the pupils. He didn't want the job of counselling or disciplining Don, or the re-training and support that he might have to give him. It was all too much for him to take on. So he reported the whole affair to the Education Department at the Local Authority and all of a sudden it was all very formal and I was the one on the carpet.' She drew a shaky breath. Tim's face showed no emotion, only the intensity of listening. 'They demanded chapter and verse of course, which is only right. But when I gave it to them, no one would corroborate anything I had to say.'

'But why, for heaven's sake. The others will have seen what he did.'

'Oh they did – pupils and staff too. But the pupils weren't ready to speak out because they knew Don would bully them all the more and he'd make a disciplinary issue out of if they persisted.' She took off her glasses and wiped them on her sleeve. 'Don was well liked in the staff room. When he's in a good mood, there are few more fun or entertaining than he is. They didn't want to upset things. And,' she put the glasses on the table, 'once I'd broken the rules, by speaking out, I was the outcast, not him. It was him or me and it soon began to look like I was on my own.'

'But the Head, didn't he know about Don's ... '

Mary snorted. 'Oh yes, he knew. That's one reason why he didn't want to deal with it himself – he'd have to admit that he'd known for some time and hadn't done anything about it.'

'What happened then?

'The LEA wrote to me to say that it had no other evidence of the allegations I was making, but that if I wanted to take the matter further, I should seek advice from my Headteacher!'

'Good grief.'

'Exactly. I was so angry when I got the letter that I walked into Harold's office and demanded to know why he had supported Don and not me when he knew damn well what was going on.' Her voice caught but she struggled on. 'He said that as far as he was concerned, I'd made the whole thing up and that I should consider my position in the school because he intended to watch me from then on.'

'Bastard.'

'That's pretty much what I called him before I left.' Her smile was weak. 'What a power trip we teachers all live on! Sad isn't it?'

Tim sat in silence for a moment, and then he smiled bleakly at the lemonade in his hands. 'Not just in the classroom I think.'

11

'That was heartfelt. Things at work difficult?'

Tim leaned his elbows on his knees and looked down the garden. 'I don't know where to start. I'm not sure that anything is wrong. I just get the feeling that something isn't right.' He leaned back again. 'Nothing makes sense.'

'For instance?'

'Well...' He paused again. *Come on boy, put it into words – sort it out.* 'James – has – is – still being aggressive. I mean I'm not some kid in his first job.'

'What's he done?'

'Well, he's called me into his office or had a go at me a couple of times for petty little things – like being 10 minutes late, and...' He was getting control of his thoughts now, '...then he ranted when I left early to check on Jennifer. All he had to do was ask Susan where I was. I'd told her.'

There was another pause then Tim went on. 'It doesn't sound like much. I suppose each time it isn't, but to be honest, I feel like I'm losing his confidence and...' He looked at his knuckles, '.... well my own I guess.'

'The man sounds like a bully.'

'Pardon?'

Mary folded her legs up onto the hammock and pulled her skirt down over them. 'It's power again – like we were talking about. By now I'm an expert – it's some people's only way of keeping power to themselves – of staying in control.'

'I can't imagine James worrying about losing control. He has a natural powerful personality.'

'Is he like this with anyone else?'

'I think everyone in the company is eligible – and I've heard of him having a go at a few other people. His secretary seems to be the only one who escapes.'

He turned his lemonade glass around on the little table. 'I'm beginning to wonder if I made the right decision to take the job. It's not the kind of work I've done in the past, but it looked like a nice chance to do some management work and still stay in touch with the mud, the vertigo and the computer screens.' He rubbed some invisible dirt off the top of his shoe. 'Maybe it's just that he's a natural prat that I have to learn to live with.'

'Maybe that's right. I mean if you can visualise him as a prat – you can gain some perspective again. What else do you know about him?'

'Not a great deal. He's not given to small talk, but I gather from the office gossip that he's married, been at Conmac for years.'

'So he's normal in some respects then.'

Tim smiled and she saw his face relax. 'I couldn't possibly guess.'

'I wonder why he's trying to crack your confidence.'

Tim leaned back with hands behind his head and stared into the middle distance. 'He's decided he doesn't like me for some reason? Or maybe he doesn't like the way I work?' Tim snorted. 'Sounds a bit pathetic, doesn't it?' He took a deep breath. 'I mean here I am, 38 years old, a professional engineer, a head of a department in charge of I don't know how many millions of pounds and my boss is turning me into a quivering wreck!' He straightened up. 'I think I'm out on site visits all day tomorrow. Avoidance is still a legitimate tactic isn't it?'

Mary laughed. 'Of course it is. Now look, I make a fantastic caesar salad and I put a pudding in the bottom oven of the Rayburn a few hours ago – I am determined to learn how to cook in that thing – and if you are brave enough to stay for supper, it means taking one of three chances.' She counted them on her fingers. 'Either the pudding will be only warmed, in which case we will have to run it through the microwave; it will be burned, in which case there will be dark smoke coming out of the chimney any minute and we will need to see what falls out of the freezer; or heaven knows it might be just right. Sounds like the three bears doesn't it?'

'I promise that if I see clouds of black smoke rising from your chimney, not to ask what's for dinner!'

'And you have to promise to call me tomorrow and let me know if you've been able to avoid James successfully! Now help me out of this hammock.'

Tim left his last site visit on Monday later than he planned and got home much later than usual due to heavy traffic on a narrow section of the A49 past Leominster.

Once he got home, he listened to his telephone messages as he undressed in the bedroom. Jennifer called to say that she, Ann and Peter were meeting with the Headmaster later in the afternoon and she would let him know what had happened. His mother called to say the same thing and there was a wrong number. He deleted the lot and throwing his clothes down the stairs made his way naked to the shower in the extension. He felt like he needed a large bottle of wine, or maybe two and he knew where he could relax.

12

Just after 8:00 Mary opened her back door to see Tim leaning on the doorframe, wearing a large denim shirt and slim jeans, a broad smile and holding a large box of books (in case there's anything you might like, he said) out of which stuck a bottle of wine. Her smile matched his. 'Let me guess, you had a better day today.'

He tossed his denim jacket on the arm of her settee and leaned back. 'I did and I know why.' She lifted an eyebrow in question. 'I was out on site all day, in the dust, with the machinery and the sun shone and I loved every minute of it.' She could only laugh at him, his enthusiasm and his delight in what he did. They opened the first bottle of wine and by the time they finished the second bottle, they were both laughing a lot. Tim had a flush of success around him that made Mary see how competent he must be and she realised how much she missed the professional atmosphere.

They laughed as though they hadn't done so in years. Which was probably true.

Tim's alarm went off minutes after he got into bed. Or so it seemed. The red digital display had to be wrong. But even after he'd put his glasses on the right way up it still said 6:45 a.m. He presumed it was a.m. He sat up one vertebra at a time; his brains felt loose in his head. Two plus bottles of wine on a Monday evening – how stupid could you get. He wasn't an adolescent and he'd been drunk enough times in his life to know when he should have quit. He wanted to chuckle, but it hurt.

He showered, dressed and put some bread in the toaster without realising he'd done it and although the toast had no taste, he got to the back door on time and in control of all his clothes. He looked at the empty drive in front of his house without comprehending what was wrong. It came back to him in pieces.

His car was still parked at Mary's. He must have been in worse shape than he realised. God, how much of an idiot had he made of himself? He looked at his watch and realised with a jolt, that unless he pulled himself together he was going to be late and he didn't want to give James anything else to shout at him about. He ran down the lane, arriving at the gate out of breath with his head pounding in time with his bashing heart.

Where the hell were his keys? Bloody hell, had he left them on the counter or at Mary's? He didn't want to wake her up if she was in the same state he was. There was a lumpy envelope on the windscreen with his name on it. Inside were his keys - good old Mary. He arrived at work, only a minute past the hour.

In mid morning, as Tim slid into the staff room to look for paracetamol, Andy Prince slid into James Racine's office. Andy was short and slight with untidy brown hair and a liking for yellow shirts and bright blue ties.

'Margaret said you wanted to see me – got a problem with your computer?'

'I've been looking at your file Andy. You have quite an impressive work history for someone your age; computer technician for a network this size.'

Andy smiled. 'Well, I do my best.'

James leaned over his pristine desk blotter. 'Except perhaps for those few weeks in America three years ago.' He paused while Andy's face tightened. Andy swallowed and straightened up as if to defend himself against odds not in his favour. 'I was on holiday.'

'Come on Andy. I've had some conversations yesterday with the police there and it seems that there are still one or two outstanding warrants with your name on them. Something to do with drugs...'

Andy said nothing and James leaned back in his large polished chair. The leather squeaked. 'I'm really not interested in what you do on your holidays Andy, but the local constabulary would be.' He patted a large brown envelope in front of him. 'However, your work here has been exceptional and we have no wish to lose you. So I am quite prepared to overlook these small matters and in fact, I have put all the details we have in this envelope, which I'll lodge with the Company's solicitors. There's no need for it ever to be opened, unless of course you wish it to be.' He paused.

'I think there's an *if* in all this.'

'Well, there is something that I would be grateful if you could look into for me.'

As he sat at his computer with a half finished design floating on it, Tim wondered if he should call Mary to see if she was all right. But he reminded himself that she was a grown up person too and didn't need him to check up on her hangovers. However, he would have liked to assure himself that <u>he</u> hadn't been too stupid. He didn't think so, but his recollections were somewhat hazy.

75

He slipped out at lunchtime, to buy his own paracetamol and discovered that his computer screen had gone down while he was away. He called Andy who arrived in a few minutes. 'What's up?' he asked sliding into Tim's chair, 'let me guess, no screen'.

'Andy, I told you that when I called.'

'Just trying to impress you with my colossal memory!' Andy attacked the keys with the speed of his experience. The screen snapped into life, but without any of the colours of Tim's usual applications. 'Mmmm,' muttered Andy 'looks like one of the screen drivers has come adrift.' He smashed a few more keys, and the screen reset itself. Andy got out of the chair. 'OK...' He grinned, '... log back in and we'll see how it looks.'

Tim resumed his seat, did as he was asked and the screen was again normal. He had to admit he was impressed. 'Thanks Andy. It's unnerving when it just disappears like that.' Andy touched his brow as he left. 'Anytime.' As he passed by the glass of James' office, he caught James' eye and gave a tiny nod.

Mary woke late and except for a very dry throat was none the worse for the three empty bottles that accused her from the counter top. She prepared her first coffee and while it was making loud noises, she padded out to the post box in her slippers. The only thing in it was another letter from her solicitor. She opened it on the way back to the house. All Joanne wanted was instruction. What was Mary going to say to Robert? What indeed? She knew what she'd like to say, but she made it a policy not to swear – at least in writing.

Still in slippers and dressing gown, she took her coffee out into the orchard. Fallen cherry blossoms covered the grass like snow. Mayflowers heaped the ends of the hawthorn branches and cow parsley swayed at the edge of the grass; its fragrance subtle and soft. A clump of wild garlic thrust delicate white globes above soft strap leaves. A few early foxgloves were open and there were bulging promises of more on the downy stems. Bluebells sparkled under the hazel trees and early wild rose buds fattened on elegant stems in the hedge.

She felt content. Life with Robert had been stable and between them they were very comfortable. But contentment? No. There was no excitement in their marriage unless you considered a week on a beach on the French coast exciting.

But this orchard was the most exciting place she could think of – it promised that tomorrow it would be different with more wonders. The hedges would reveal more flower treasures, tiny birds or colourful insects. If paradise was to be found on earth, this was a strong candidate. She stopped at the top and looked back to the house. She wanted to be here and she wanted to stay here. She did not want to give up any part of it, ever. Be damned if Robert was going to make her do so.

She waded back to the house through the flowering grass and brought a pad of paper and pen to the table at the back door. Her letter to Joanne was business like, but firm. She was not prepared to re-negotiate any agreement. How and where he got the funds to meet them was for him to decide.

In her heart she knew that she might have to compromise on the total amount that the agreement had been based upon and to accept reduced payments, but for now she would keep that to herself. In the meantime, she asked Joanne to get her a copy of the last published accounts and the last unpublished accounts of Robert's company. She wanted to know just how things had changed for him.

The evening was fine and warm. Tim put a pair of folding aluminium ladders over his shoulder and walked down the lane. He could hear that bird again; its beautiful sound rising and rising. There were more of those big white plates of flower, releasing a clean smell into the evening air. New soft grasses swished against each other and the laburnum was beginning to bloom over the hedge. He knew that one. Invisible insects rose to hum the flowers. Relaxation drifted up his body like a wave. *Please let it always be like this.*

Inside his thoughts a small ping made him pause; then he heard a rustle in the hedge. Perhaps the birds were nesting. Then he heard something hit the tarmac and saw a small object bounce into the grass. He stopped and in a few seconds, another came over the hedge. He saw it this time; it was a snail. As he watched it bounce off the hard surface another one followed it.

He leaned over Mary's gate. 'Is that you sending those poor creatures to their deaths on the public highway?'

'Oh Tim, you gave me a fright! I'm trying to get the slimy beggars off my hostas! Look what they've done!'

'But don't they just come back?' He closed the gate behind him.

'Oh, perhaps they do. I shall have to ask at the next garden club meeting. But what are you doing with ladders?'

'I've discovered that there is not a scrap of insulation in my loft and so I'm about to order some. Do you have any?'

'I have no idea.'

'If you don't, I can order some for you at the same time. I shall need to poke my head into your loft to find out.'

She laughed. 'By all means. I think you can get your head through a hole in the landing ceiling.'

He opened up the ladders and with a torch in his hand, disappeared head and shoulders into the darkness. 'Just as I thought – not a thing. You wonder how people bright enough to put in central heating, failed to understand that it was important to keep the heat in the house.' His muffled voice descended the steps. He shifted around on the steps, making them wobble. Mary grabbed the sides to steady them. 'Well, I'll be damned ...'

Mary caught the excitement in his voice. 'What?'

'Come up and have a look.' He reached down and helped her up the other side of the steps. When she got her head through the little hole, he could feel her breath on his face in the darkness and he whispered, 'Turn around and I'll show you.' The ladders wobbled again and he caught her hand to steady her. He shone the torch over her shoulder onto the roof slates beside a crooked timber. They focussed on a small dark patch. 'Bats!' he whispered still holding on to her. She gripped his arm in surprise. He could feel her hair touching his cheek.

'Bats? What are they doing here?'

'Roosting I guess. They like quiet dark places like this.' They watched the little creatures wiggling in their sleep swaying upside down from the purlins. One here and there would unwrap its wings and lift its head to look at the light.

'From the tone of your voice, you don't consider them to be vermin, then,' Mary whispered.

'Oh no! They're protected and can't be disturbed. You're very lucky to have them. They'll eat insects and stuff – but I don't think they eat snails. You don't use chemicals do you? '

'I might have if you hadn't said that.' Mary looked at the warm little cluster. 'They're so furry, like mice. '

He shone the torch on the floor of the loft. It was covered with black droppings. 'It looks like they have been roosting here for quite some time. Maybe even breeding.' He shone the torch back onto the bats that were beginning to move on the roost. 'I don't think I've ever seen them so close. Aren't they wonderful?'

Mary had to admit they were. They closed the loft hatch with great care.

Outside again, Tim laid the ladders down and rubbed his shoulder. Mary put some glasses on the table and opened a bottle.

'Forgive me, but if that's wine, I may just have to decline.'

'You poor thing – no it's not wine. It's non-alcoholic you'll be glad to know. I don't think I was as tipsy as you were. But then these things are relative after all.'

'Was I really a mess?'

'I wouldn't have said "mess" exactly. Nearly a mess yes, but a full mess, no. And funny with it. I haven't laughed so much in years.'

Now he was embarrassed. 'Sorry, I was probably being a complete adolescent.'

'Don't be silly. What are friends for?' She poured two very big glasses. 'Here you are.' She handed one to him. 'We need rehydrating. Now come and look at the orchard. It was spectacular this morning.'

In the gathering dusk, they walked under the ivory blooms. Now the apple blossoms were beginning to open, competing with the last of the cherry petals.

Suddenly, Tim put his arm across her shoulders, 'Stop a minute.' He whispered, bending to her level, and pointed into the trees. A silent movement caught her eye. 'It's the bats.'

They stood still in the dusk as the tiny animals swooped and flitted silently around them, through the branches and over the grass – grazing in the twilight - pointy wings unmistakable in the low light. Hardly daring to breathe with wonder, they watched the bats flicker above them and then move on to another feeding ground.

Tim had forgotten that his arm was still around her and was embarrassed when she turned in its arc, then startled when she put her arms around him in a brief hug. 'What a wonderful gift! Thank you.'

He breathed into her hair and replied with a quick clumsy embrace. 'What are friends for?' As he walked home he realised that no one had ever hugged him in friendship before.

13

Phil's keen this morning, thought Mary. He was early and got out the mower before Mary could say hello. *Must have something to do with the weather.* That was not altogether unreasonable. The sun was warm and there was a possibility of great heat later in the day. One could be forgiven for thinking that summer had arrived.

Mary intercepted him as he pushed it to the front lawn. 'I've been wondering if I should leave the back grass to grow long.' He narrowed his eyebrows in an unspoken question. 'We saw some bats flying there last night and it seems to me that since they eat insects, long grass might be beneficial. What do you think?'

'Who's "we"?'

'Tim Spencer and I. He lives in the next cottage up the lane. I think he was going to see if you could spare him a few hours. Has he called you yet?'

'Not yet.' It was almost a retort. 'Maybe he thinks he can manage on his own.'

'Oh, he's got lots to do up there. The place hasn't been looked after for years. Have you seen it?'

'No.'

Mary did not miss the change in Phil's voice. What is the matter with him? She ignored whatever message he was trying to give her. 'I'll remind him next time I see him. But you'll have to excuse me this morning. I'm off to the Records Office today. Do you think you could weed a bit of the vegetable plot if you have time? Lots of things are coming up now and I haven't any idea where they are among all the weeds.'

Phil did not comment, but pulled the rope on the mower and it sneezed into life.

The idea of family inheritance of Rosemary Cottage and Jennifer's observation of the girls who may have named it intrigued Mary. The girl at the Records Office desk, still wearing the nose stud, but today a grey blouse with her long grey skirt, recommended maps of Eaton manor and the area around.

She began with tithe maps of the 1840's and the cottage was there in its present shape. An enclosure map of 1821 indicated that it was outside the area to be affected by the Acts. There was no reference to Rosemary Cottage on a manor map of 1750. Perhaps the land had never been part of the manor and that would make it more difficult to trace. She seemed to be getting nowhere. She re-rolled the fine, sketched map and looked up to see the girl in the grey skirt bringing a ring binder with frayed corners to her table.

'This index might be useful. It has records of land sold by estates and general rent matters in the parish in the late 17th and early 18th centuries. Eaton Manor is listed so you might find what you are looking for there.' The nose stud winked in the fluorescent light.

The index provided brief descriptions of papers and maps in the archives and Mary located something that related to Eaton Manor before 1750. When it arrived, it was in the form of a narrow hardback book listing all the estate property. In fine penmanship were recorded the sizes of plots and fields and what might be a rateable value beside each. The book contained records for three years: 1685, 1701 and 1710. In each year, some plots of land had been sold and the names of the purchasers and the price paid were listed. Rosemary was not among them. But it seemed, from some pages at the front of the book, that there had been an earlier assessment and therefore another record book.

Mary inquired and soon several loose pages arrived. There was no cover or introductory pages to indicate their date, but she recognized the field names from the previous surveys. Then she found a loose note to say that a plot of pastureland, unnamed, had been transferred to Wm Fletcher – no value was recorded. No buildings were named but the land was described. None of the reference points were familiar, but Mary recorded the details in her notebook. There was no date on the transfer, but the name Fletcher rang a bell and she recalled that the vicar was called Fletcher and that Jennifer's discovery had involved someone called Fletcher. Maybe she was just confusing herself. Mary pulled out the family tree sheets that Jennifer had recorded.

From their work in the parish registers, she saw that Wm Fletcher Jr and his wife Alice had lived in the parish sometime between 1678 when they were married and one had to assume, if Jennifer's theory was correct, they were living at Rosemary Cottage, until 1700, when their daughter Mary should have taken over the property.

Mary stared at the estate papers and even went through them all again seeking some possible reference to Rosemary Cottage or a date, or even another reference to Wm Fletcher or Wm Fletcher Jr. But there was nothing to be found.

She leaned back in her chair and blew out a long breath. The man across the table looked up. 'No luck?' he inquired.

'No I am afraid not. So near and yet so far.'

He lifted the sand bags off the corners of his bumpy map and it rolled itself into a loose coil. 'It works that way some times.'

But Mary jumped up. Of course. There might be another map to go with these notes. The girl in the grey skirt tutted between her teeth and thumbed through a ragged card file index, the shiny stud winking on the side of her nose. 'I don't think there is.' She pursed her lips as she considered. 'But let me look. Well, there is this, but I don't think it's quite what you are looking for. It's a sketch map of that area from about 1670 or so and marks a place of execution. But it is of the area you want. Do you want to have a look?'

Mary unfolded the tiny map. The folded edges were beginning to part and the sketch was faint on the yellowing paper. There were few landmarks on the map, but she was able to identify the old manor house that had been the main building on the estate and the road that still ran past what remained of it. She traced the road towards the top of the map. A tree was sketched on one side and a small stream ran across the lane. A hill was marked; that could be the hill where Tim's cottage now was. Between stream and hill, in the little hollow where Rosemary Cottage might now stand, was a faintly sketched skull and what looked like a gallows. There were little sketches of men loading a hay wagon and cutting corn along one side.

The map bore a faint date of 1670. What had happened? The archivists recorded this sketch as a map of executions. Had there been executions there - by hanging? Hangings were public events. Why would one occur in the remote countryside?

With a hand that was close to trembling, she reached for the notes she had made on the land transferred to Wm Fletcher. The land was past a large yew tree that stood on the left side of the lane. It began where the land fell from the hill, and was contained by the lane until the watercourse crossed it. It followed the watercourse to the boundary of the field known as Cows Meadow and along the foot of the hill back to the lane. Mary traced the perimeter of Rosemary Cottage in her mind. The big yew tree was long gone, but the hill and stream were still there. Not only that, it fitted the little map in front of her.

As she stopped the car on Rosemary's gravel drive, Mary choked on an intake of breath. There was not a green shoot to be found in the vegetable plot. What on earth had Phil done to it? There was a note on her outside table held down by a broken plant pot.

'Couldn't find veg seedlings up yet. Weeded so you can see them when they do. P.' Mary looked at the forked earth. Nothing. He'd pulled up every living thing.

She opened the back door to the cottage full of anger and frustration and was surrounded by the hum of bees that flowed out around her. She dropped her papers and ran back into the garden batting at her clothes and hair. The bees swarmed into the orchard and reformed in an apple tree. She crept back to the house and yanked open the door to the kitchen sink cupboard for Harry's large tin of insect spray. With both hands on the can, elbows locked, she advanced through the kitchen to the dining room feeling like a character from James Bond film – ready to shoot at the slightest hint of movement. Blasting lone insects as she went, she reached the library door. The invasion of flies last week had come down the library chimney – this was the probable point of entry. She put her ear to the door. Silence. She opened the door and followed the can of spray into the room. Nothing. How did they get into the rest of the house if the door to the library was closed?

Mary slammed the door of the washing machine at the same moment there was a banging on her back door. It was Harry. In spite of the gathering heat of the morning, he was wearing a wax jacket and hat.

'I brung you summat'. Mary looked puzzled as he opened the jacket, reached into the long poacher's pocket and brought out a black and white kitten. 'Don' know if she were the one y'wanted, but she's healthy an' all'. He handed the mewing bundle over to Mary and reached back into the pocket. 'An' here's th' other.' He put a little tabby kitten on top of her sister in Mary's arms. 'Hope they's OK.'

Mary found words at last. 'They are lovely and yes, of course they'll be perfect. Thank you so much. I'd have come to collect them if ..... Aren't they sweet?'

'Guess so – cats been livin' in the barn mostly. Keep the mice down an stuff.' He saw the can of spray on the counter. 'Been usin' the fly killer?'

'Well, yes I have.' She stroked the squirming pair of kittens whose tiny needle-like claws clung in desperate terror to her jumper. 'There were bees in the house when I got home yesterday. I got most of them out before I had to resort to the spray. I was glad to have had it though.'

'They get in through the chimney again?'

'Well, no. The door to the library was closed. I haven't any idea how they got in.'

Harry shifted from one foot to the other. 'Well, I'd best be off – keep the tin, y' might need it again – never knows. Kittens'll need wormin'.' And he was gone.

'Thanks,' Mary called after him.

Tim concluded his Thursday morning staff meeting at the stroke of 8 o'clock and as he stacked up his papers, Bryn asked, 'Where's the old troll today?'

'If you mean James, I have no idea. I've haven't seen him for a few days.'

Susan wedged the last cup onto a tray. 'Margaret said something about site visits – some old places in west Wales somewhere.'

'What kind?' Tim stacked up his papers

'Possible renovations, stabilization, that sort of stuff.' Susan laid her notes on top of the coffee cups and picked up the tray.

Bryn opened the door for her. 'Ever notice that James always gets those beautiful old properties – I'd love to see just one.'

'Not true.' Derek spoke over Tim's shoulder, 'Howard's had a few, haven't you Howard ...' Howard was walking away and didn't appear to have heard.

'Well, it's new plans and quotations for me.' Tim sighed. Susan smiled up at him.

Andy was drumming his fingers on Tim's desk when Tim dropped his notes into the basket on his desk. 'Come on, come on,' Andy was saying as he waited for a programme to stop loading. The little door slid open with a quiet whir and he retrieved the shiny disk. 'That should do it.' He grinned at Tim as he poked the little door shut again. 'You won't notice any difference. Just a little maintenance to make things a bit more smooth.' He wiped Tim's seat with an imaginary cloth and spun it around. 'All set guv.'

Andy always made Tim smile. He appeared never to have a care in the world and loved what he did – from un-jamming printers to staying the night to run massive back up and archive programmes. He wasn't the usual computer nerd.

'Thanks Andy.' Tim took over the chair.

'Fancy a drink after work?' Andy twirled the disk around his index finger.

Tim reflected for a second. 'Sure, why not?' Tim needed a new social life; he knew that. He could tolerate a few hours in a loud pub. The friends he'd called friends once, evaporated when he told them where he was moving. They were pleased for him – envied him even, they said. Promised to visit, but he heard no more.

Tim met Andy at a bar in the town centre – lively, loud and young. Lights flashed, music thumped and people shouted at each other – everyone was having a good time. Tim felt the stuffiness of the last few months begin to soften around him.

Andy seemed to be a regular – everybody knew him and in spite of himself, Tim relaxed in the spirit of the place and the people in it. Andy introduced him to one pretty girl after another and Tim tried to remember their names. None of them looked old enough to be able to order their own drinks, and for a moment he felt closer to 40 than he'd ever done.

'Over here,' Andy yelled over the music and pushed through the throng to a table by the wall and all at once they were able to speak and be heard.

''nother drink, Tim?' Andy drained his glass and picked up his next.

'No thanks, I've still got to drive home. Everybody knows you Andy – come here often?'

'Yeah, most nights I guess. My flat's in town, so it's easy to crawl home and most of the people I hang out with slither in here sooner or later. But you must miss all this – lived in London, didn't you?' A pretty girl brushed by the table and Andy caught her around the waist. 'Hello darlin'.' He spun her into his lap. 'Darlin' this is Tim. Why don't you take him for a dance or two while I get a drink?'

'Sure.' She smiled at Tim, but the sound system crashed into life again and he missed her name. The music felt good; she had a pretty face and a nice figure. Looking at her reminded him that he could begin to look again. He didn't have to live the rest of his life alone. They had a few dances; she was warm, soft and sweet. Parts of him that he thought had died woke and he knew he could learn to enjoy women again if he tried. He bought her a drink, put his arm around her and looked at her again. She seemed to be about 12 years old and he felt he was in the wrong decade. So he walked her back to Andy's lap, confessed to feeling tired and said his goodbyes.

He wasn't ready yet. There were still things he needed to shed. He needed more time. *Why for God's sake?*

14

Tim stared at the drawings on his screen but saw nothing. The view of the car park outside his window was unchanging and it was too soon for him to feel in a rut. The drink with Andy and the short visits with Mary were about all that put any sparkle in his life. Macie was gone – but he gave himself permission to be relieved. Jennifer was more or less sorted out – at least according to the latest information. His mother and father had postponed a visit for a while – thank goodness. He felt as if the wheels of his life and career were spinning in mud.

He'd enjoyed his drink with Andy. Andy was clever and fun once they got to know each other a bit and the girls were pretty and probably willing. His former social life revolved around Macie and her friends – most of them married - and their talk of mortgages and having babies made him want to gag. He needed to start again – to enjoy himself – it was a skill he'd neglected for years. He decided he'd ask Andy for the name and number of that girl.

In mid morning Susan arrived at his desk with another stack of files. 'I hope you like dusty old files, because there's lots more where these came from.' She dropped them on his desk and dust puffed out from between them. He gave her his best smile. 'OK,' she whispered, 'I'll make the coffee.'

These files were a mixture of old quotations that hadn't been accepted and some that had. He looked down the names on the tabs and pulled out the one marked Royston Construction.

Tim spread it out on his desk. Royston, based in Leeds, wanted some small steel to make racking and this had been provided and paid for. There should have been nothing unusual in that, except that the steel requirement was very small dimension and the quantity was too. Conmac specialised in industrial sized girders and beams. Why were they supplying something so small?

Howard walked by Tim's desk, looking as if he was on another planet and Tim called to him twice before Howard responded. 'Has Conmac ever supplied small dimension steel?' Howard looked blank. 'I've got an order here for some racking from Royston Construction...' he flipped up the order page, '...four years ago.' Howard's colour deepened and he gripped the papers he was carrying so hard that they all wrinkled in his fist. 'Never heard of them...' His voice was faint and he turned and hurried on.

Tim looked at his retreating back. What was going on? It was an innocent question. He looked back at the file. The order wasn't really an official order, but rather a letter handwritten on headed paper. Not really even a letter, just a list of what was needed and a signature at the bottom.

The remaining papers were a shipping note and a copy invoice. Tim took the order list down to the loading office. No, they said, they don't make or handle these sizes. 'But,' the loading manager banged his big gloves together, 'it could be found somewhere in the industry and sent on, I suppose.'

Tiny pricks in her scalp and frenetic snatches on the duvet cover woke Mary in the morning. Rising with effort out of the layers of sleep on top of her, she found Rosie padding her hair and purring with delight while Marie chased imaginary insects among the honeysuckle flowers on the cover. Sleeping-in was about to be a thing of the past.

The last thing she remembered the night before was tucking two sleepy kittens into a towel lined box beside the bed. They had clearly decided that the duvet was a better offer. There was little doubt as to who was going to be making the decisions about their welfare. She enticed them downstairs with a piece of paper tied to a string.

The cupboard however, yielded a distinct lack of cat food and while the temporary litter tray filled with shredded paper had been used, it would not be satisfactory for long. She looked at them both.

'The time has come to establish some routines here.' Rosie yawned and then began some serious face washing. Marie made an attempt to scratch her shoulder, but missed and fell over. 'I'm going out to find appropriate provisions for you two. While I am gone, I expect you to look after things.' She secured the ancient cat flap left by the last owners, but they were much more interested in the remains of last night's tin of salmon that she put on a saucer in front of them.

When she returned late in the morning it was with cat food, litter, trays, bowls and a large assortment of cat toys. She was going to dote on these cats and didn't care who knew it. She also brought in a large box that she put on the counter. Spooning some proper kitten food into two new bowls she confessed. 'I don't admit my failures to everybody – although I did tell Sandy – but my bread making abilities appear to be limited, so....' She opened the box with a flourish. The bread maker did not seem to interest them at all although the box was going to provide hours of entertainment.

Regardless of what the kittens thought of the matter, Mary was delighted, when a few hours later a wonderful, perfect loaf sat cooling on the counter top. 'Look!' She was triumphant. 'All I did was put the ingredients in and start it up!' The kittens preferred to chase tails; their own or each others' it didn't matter. 'Well, I'm impressed, even if you aren't!'

In fact she was so impressed she made two more loaves.

The success gave her such a feeling of strength that she began to see what it was like to be in control again. So she also ordered the lime putty for her living room wall and replanted the vegetable plot.

Mary held her mobile phone at arm's length so she could just see the numbers and pushed the little keypads. 'Sandy! It's Mary. I hope I haven't interrupted your tea or anything.'

''Course not Mary. It's good to hear from you, but you sound funny – are you OK?'

'Yeah I'm OK, I'm lying on the floor with my knees up because my back is killing me. I've been in the garden all day and I am exhausted.'

'I'm beginning to worry that you have bitten off more than you can chew with this place of yours. I can't imagine spending a whole day working in mine – half an hour maybe – don't you have help or something?'

'Phil comes in once a week for a few hours, but it was nice outside today and I kept finding things that needed doing, so I just kept going.'

'Now that does not sound like the Mary I used to know. But look, here's some gossip if you want it: I ran into Robert today. Are you two speaking to each other yet?'

Mary rolled over onto her knees. 'No 'fraid not. The bastard is still playing dirty games.'

'Mary. I don't think I've ever heard you swear in my life.'

'Well, you've never had to deal with Robert. He's trying to undo our agreement, so that I'm left with no income, but apart from that he's being normal.'

Sandy managed a laugh. 'If it's any interest to you, he didn't have that posh lady friend welded to his arm.'

'No it doesn't interest me in the slightest.'

'All right then, what about you? Have you met anything interesting – or are you really out in the sticks?'

'Well you will have to come and make that judgement for yourself, but I've met my gardener, my nearest neighbour and the farmer down the lane.'

'Well, I'd leave the farmer alone unless he's landed gentry – there's nothing in farming these days to look at the national press, and skip the gardener – no money in gardening, but what about the neighbour? What's he like – it is a he I take it?'

'Oh yes, he's a he.'

Sandy's saucy giggle tickled Mary's ear. 'Come on, tell all then.'

'Nothing to tell; 30 something; quite good looking – a structural engineer in Hereford – and that's about it. Nice guy – a friend.'

'Single?' The implication in Sandy's voice was obvious.

'Yes, well I think so – but come on Sandy I'm older than he is.'

'So what and by how much?'

'Well, about 7 or 8 years I guess.'

'For heaven's sake Mary, clear your brain – you can start again you know – there's no earthy reason why you can't be happy. Go for it girl. Enjoy yourself. You don't have to marry the bloke.'

Mary had to laugh. Sandy could simplify the most complex things in life. So without asking if there was any news from the school, she changed the subject and they gossiped about other things. Then, having told Sandy about the kittens and the bread maker which seemed like such microscopic topics of excitement, she sent her love to Jim and poured some brandy into the bottom of a large glass. She slid herself into a tub of bubble bath where she stayed until the water was cold and it was dark, then went straight to bed.

The kittens nested as usual at the bottom of the duvet and when Mary looked up near the end of a Hay on Wye novel, she found it was close to midnight. With the light out, she was asleep in seconds.

Some hours later, her back was again stiffening and she tried to make herself comfortable, pulling the duvet around her to make a nest in her bed, but the discomfort gradually woke her.

Through the last layer of sleep frantic gauze-like swirls circulated in her head; dark fragments of trees, grass and clouds whirled around her. She tried to pull herself from under the last skin of sleep that held her down. All around the air was dark, heavy and cold. Wind gusted across the back of her head, thrashing her hair around her face and blew the hoot of an owl into tiny pieces of sound. Pushing her hair back she saw her breath in short white puffs. Silver moonlight flickered on a hedge, its bare sticks thick with hoar frost. The light skittered across the hard road into the pasture and away into the night.

In a gap in the gusting wind, she heard a horse galloping hard down the dark lane toward her. Grasping for the hedge, she saw its hooves crashing on the hard packed surface, sparks flying from the stones. She pushed against the sharp frozen twigs to give it space. The cold frost stung her hands and a thorn in the hedge scraped her arm. Horse and rider's eyes were wide and white. Mane, tail and cloak snapped in the desperate wind. Terror was scratched across the face of a hatless young man. He flew past her riding hard. The turbulence of the air and the noise of desperate escape billowed around her and then the shouts of other riders 20 yards behind overtook her. She struggled again against the hedge. The freezing wind blew her nightdress and she clawed it against her leg. The three pursuers were on finer horses and overtook the solitary rider a hundred yards past her in the dark lane. One of them swerved his mount in front of the young man's beast; another grabbed its bridle. It stumbled.

The third rider came along side and lifted a long heavy stick. Mary heard the sickening crunch as it struck the side of the young man's head. Man and beast fell to the ditch. The horse screamed and there was silence. Neither of them moved again.

The two riders pulled up, circled back, looked at the still man and dead horse. Without speaking they turned their mounts around and lashing them hard disappeared into the night. The third man dismounted and stabbed several times with the heavy stick. As he lifted his head, Mary saw that he too was young. He re-mounted and rode back towards her; the horse blowing noisy blasts of breath into the dark air. He stopped in front of her and stared at her; his face expressionless; his eyes clear and dark. Then he turned the horse and rode after his companions.

Mary slid into the grass under the hedge. He heart was pounding in terror, breath coming in huge gasps. She was covered in sweat but it was cold. There was no strength in her arms – they hung beside her – she couldn't move them. In her head, she knew that she had just witnessed a murder.

15

It rained on Sunday. Long, smooth, solid, cold rain. All day. Daylight hours went by without any change in the depth of light to indicate that time passed. Mary played with the kittens, who should have thrilled her, but who only amused. She made bread. The loaves were heading for the freezer now. But nice as it was, she couldn't eat. There was no joy in the rich smell. Hunger did not entice her. Her mind flapped inside her head.

There was no reason for it, but there was – there's always a reason: a memory, a significant date, a time of day, a smell, an object. There were always reasons. Too many reasons. For her it was the past. The recent past.

She tried to focus on the future, on reality, problems to solve. She needed a plan in case Robert refused to continue their financial arrangement, as he was bound to do. But her mind was incapable of logical reasoning.

The executions on the site of her cottage begged to be researched, but for that she needed the Records Office. She needed to understand what that vision of the murder meant – was it a dream or her mind dissolving? She couldn't face the understanding. The scratch on her arm she did not want to understand.

She was tired of baking, tired of reading, tired of thinking. She was just tired. The kittens were asleep. She poked the television remote. The evening choice was so excruciating she turned it off again as if she might become infected with something nasty. She picked up a magazine from a pile beside her chair. Tidy up? Oh hell, why?

There was a quiet tap at the back door. As she rose to answer it, it opened and Tim's voice called, 'I've come to relieve you of your valuables.'

The sound of a friend should have made her feel better but it didn't. She didn't want company, but a voice called for him to come in. It must have been hers. He dripped on the kitchen floor from the brim of a wax hat, a bright red anorak and green wellington boots. 'Good grief,' her voice said when she saw him. 'You're soaking.' Out of his wet weather gear, he looked more like Tim in slim jeans and a big casual shirt, glasses spotted with rain and drops on the ends of his curly hair. He grinned at her and handed her a bottle of wine. She willed her face to smile back.

'I realised that I hadn't seen you for days and - what is that smell – is it bread? You aren't lighting bonfires again?'

'Oh shut up.' Her face smiled by itself. 'Yes it's bread and it's just finished so it isn't burned. But, come and have a look at these.' She led him into the living room where two little furry bundles were asleep in a little box beside the open fire, soaking up the heat. They loved him the minute they opened their eyes, climbing up the legs of his jeans and leaping at him and each other from the back of the settee. He teased them with a piece of paper and a strip of bark from the wood basket.

Mary brought fresh bread and the wine on a tray. 'There's no doubt they love you. I'll have to count them when you leave to be sure I still have two.' She poured the wine and they buttered huge slabs of warm bread. Time began to develop some scale in her mind. 'Have you had any more grief from James?'

Tim mumbled through a mouth full of bread, 'No. I'm planning to keep my head down with a great stack of old quotations and a greater stack of new work. ' Rosie sat on his shoulder watching the corner of his mouth. 'And when he's in the office, I plan to do as many site visits as I can.'

'Ouch!' Marie was trying to climb up Mary's bare leg. The tiny stabs of pain moved some of the grey wool aside. 'What are the old quotations for?'

'I'm fitting them around other work, but I'd like to see why Conmac failed to get the contracts. Like, was it price – which is probably the reason – or quality, or timing, or was it something else.'

'How many?'

'There could be hundreds if I go back far enough. And then I want to look at a few more that were successful, just to compare.' His eyes twinkled with mischief. 'Who knows, more site visits might be necessary.'

Mary could just about remember what that kind of joy was like. 'What about the rest of your team? Are you going to involve them?'

'They have their own work at the moment, but maybe in time. Susan is the only one who's helping me. She knows where the papers are buried.'

Tim buttered another piece of bread that he passed to her and then one for himself. 'I did see Howard talking to James today and that seemed curious. They have these chats often. Not that they shouldn't of course, it's just that Howard looked so worried about something. If I'm being charitable, and if it's a discussion of company or departmental business they might have included me – so I have to assume that it was something else – but I have no idea what.'

Somehow she ate the bread. Her mouth enjoyed it even if her stomach didn't notice. 'It sounds like you have it all organised. Speaking of organisation – how is Jennifer?' Her mind was flying off in another direction and she attempted to drag it back. But it had already gone.

Tim stretched his long legs out in front of him and leaned back while Rosie climbed down them, tiny claws spread. 'Well now there's another story. According to my mother – and you have to take this as being a bit over emphasized – Jennifer was amazing. She insisted on doing all the talking and had the plan so well organised that all the poor old headmaster could do was agree. She told him what she wanted – or more to the point - didn't want, but that she would take the examination and all the others only if that was agreed to. She even pointed out that the head would not look too good in front of the press if he refused her the right to take them. I guess all he could do was close his mouth and nod his head.'

Mary laughed but there was no humour in the sound. 'Well done to her. Jennifer is the kind who will thrive on being in total charge. I must drop her a note sometime.'

'She'd be delighted to hear from you, but don't be afraid to give her a call. You may get stuck talking to my sister-in-law, but I think you're a match for her.'

'Oh thanks.' Something offended her.

'But what's been happening with you?'

She curled up on the settee, feet under her skirt, glass cradled in her hands. Its smoothness was stabilising. 'I found out something interesting about the cottage site at the Records Office. It seems like this might have been the site of executions around 1670. There may be a direct link between the site and the family tree that Jennifer put together. What I can't link yet is the executions and the family.' The greyness returned and felt heavy – very heavy. She thought she heard the horses again.

'Executions! That's amazing. Do you think you will? Be able to connect things, I mean?'

'Maybe, but I'll need some more time. Since then, and except for these two little things, I've had a depressing week. Nothing I can put my finger; I've just felt a bit low.' The two little things in question had retreated to their box and were washing each other's ears.

He didn't question her, so she went on.

'Phil saw fit to weed all of the plants out of my vegetable plot, including the seedlings that were just coming up, so I've had to replant. Then the cottage was full of bees when I got home from the Records Office on Wednesday and I have no idea how they got in unless they have learned how to manipulate the cat flap. And I haven't been able to work out what to say to Robert when he rejects the 'no' I sent to him – as I know he will - and now it's raining.' Her voice began to trail off.

He reached down into the kittens and began to stroke them. They purred once each and fell asleep. 'I know it's none of my business and you can tell me so, but what happened between you and Robert?'

Her mind grabbed and focussed. Some thoughts would have clarity for the rest of her life. 'For years and years nothing happened – and maybe that was part of the reason it fell apart.' She took a deep breath as if she were about to plunge into something deep and then did exactly that. 'We worked hard to set up the business. But I told you about that.'

Tim nodded. Her voice carried on of its own accord. 'He worked incredibly hard – much harder than I did in teaching. I used to work in the office during half terms and summers in the early days, so I know.' She shrugged her shoulders; the weight was still there but perhaps it was getting lighter. 'As the company got bigger, it needed full time support, so I stopped being involved as much as I had. I was left out - maybe that was the problem – or part of it – we saw very little of each other.' Her eyes glistened and she took a deep shaky breath. 'Then one day he came home and said that he was going on holiday, but that he taking a woman from the company office.'

'Did you have any idea that …?'

She felt that she was unloading a lorry. She shovelled faster. 'None whatsoever. I was stunned. No, first of all I was so angry that all I could do was scream and shout. I had never been so angry. I scared myself.'

Tim picked up a log from the basket and put it on the diminishing fire. 'How did Robert take it?'

'He just walked out. We've not shared a house since then. Then I went through all the usual things – begging and pleading, being hurt and, to my shame, being feminine. Then angry again and now just miserable.'

They were quiet for a moment; then Tim looked at her and his eyes softened. 'But there's something else isn't there?'

She looked at him in surprise. 'What?'

'There are still little crease lines across your forehead. They're not there when you're relaxed.'

She rubbed her forehead. 'Well, yes.' Her mind picked up the shovel to off-load the big stuff from the lorry. 'I'm beginning to wonder if I'm losing my grip on reality.' She wanted to tell him what she had seen. But something stopped her and she put the shovel down. It would mean admitting that she was closer to the edge of sanity than she was prepared for.

Tim leaned forward – eyes focussed with concern.

'Days go by and I feel wonderful. Then without warning, I feel like nothing will ever be right.' He got up, sat beside her and put his arms around her. He pulled her against his shoulder and she came, curling up small in his hug. 'I feel like I've got what I want in this cottage, but it doesn't seem permanent enough for me to believe in it.' Panic began to rise in her – breaths came short and sharp. But the warmth of him – the heat.

'It's as if it isn't real; that I'll have to go through all that loss again. I know it's just stress – I'm just not able to handle things – broken bits of my life are.... I'm afraid that if I look to the future, and something happens...' her voice began to break and her head dropped forward, '...well, it feels like I'm living in a house of cards and it will all fall down and – I'll be left with nothing – nothing at all.'

Tim tucked her under his chin as sobs buckled up from beneath her heart. He put his cheek on her head and held her closer. He whispered into her hair, 'I know what it's like to stand at the edge of your life and watch it beginning to crumble under your feet. I've been on that edge too - waiting for the rim to suck you into the unknown.' He brushed her hair back from her face. 'I know how much strength and damned plain luck it takes to stop the collapse. I know – and all I can do is hold on to you and be here to pull you back. And give you what I can. I'm here.' She lay on his chest, the sobs now painful grateful hiccups.

'I want to take all that pain away,' he whispered over the top of her head. 'I want to see the Mary I know. The one who makes me laugh, fills me with wonderful food and gets drunk with me. The one who watches bats in the orchard and shows me how wonderful the apple blossoms are. This Mary is the one who sees off a swarm of bees single-handed, is prepared to re-plaster her living room wall and replant her garden. She'll be OK.' His voice buckled and he swallowed hard. 'You're not losing it – I'm sure of that – because I know there's a strong person in there. Think of the things that are real.'

When she stopped crying, they found one tissue between them. Mary blew her nose and he drew her back onto his chest. She lay against him for a long time and he stroked her hair. They talked about nothing in particular – some things personal, some not. His warmth put colour tints back into her mind. He at least was real – something close to her had depth, space and form. She could smell him. The grey wool in her brain faded; crisp and dusty it broke and slowly drifted away. 'I don't know how you do it,' she wheezed through a stuffy nose, 'you've just taken me from the depths of despair and made me feel normal again - I don't know who I was before. I feel like the rain has gone, that the sun is out there somewhere.' She straightened out the tissue.

He kissed the top of her head and smiled. 'I have that effect on people. Most people don't know who they are when they've been around me a while.' She smiled – a real smile – one from within and looked up at him. He lifted her chin with his finger. *I shouldn't be doing this.* Then he leaned down and touched her nose with his lips. *This is madness.* His lips brushed hers. *Stop.* He kissed her. It was soft and simple. *Oh what the hell.* The kiss tasted sweet and warm, of fruit, red wine.

She reached for him, needing more of his warmth. 'I can't imagine what I look like,' she wiped her eyes, 'but I think I know who I am now.'

He kissed her again and she lay on his chest. Then he rubbed his cheek on the top of her head. 'There are some things I don't know how to do very well – like tell you what I'd like to happen next.'

She put her fingers in his curls. How strange they felt. Soft like a child's, still moist from the rain. Different, new. A voice that sounded a lot like Sandy's said something she didn't quite catch. She traced his jaw with her finger. 'I think I know.'

He laid his head on her hair and drew her back against him. Then she felt his chest vibrating and realised that he was stifling a chuckle. 'What are you laughing at?'

He tucked his face into her neck. 'I don't suppose you have a condom anywhere?'

She felt the hot flush of embarrassment rush to her face. 'No, I, well, I thought...'

'Well, I assure you I didn't come down here with sex foremost in my mind. I don't usually...' His voice drifted away. Then he leapt to his feet. 'Wait. Wait just a minute...' He disappeared into the kitchen and returned with his hat and a silly grin.

'What on earth...what good is that going to do?' She caught his sense of the ridiculous. 'You don't mean...' She started to giggle and swallowed it back.

'Don't laugh. I have to have these specially made.' Sitting down beside her, he felt around the band inside the hat. 'No delusions of grandeur I assure you.' He turned the hat in his hands. 'It was too big and I needed to pad it out... The hat, I mean.'

Mary had her knuckles in her mouth. 'Aha.' He pulled out a small packet. 'It's old, but....' His eyes glinted with humour.

Choking with laugher, she clutched his arm. 'I don't care...'

16

Something wasn't quite right. Mary struggled through a heavy layer of sleep that covered dreams she couldn't remember. Surfacing to murky daylight she realised she was on the wrong side of the bed and then remembered why.

She stretched out as far as she could under the duvet, bouncing first one kitten and then another out of their puffy nests. 'Sorry little ones.' Two sleepy faces looked at her without expression. 'Don't either of you say a word.' The other side of the bed was empty. The clock said 6:25 and there was a slip of paper leaning on the base of the lamp. Struggling to focus her eyes without glasses she read: 'glad I didn't wake you as I left. will call tonight. will put the key through the cat flap. T'

His handwriting was neat, full and round, almost printed, controlled and professional. There were no capital letters except for his initial, letters and lines perfect and straight. *A lot like the man himself.* Clutching the duvet around her she realised she had nothing else on. She stretched out again savoured the luxury. There was a taste of freedom on her tongue.

The last time I did this..... It was nothing like this – no laughter, no sympathy – just... just what? Lust? Angry, good God damn, get-even lust. Nothing 'feel good' about it – before or after. She pulled the duvet around her and sat on the edge of the bed. *This couldn't be more different. I'm a fully paid up member of the adult human race – there are no other people to be hurt and damn it, why not – if that's what we both wanted. And we had. And am I justifying what I did or ....?*

She felt the floor for her slippers, but they were on the other side of the bed. *I should be feeling guilty or sick or remorseful or worried about what will happen next. But I don't. I just remember the warmth and the laughter. For the next few minutes, I just want to feel good about myself.*

Through the crack in the curtains she saw that the sun was up; the clouds of yesterday had gone, metaphorically as well as meteorologically. Today she would search the Records Office through every piece in its library if necessary until she found the connection she was looking for. Opening a dresser drawer she took out all her underwear and one at a time, folded them into two very neat piles – one large and plain and one small and lacy. Taking the stack of large ones to the bin she dropped it in. Then she let the duvet fall to the floor and went to the shower.

Not bad shape - could lose a few pounds, well be honest, a stone. She pulled at her cheeks. *Face good shape, skin not bad with a little make up. Horrible stuff beginning to accumulate under the chin and – good God, cellulite!* There it was, between her breasts, on her chest at her arms, down the back of her legs. *Who am I trying to fool?*

But Tim hadn't minded. Or had he? Oh God what would happen if he didn't like what he'd found? Had she lost what could well be her best friend in a moment of deluded freedom? Freedom for its own sake did not come without costs.

Tim got to work early. He couldn't understand what he felt. He'd not once even thought about it before it happened. Not once. He didn't think of her like that. He didn't think, period. He should never have held her – that's where it started. But how could he have ignored her for God's sake? She needed a friend - and friendship was about touching. He'd learned that from Mary. But where did friendship end and lust take over and what happened when it did? He could have stopped – he didn't have to go through with it. Because he wanted her, that's why. Pure and simple. Just sex.

He made himself a coffee in the quiet little staff room; the computer screen on the desk in the corner glared at him and under its accusing stare, he returned to his own desk. He knew he was smiling even though he didn't feel like it inside. He looked at the office copy of James' schedule for the week on the system, programmed his own trips out to avoid the old bugger as far as possible and saved it into Susan's copy. Tim leaned back in his chair, feet on the edge of the waste bin, and a trade paper over his knees.

'Tim?' A voice drifted in to his range from somewhere behind. It was Susan with his e-mails and post. 'Are you all right? You look a bit - well, I don't know ...'

Everyone else was at work and he hadn't heard any of them arrive. His smile widened. 'Fine thank you and yes, before you ask, I will have another coffee.' He pushed his cup towards her. She sighed in mock disgust. 'I promise to make you one this afternoon,' he pleaded. She took it and smiled back.

As Susan waited in the little staff room for the coffee maker to finish, Margaret came in carrying a small silver tray on which was a cup and saucer. 'Is that for James?' asked Susan. 'Why don't you make him get his own?'

Margaret smiled. 'I know it's old fashioned, but I don't mind.' She looked at the two cups in front of Susan and asked with a mischievous grin, 'Is that one for Tim?'

Susan laughed, 'OK. Caught out.' The coffee maker finished its gurgling noises and Susan poured the three cups and then found another one for Margaret. 'Tell me Margaret, does Tim look all right today?'

'Why do you ask? Is he not well?'

'No I think he's OK – it's just that well, he looks like he's been somewhere else this last week or so – you know, in his head.'

'I think that you have a soft spot for him don't you?' Margaret asked with a gentle smile.

'Yeah... well... You have to admit that he's very good looking.' Susan poured milk where it was required.

'He is that to be sure. But I have a feeling, my dear that he is spoken for.'

The box of milk slipped through Susan's hand, hitting the counter top with a smart smack. 'What? He's never said there's anyone.'

'I know, but - it's just the look in his face and behind his eyes. I think there's more to Tim than just what you see.'

Susan looked Tim full in the face when she set down his coffee.

The card index system in the Records Office was old and dog-eared. There were a couple of references to executions – one of them being the map Mary saw last week. The others were papers written by learned academics concerned with local history. None mentioned the execution at the site Rosemary Cottage, as she assumed it to be.

Mary looked again at the indexes for the parish, then realized she was reading none of them. Visions of Tim covered the print. She wondered how he felt this morning. Would he have the same beautiful feelings she did, or not? Perhaps his feelings would be quite different. Maybe he felt it was wrong. Maybe that's why he hadn't stayed. She didn't know when he'd left – had he been in a hurry to get away? Perhaps that had been the ending and not the beginning.

She went outside for a quarter of an hour and walked in the grounds. Panic began to rise but she pushed it back with logic. *Wait until we can speak to each other. Wait. Wait and see.*

Back at the long table, she thought again about the map. What crimes were punishable by execution in those days? She listed what little she knew on a sheet of paper: murder, theft, religious deviance, and rape in all likelihood.

The grey archivist showed her where the records of the Assize Courts were indexed. These courts, she explained were the ones that dealt with the very serious crimes – the kinds that might have brought a death or prison sentence for a guilty verdict. She handed Mary a thick book, 'This one covers the dates you are interested in. It is indexed by the names that appear in the record in some capacity, such as accused, barrister, that sort of thing and also by date. You may find one list more useful than the others.'

Mary opened the book and worked through the indexed names looking for Fletcher. There was nothing listed. She checked the date on the spine of the book 1650 – 1700. It was the correct period. She checked the date index and went through the 20 years from 1660 to 1680 to include the date on the map and the probable date of transfer of land to William Fletcher. The list of crimes to be heard was quite inclusive; there were trials for theft, murder and rape, but also poaching, and counterfeiting. Even some land disputes were heard by this court. And, she was surprised to find that convicted witches were hanged; death by burning was a more common on the continent the archivist explained.

Mary leaned back in the hard leather chair and pushed her glasses up onto her head. She rubbed her eyes and closed them to rest them from the close print of the index. She wondered what Tim was doing. What was he feeling? Why had she encouraged him? What would happen now? The same questions again. She forced herself to continue with the index.

There were no trials involving anyone named Fletcher in any capacity to be found. Her options receding, she checked the trials of 1670 again. That was the date on the map. If there was anything to be found about it, it would have to bear a date near that time.

The trials in the two sittings of the court in 1670 dealt with the usual events, and those that did result in executions were hangings held in the castle grounds. She continued into 1671. Here there were again two sittings of the court, the early one showed nothing unusual, except that the number of hangings was greater due to several women being accused of witchcraft and being hanged when they confessed. Mary wondered just what confession in this sense meant.

The second sitting, showed no hangings for this conviction, but did include an acquittal of one John Roberts accused of arranging an execution for witchcraft. Although it was not what she was looking for, Mary felt intrigued why anyone should be able to arrange for what looked like a private execution.

The papers when they arrived were of various sorts. In a statement made by someone called John Cooper, she found: 'John Cooper says that John Roberts did unlawfully kill two god-fearing women of the crime of witchcraft. Victims they were and not condemned, nor confessed.' She looked at the index: 1671

On scrap of torn paper was a part of a statement by a cleric who had prayed for their souls and who had heard their pleas that the women were innocent. Mary raced on.

The court verdict was handwritten on a small piece of ragged paper. 'Verdict: not guilty, but the said John Roberts shall give Wm Flitch in recompense [land] to the value, etc and shall have no jurisdiction for it.'

The name Flitch leapt out at Mary. Could this be William Fletcher? Who was John Roberts and why had he executed two women? Were these two women Rose and Mary Fletcher. If he had not done so, why was he prohibited from any jurisdiction over William Flitch or Fletcher? And who was John Cooper?

She put the papers back into their plastic sleeves and returned them to the archivist. What else could they tell her? The girl in grey took the documents. 'Did you find what you were looking for?'

I've probably just lost it. 'I may have, but I think that there are more questions now than there were when I started.'

'It's often that way. Have you looked at the court leet or court baron records by the way?'

'What are they?'

'Well, they are records of manorial courts. A landowner often had disputes to settle in one way or another on his or adjoining land and rather than deal with it himself, he put together a court of respected – or maybe just sympathetic – men who settled things for him. You never know there might be something.'

Mary looked at the large wall clock. It was already nearly 4 o'clock and her head was beginning to ache in sympathy with her back. Tim had said that he would call. She needed to speak to him and she needed to hear what he would say to her.

'It's a bit late to start on them now. I'll look at them the next time I'm in.'

Mary was so deep in imagining what she would say, what Tim would say, she nearly missed the turn to Croftbury. When she finally arrived home, two kittens informed her they were starving and mal treated and had discussed moving back to Harry's where at least there were mice. She ran a hot bath while they ate and reconsidered. Her back was tense from bending over the high table in the reading room. She needed wine, candles and bubbles, and the telephone near enough so she could answer it if he called.

Sinking into the delicious soft water, she pulled the bubbles up to her chin and blew a channel down the middle as far as she could. She washed her hair, drank half a bottle of wine and rearranged the bubbles. Then she blew another pattern over the top; leaned back, closed her eyes and considered her situation.

From a selfish position, she was glad that it had happened just as it did and she admitted that she hoped it would do so again. But – and this was a big but – she had to maintain some kind of detachment. Oh God's sake, just how possible did she expect that to be? How far could this friendship go before it became something else?

'I don't want the something else – not just yet. I want to be me first.'

A knock on the back door made her slosh water out of the tub. She dripped to the window. Opening it she called down, 'Who is it?' Tim's voice came up in reply. It couldn't be much past 5:30. He was early and she wasn't ready. 'Come in – the door's open. I'll be down in a minute.' She wrapped a big towel around her hair and pulled a long fluffy bathrobe over her sticky body. 'Don't go away,' she ordered the bubbles. 'I'll be back.'

Tim was standing in the kitchen. 'It's my turn to get yanked out of the tub.' She smiled at him, but he did not look amused. Her heart went cold and she could feel things beginning to dissolve. 'You'd better come in.' He sat down on the settee where he had been last night and put his arms down between his knees. They both spoke at once, 'I ...'

Mary stopped. 'You first.' *I need to get this over with. If this is the end to my wonderful beginning I need to hear it.* She clutched the back of the other settee and looked at him.

He looked up at last. 'I came to apologize.' She opened her mouth to speak, but didn't. 'What happened last night should never have happened and I am very sorry.'

'Tim. What happened last night was my choice.'

He took a long breath. 'No, I feel as if I've done you an injustice – taken advantage of you or misled you somehow...'

'Tim, you did not take advantage of me or of anything else. I could have stopped it all in a second and you are not the kind of person who would have been offended by that – I know you at least that well.' As usual she said too much.

'But... I find this very hard to explain – even to myself – but I'm coming to think of you as a very good friend.' He rubbed the bridge of his nose under his glasses. 'God, I can't think if I've ever had a good friend. Look I'm not putting this very well.' He drew a long shaky breath. 'Mary, I'm not ready for anything more than friendship in a relationship. It'd be very wrong of me to let you think it was...' his voice trailed away.

The towel started to slide off Mary's head. She pulled at it and rubbed her hair. 'Tim,' her voice was quiet. 'Last night was wonderful.' He looked stricken, like a man being sucked under the surface. 'But I'm not ready for any committed relationship either.' His expression changed to surprise and she felt the ground stabilizing under her. 'I realized today, that just because we've shared a few bottles of wine and made love, we don't have to live together. Good God, what I need right now is my independence. I have got to be strong enough for it. You helped me see that last night.'

'But having you as my friend is important to me. I feel as if I've put that friendship at a huge risk.'

She sat down opposite him. 'Then I have to take my share of the blame for that, but tell me - where is it written that friends can't laugh together, get drunk together or maybe even make love now and then? Neither of us wants a heavy commitment here.' She rubbed more drips from her hair.

'But can we still be "just friends" if we – well...?'

She looked at him and willed her voice to be gentle, 'Tim, I heard what you said to me last night, about wanting to go on laughing, watching the bats, getting drunk. I want that too.' She looped the towel around her neck. 'We're grown up people and I hope we can deal with the way this develops – if it develops at all. In the meantime, I promise not to make demands that go beyond friendship if you promise the same.'

A slow smile creased his face. 'I hoped you'd say something like that.' He pulled down on his tie. 'Is there room in your tub for two?'

17

This time Mary felt embarrassed. Taking her bathrobe off was embarrassing. Getting in the water was embarrassing. She knew he was seeing her naked and she remembered the unpleasant things she'd discovered about her plump, cellulite packed body. She hurried to cover herself with bubbles. This wasn't fun. She looked at Tim at the other end of the tub, pleated into a pointed package, knees and elbows trying to find somewhere to relax with the taps in his back. He looked uncomfortable too, but as they sat looking at each other with knees touching, it began to seem funny again.

Mary leaned back in the warm water. The depth of it bounced her like a cork to the surface and she grabbed for the side of the tub to prevent being turned upside down. The resulting splashing and grabbing made them laugh and considerable soap and water ended on the floor. With less water in the tub, stability improved and Mary filled the singular wine glass. Maybe friendship could survive sex and a tub of bathwater on the floor.

'You were saying...?'

'It's been hard to talk about Macie, but... I'm boring you silly...'

'What are bathtub friends for? Turn around, I'll scrub your back.' Mary grabbed the orange fish-shaped sponge as it bounced close to the edge.

He looped his legs over the side of the tub; slid around and folded them back in again. 'She... well she sort of took over my life. That's nice – what is it about a back rub? I've had jobs all over, middle east, Africa, America, then a good one in London, and a flat not far from my family – not that that was a critical issue. It must have looked like I was ready to settle down at last. Maybe I was just tired. I'd not been in the flat or the job very long when I met Macie. She's a friend of Ann's – well you can see how these things unfold. It sounds so ordained when I talk about it now.'

He handed the wine glass back to her over his shoulder and she filled it up. 'What did Macie do, as a job, I mean?'

'Climbing the ladder at some PR company. To be honest I took little interest. It's not the kind of business I claim to know anything about and I didn't really care either. Sounds unfeeling to say so.'

'Not really.'

He turned sideways in the tub and hung his legs over the side. 'Everything I felt about my job, her job, the flat, London, our relationship, was very little.'

'And yet you don't sound as if you were very unhappy.'

He handed her the glass, bubbles dripping off the stem. 'No I can't say that I was unhappy, but I wasn't ecstatic either. It was a sort of nothing. Hard to describe. '

'It's life just going on by. Nothing ripples the surface and nothing happens underneath either.' The sponge swayed on the surface.

He smiled. 'You've been there too haven't you?'

She nodded and drops of water fell from her hair. 'So what happened to change it for you?'

He blew the bubbles off one knee, then the other and pulled his legs back into the tub. 'I remember it like it was today. We were at a black tie do – a corporate Christmas thing – a big affair – last December.'

The thought of Tim in a dinner jacket made the breath catch in the back of Mary's throat. She had to concentrate hard to hear what he was saying.

'Everybody dressed to the nines – drinking, eating, dancing, looking like we were having a fabulous time. Macie's friends were talking about having babies and telling me that it was only a matter of time until I could enjoy all that crap as well. The guys were discussing the stock market or something. And I looked around and felt so lonely that I just had to leave.'

'A pub.'

'Pardon?'

'I was in a pub when I felt it. Just the same. There's noise and mayhem all around you - you can hear the noise and it cuts off all your screams. You feel like no one can even see you and worse – no one will notice if you aren't there.'

'What did you do?'

She floated the wine cork through the bubbles toward him. 'I did nothing. I just went home, had a good cry, and forgot about it. Except that I didn't really. How about you?'

'Well, I got the trade paper, found another job – in Hereford – then I told Macie it was all over, that I'd put the flat on the market and I was moving away. Then I drove into the Surrey hills somewhere where it was so dark I couldn't see my hand in front of my face. I sat in the car all night – damn near froze to death.'

'Wow. Just like that?'

'It was cruel and I'll have guilt feelings for the rest of my life. She was devastated. She pleaded with me, my sister-in-law, my mother, everybody we knew. God but I had to be stubborn about it. I came so close to giving in, so many times.' He pushed the cork under the water and then watched as it popped to the surface again. 'And I still feel bad about it.'

'So this is quite raw still – it's only been, what...' she counted – fingers fat with soap, '...four or five months?'

'Yes, but I don't regret any of it. I love the cottage I live in, I like living near you, the job is pretty good, it's a beautiful part of the country and it's good not to have my mother popping over every fifteen minutes to be sure I'm eating all right. I just feel bad for Macie.'

'Why should you? Decisions are never guilt free. The one making the decision has the advantage, so the other one has the harder part to play. That's just the way it is.'

He made a pile of bubbles and dropped the cork into the middle of them. 'But you were the hurt party when it happened to you.'

'You have enough honour to feel guilty about it; it does you credit. But if it was the right decision then, it is still the right decision now. She'll recover or hate you forever – well, I think so, if my experience is anything to go by.'

'I don't feel as if I've come out of it very well though.' Gloom seemed to coat each word.

They were silent for a minute. Mary laughed. 'Look at us. I can't believe I'm sitting naked in a tub with a man I only just know, discussing my ex and his.'

Tim grinned. 'Come on; let's go up to my place. I'm starving and it must be my turn – just bring a loaf of your bread will you?

Mary woke on the wrong side of the bed again - and it wasn't her bed. She smelled coffee. Tim stood beside her in a dark blue dressing gown holding two cups. Steam rose and with it, the clean early day aroma.

'Good morning.' He smiled and tried to blow a curl out of one eye. 'Coffee?'

'Need you ask?' She pulled herself up onto the pillows and he handed her a cup, then got back into bed himself. As she sipped the black brew and she felt some sense of normal life returning – in all kinds of ways. 'Tell me something...'

'What's that?'

'What side of the bed do you sleep on?'

'This side, why?'

'Well, that's the side I sleep on too. Can we agree that when we are in my bed, I sleep on my usual side and when we are in yours, you do?'

'You are nuts.' He wiggled down beside her until his head was on her shoulder.

'Good, that's settled then. Now, what are we doing up this early in the morning?' She twisted one of his curls around her finger.

Tim laid his laptop and briefcase on the floor of the back of the car. 'Sure you won't come? I expect that Leicester is pretty this time of year.'

Mary leaned on the car's shiny wing. 'Lovely idea, but I've got responsibilities at home. Two kittens in case you'd forgotten, and I've got some research into an execution to finish.'

Tim got in and shut the car door. 'Much more interesting that a crusty engineering office. See you later.' He blew a kiss through the window.

She was very much on his mind as he worked his way toward the motorway. This arrangement was totally idiotic. How on earth could he keep detached? The concept of being sucked in again was a lot like the panic he knew only too well.

The sound of his mobile startled him. He pressed his ear piece. It was Susan.

'Tim. Your appointment in Leicester just called. They've got a crisis meeting on and have to cancel this morning. Do you want me to re-schedule it?'

'Damn. Yeah, re-schedule it please and call those two companies in Leeds. If they can see me I'll go there today instead. I'll be at the M5 in about 10 minutes. Can you let me know by then?'

She sounded puzzled when she called back. 'Evans can see you about 11, but I can't find a number for the other one. It's not on the database.'

'Tell Evans I'll be there about 11 – I think I can make it in time. See Howard if you can't find a number for Royston in the file on my desk. We did some work for them a few years ago and Howard handled it.'

Tim was on the M5 when she called again sounding more puzzled than before. 'Tim, is Howard always like that?'

'Like what?'

'Disorganised, flapping around. He shuffled every paper he had on his desk when I asked for the telephone number.'

Tim laughed. 'Well he can be like an old woman some times. Anyway, did you call Royston?'

'No. Howard couldn't find the number and believe it or not there isn't one on their letterhead. I've looked at the directories and they don't have any listing for Royston – old or new.'

'Odd. Never mind, I've got the address; I'll just call in on spec while I'm there. Call me if anything comes up.'

Andy wasn't surprised to hear James on the other end of the telephone. 'Morning, boss.' He tried to sound glib but he knew what was coming.

'Andy I need you to alter some data for me. I'd like some of the figures changed in the quotation number...,' there was a pause during which Andy heard papers being turned, '.....2601-10'.

'Just what do you want amended?' Andy looked around his part of the open office, and chose his words as he typed in the numbers. The document appeared on his screen.

Two kittens were at the back door, waiting to give Mary an incredible tale of neglect when she went in. She threw her little overnight bag onto the kitchen counter and listened to their sad story as she opened a fresh tin of kitten food. In minutes they were busily quiet again; tails straight out behind them like a pair of tiny exclamation marks.

She brewed coffee and sorted out the morning post. Most of it went for recycling, but there was a note from a former colleague that would require a short reply and it was time she made some decision about Robert. She knew what he would say and it would be as well to be ready. The kittens turned their attention to a bowl of water while she sat down to the kitchen table with a pad of lined paper.

With nothing to commit to paper she doodled on the pad until the coffee was ready. Tim was all that came to mind. She liked being with him. They enjoyed each other, but they had agreed that the idea of creeping commitment would remain undeveloped. This was crazy. Maybe if they were careful and reserved some space and time for each of them... They needed, and they both wanted, time alone. She poured the coffee. Who was she trying to fool? What she really meant was that she would have to allow him time alone for his sake and for hers.

Would it work? They - no she - could only try. She smiled to herself. Improbable, but if she were careful not to let emotions intrude too far, then perhaps.

She returned to the scribbled on page. But now what to tell Robert? She made a couple of feeble points. When she finished, she would go back to the Records Office and find those court records, whatever they were called.

She jumped when the phone rang. When she answered, the reply was a succession of gulping sobs, and finally, 'Mum?'

Leeds was foreign territory to Tim and the Satnav struggled, but with a great deal more luck than good planning, he found Evans Brothers in a new industrial park. Trees only a few years old, still supported with ropes and stakes, were beginning to green around him, defying reality and trying to look established and happy. The modern office reception was carpeted; huge plants glowing with unnatural green health gave the impression of a protected rain forest.

The receptionist seated him under a palm tree and a moment later an astonishingly pretty young woman arrived and with a huge smile welcomed him. She introduced herself as the office manager and leading him to the stairs, chatted about the drive from the western Midlands – one she did often – she had family at Shrewsbury – and the state of the weather. He looked at the back of the slim skirt swishing in front of him as they went up the steps. She sat him in an open conference area and he watched with admiration as she walked down the office corridor to get his coffee.

Still feeling good, he had a very constructive meeting with one of the senior managers and one of the project engineers. They were pleased Conmac had taken the trouble to discuss their requirements and promised to contact him when they again needed a quotation.

At the meeting's end, Tim asked the lovely office manager to check the post code for Harvard Road where, according to their headed paper, Royston had offices. His Satnav had not been satisfied with what he had put in. She found what he needed; it had been his error. 'It's not very nice over there.' But with the same wondrous smile, that made his tongue dangle, she gave him some general directions to get there. Reluctantly he got back into his car.

'Kelley?' Mary tried to break into the sobbing. Panic began to take over her own voice. 'Darling – try to calm yourself – I need to hear – what's wrong...?'

The racking sobs became blubbering and then random gulps. 'Mum, oh Mum, I don't know what to do.'

'Kelley, you have to tell me what's wrong – I can't say any of the right things if I don't know what's...'

'Mum, I'm pregnant.' The crying started again.

The area was as the office manager described - not very nice. It had been a thriving industrial area but now, once elegant, brick-built Victorian buildings loomed over the narrow streets making them dark and unhappy. Harvard Road was deserted and most of the buildings were unoccupied, boarded up with wooden hoarding or steel shuttering plastered with flapping fly posters and colourful graffiti. Scattered among them were small factory outlets for carpets and fabrics, a discount warehouse and a small shipping company, with a dented van parked on the pavement. On one corner there was a black yard behind a steel mesh fence topped with razor wire. He saw black oily steel sheeting and large automotive parts, heavy military equipment and broken vehicle bodies. He wondered why there was need for the razor wire – who would want to steal tank tracks except some cash-struck small time third world wannabe. Even here there was no one about, however etched in the glass above what was likely to be an office was the number 47.

For no reason that he could name, he slid his laptop under the driver's seat and locked the doors as he got out. The office had the remains of a once fine panelled counter inside the door, but it was clear that the office hadn't been painted since any of the King Georges were on the throne. Daylight was unable to make much advance through the grimy but elegant stained glass fanlight and artificial light came from a single bulb hanging from a fine rose in the high ceiling. A greasy man looked up from the Daily Sport and said something that sounded like, 'Yeah?'

Tim felt as out of place in a clean shirt and tie as it's possible to be. 'Sorry to trouble you, but can you tell me where to find Royston Construction; it's supposed to be at number 51?'

The greasy man did not answer, but looked Tim up and down, then folded his newspaper before he spoke. 'Royston?'

'Yes, do you . . .'

'Never heard of it.'

'Then can you tell me which direction number 51 will be from here – left or right?' The man nodded to the right. 'Thanks.' Tim got back in his car, grateful to feel safe and without putting on the seatbelt, rammed the car in gear and drove on looking for anything that would identify Royston. In the rear view mirror he saw the greasy man standing on the pavement watching him.

The building of dark bricks continued from number 47 to the next side street - its doorways boarded and deserted. Broken glass poked empty sockets in windows of the two upper floors. At the corner, he came to the mirror image of number 47, with 57 etched in its fanlight. He reversed into the next side street to turn around and try again; then his mobile rang.

18

Mary hung up and was surprised to find her hand wasn't shaking. Everything else in her felt like porridge. A pregnant daughter was not the catastrophe it might have been a generation ago. She could postpone dealing with the implications of that until later. What knocked the knees from under her was her daughter's screaming unhappiness and desperate begging: 'Mum please can you come... I need you.'

When had she last heard those words? Had she ever heard them? They should have given her joy, but they filled her with dread.

She put some clean underclothes and makeup into the little bag she'd taken to Tim's, put a pile of biscuits and a bowl of water in front of the kittens and drove toward London.

Almost before Tim could answer it, James' voice slammed into the side of his head. 'Tim, where the hell are you?'

Tim's head almost hit the steering wheel in surprise. 'Leeds. I said I was...'

'Leeds! What in hell are you doing in Leeds?'

'Trying to find Royston . . .'

James' voice almost broke. 'Never mind goddamn Royston! Just get back here.'

'It'll take me a couple of hours.'

'Well put your foot down, just get back here. Now!' The line went dead and so did Tim's hand. What on earth now? He called Susan's number.

'Susan? What the hell is up with James?'

Susan was surprised. 'Nothing so far as I can tell Tim. What's the matter?'

'Well, he just called me, demanding that I get back there now. Sounded like trouble. Didn't he know where I was today?'

'Yes, he asked me a few minutes ago and I told him. What's happened?'

'Susan, I have no idea. If he wants to know, tell him I'm on my way but call me if anything else happens will you?'

Tim put his foot down as instructed, but with a thick sense of foreboding and at 10 to 4 signed back in at the front desk. He stopped at Susan's desk. 'Anything new?' He nodded in the direction of James' office.

'Nope. Been as nice as anything all afternoon.'

It was after 10 when Mary got into the lumpy bed with the thin mattress in Kelley's small flat and called Tim. He answered on the first ring. 'Mary? Where are you?'

'I'm in London – family emergency.'

'I'm sorry... what's happened?'

'You first. Your messages sounded terrible. I'm the one to be sorry for not getting back to you sooner. Whatever is the matter?'

'I don't know... I don't know what's going on, but I have this terrible feeling between my shoulder blades, if you know what I mean.'

'Tim, I'm not following you. Start at the beginning.'

'Well, someone corrupted a quotation of mine today, with the result that the customer – a big construction company – got a very buggered up price. They were only too pleased to accept it and the cost to the company is about ¾ of a million. Of course, James is assuming great pleasure in blaming me for some colossal degree of incompetence. It has my signature on it – I signed it off but I know it was right when I did it.'

Mary could hear his breath coming in rapid gulps. Hers was doing the same. 'How... how? Who?'

'I've no idea. I think that someone has cracked into my computer files and changed it. God - that sounds like paranoia doesn't it?

'Oh Tim. What can you do? Can it be put right?'

'I've changed my passwords again and James is working on it – says he's talking to the company. For once I have to hope he can do it.' There was a pause and she had to struggle to hear him. 'I wish you were here, I need a warm hug right now.'

Mary felt her throat fill. 'I wish I were too.' She wished with all her heart that she could.

His voice sounded weak. 'But what's happened to you? Why London?'

Mary put the phone to her other ear and tried to get comfortable on the bed settee. 'It's nothing too serious – I'll tell you all about it when I get back. It all happened rather suddenly and... I'm sorry I didn't have the chance to tell you...'

She thought she heard his breathing moderate. 'Would you like me to check the kittens?'

'Would you? I've left them a pile of dry food, but... yes... thanks. I'll be home in the morning and promise to tell you all about it.'

'I'll bring them up here. I need something warm and cuddly right now. But I still wish you were here.'

'Call me in the morning... first thing... promise.'

Mary propped herself up on her pillows and squinted into the early city sunlight from the window. 'Tim. You sound better this morning – I felt terrible not being there for you.'

'You had other things to deal with. I didn't sleep much, but I did a lot of thinking. I've got to find out what's going on.'

'Can you get away for lunch – same time, same place?'

'Yes. Can we make it 2 – I'm on a site visit this morning.'

Tim was glad of the site visit. It meant that he didn't have to face James and it gave him a few hours doing what he liked best. At about 11, his mobile rang and he thought for a fleeting second it might be Mary. But Susan's panicked voice cried, 'Tim, where are you? The engineers from Telfords are here to see you. You have an appointment at 11.' Tim's heart hit the floor of his stomach.

'They can't be. I have a site visit this morning. That meeting with Telfords isn't until next week.' His mouth was dry and he swallowed, but it made no difference.

'Not according to the diary I've got in front of me. They say you set it up yourself on short notice.'

Tim struggled to remember. His mind was collapsing. 'I haven't spoken to anyone from Telfords. The meeting was set up some time ago for next week. I'm sure it was.'

'What do you want me to say to them?'

Tim's mind raced through his options as he spoke. 'It'll take me an hour to get back to the office, so there's no way I can pretend to be a bit late. You'll have to apologise for me and look, don't take the flack yourself, blame me and I'll sort it out when I get back.' He rang off and having no control over what he was doing or saying, concluded the site visit and collapsed in his car. What was Telfords doing in his office? He checked the print out of his diary Susan gave him last night. There was no meeting with Telfords on it. He was meant to be on a site visit. What was going on?

Mary's heart crumbled as she saw Tim approaching the bistro. His face was strained. The tension in his jaw and neck was obvious. She opened her arms and he laid his cheek on the top of her head. He hugged her for a long minute; she could feel that he was trembling. 'Tim, whatever is the matter?'

They sat at an outside table with a huge green umbrella over it. 'I ordered what we had before. I hope that's OK.' He nodded and his hands trembled as he reached for his drink. 'Another cock up, I'm afraid.' He took a long drink as if to put out a fire inside. His eyes were wide. Confusion? Panic? 'There's been a mix-up with my diary and I wasn't at the office for a meeting with some very big boys from Telfords this morning. But honest to God Mary, my diary doesn't have any meeting on it.' He pulled the print out from his shirt pocket and handed it to her.

She looked at it. 'This isn't just a mistake is it?'

He turned his drink around and around. 'No. I know I didn't change the date – I know it.'

He lifted the top of his baguette and looked at the filling as if he didn't expect it to be there. Then he seemed to draw himself together, smiled and for a moment the world looked normal. 'But tell me – is everything all right in London? What happened?'

Mary inhaled as deeply as she could. 'My daughter called – she's pregnant.'

'I didn't know you had a daughter – do I take it this isn't good news?'

Mary cut the end off her baguette. 'She was nearly hysterical at the idea – she's a career girl you see – 22 years old and far too young to be burdened with a child.' She sipped her drink. 'But the boy friend – who I didn't meet – and his family and Kelley's father and every aunt, uncle and cousin on the planet is delighted.'

'But you didn't know.'

Mary swallowed hard. 'No. When Robert and I split up, Kelley took her father's side – completely – to the point of blaming me for everything. Once we stopped shouting at each other, we stopped communicating at all. We've not spoken for months.'

Tim stroked her cheek. 'And now?'

'She needed her mother I guess.' She attempted a smile. It didn't hurt and she felt a little better. They tried to eat.

'But Tim, your problem's more important just now. I've got time to get used to mine. Is someone is doing this to you on purpose?' She patted his hand.

'Oh, I have no doubt.'

'Then we have to find out who. Who could want to do this and why? Is it James?'

He clutched her hands in his like someone with vertigo on a ledge. 'I really don't know. He has access to my electronic diary so he knew where I was and why...'

'What about your own department?'

'Howard's the only one to have shown any kind of hesitation to me. Bryn is as keen as mustard and wants to get ahead. Derek has all the work he can manage and he won't be about to sabotage anything. Susan thinks I walk on water.' Mary's heart tripped. 'The other engineers and estimators live in this troglodyte world staring at computer screens all day, crunching numbers and drawing little lines.'

'Whoever it is needs to be able to manipulate the computer system. Yes?'

Tim nodded. 'I don't think James can. Andy's our IT man, but he's sort of a friend. I don't know Mary, I just don't know.'

'I wish I could have been there for you last night – you needed a friend and I feel like I let you down.'

Tim squeezed her hand. 'I'm a big boy, but I won't deny it, I was in need of a hug just then. Look, this is something I have to face. Can you just be there to listen to my whining?'

'Whining is allowed when someone's out to get you. I've got to do more than just listen.'

He straightened up and waved the bill at the waitress. 'Listening is what I need – so I have some touch with reality. What's important now is how you are feeling about – gosh, being a grandmother.'

'I don't know how to feel – not yet anyway. But that wouldn't have entered the equation for Kelley. She wanted someone to take her side, but I couldn't. All I could do was go – and be with her and calm her down a bit.'

Tim put his arm around her as they walked to the car; hers around his waist He gave her a squeeze. 'How is she now?'

116

They walked to the car park and she leaned on Tim's car. 'Well, she's talking to the boy friend and they're considering what they'll do next.'

'What about you?'

'I have very mixed feelings. I'm only 45 and feel a lot less. I'm not sure I'm ready to be a grandmother. To be honest I don't know how to be a grandmother.' Her voice was tight.

Tim hugged her and kissed her hair. 'You look nothing like any grandmother I've ever seen and you don't look old enough to be one either. As far as it's possible for a man to understand, I'll try to and I'll be there for you if you need me.'

Why is it he always can say the right things, she thought. She reached up and kissed him. 'Thanks. Shall I wait at your place for you tonight? I'll worry about you all afternoon. Do you really have to go back?'

'I've left Susan sitting on the time bomb and I'd better do the gallant thing and rescue her - much as I would like to ride into the sunset with you. You've got the key? It would be nice if you were there.'

She drove home feeling terrified, useless and quite sick - for several reasons all at once.

19

'I don't understand it.' Susan sounded as if she'd cry if she said any more. She and Tim sat at her desk, staring at the computer screen and then at the printout he'd flattened out in front of them.

'It's OK Susan. James's out on the golf course snobbing with some very big clients. He won't be back today. Just as long as they let him win once in awhile, he'll stay happy.'

She smiled bleakly. 'All I could do was apologise and get them out of the building as fast as I could. I don't think that James knew they were here. I promised that you'd call them and sort it out.' He wanted to give her a hug to reassure her. But knew he couldn't.

'You did the right thing, Susan. I think someone is starting to cause deliberate trouble for us – well for me. I'll deal with Telfords – have you got the names of who was here?' She handed him three business cards. *God, they were the heavy weights.* 'Thanks – I'll speak to them and set up another appointment. But right now I want you to change your password and get everyone else in the department – everyone – to do the same. We've got to stop whoever's playing silly-bugger games. Then we'll try to keep today quiet. I don't want you in the firing line if it gets out.' She nodded and there were huge tears at the corners of her eyes.

Tim spent a part of the next hour walking up and down a secluded part of the car park with a mobile phone to his head. He made grovelling apologies and promised to come to their offices at a time that suited them – at this point, he'd do just about anything to keep it all quiet. To some degree he succeeded.

When he got back to his desk, the office was still calm and it was almost time to close things down for the day. For the first time, he wanted to be at home more than anywhere else on earth.

Mary looked for something suitable among Tim's CD's. She smiled. It was amazing what some people found attractive in music. She checked the casserole in the oven and finished setting the table. When she heard his car crunching on the gravel, she uncorked a bottle of chilled white wine and was pouring two large glasses as he came in the kitchen.

'Oh, wonderful.' He dropped his briefcase inside the door. He kissed her and took a large drink. 'Oh I needed that. But first, are you all right?'

She licked wine off her fingers. 'You're amazing. You've had a couple of days of hell and your first question is how am I?'

He pulled his tie off and undid the neck button on his shirt. *Why is that so erotic?* wondered Mary and pulled her concentration back to what he was saying.

'I still want to know.'

'It'll rather changed my life, I suspect, but I'm not sure just how. So, yes, for the moment, I'm all right. It'll take me a little while to decide how I really feel. But tell me what's happened this afternoon.'

'You won't believe it, but nothing happened.'

She raised her eyebrow over her wine glass as he led her into the living room. 'James was out all afternoon – golfing somewhere.' They settled down in the oh-so-comfortable settee. 'So Susan and I had a look at the diary and surprise, surprise it was quite different from the print out you and I looked at.'

'So someone is doing something, somewhere.'

Tim spread his hands and lifted his shoulders in a gesture of helplessness. The timer pinged in the kitchen. 'Does that mean that dinner's ready?'

'No. It means I have fifteen minutes to put the salad together.'

'Good, that's fifteen minutes for me to change.'

Dinner was animated. They discussed. They speculated. They imagined the possible and the impossible. They analysed everyone in the office and they filled the gaps with the tiny snips of gossip that Tim could remember. As they put the dishes in the dishwasher they concluded that they were no further ahead than when they started.

As they sat together on the settee, he pulled her toward him and put his face into her hair. *She makes me feel calm.*

Mary wasn't prepared what met them when they opened her back door. It was a stench capable of blistering paint.

'Damn it. Now what?' She shouted at the house. Gagging, she pulled the big coat Tim loaned her over her face. Tim pulled the neck of his sweatshirt over his nose and pushed in ahead of her. 'It smells like something's died.'

He searched the house for the source of the smell, while she put the kittens back into Tim's car then opened every window in the house. In about half an hour they found two dead and decaying rats under a loose board on the floor of the airing cupboard. Tim lifted them out with a shovel and tied them in a bag.

'Even in a bad dream I couldn't imagine how they got there or how long they've been there. I bet it hasn't been long. They'd start to rot pretty fast in the heat. I'll call the pest control people in the morning for you.'

'No, I'll do it.'

He looked down at her, then at the bag in his hand. 'Sorry.'

She realised she'd spoken without thinking again. 'No, I'm sorry. You were just sharing a problem. What I meant is that you'll have enough to do tomorrow.'

They buried the beasts in the bag in a deep hole at the top of the garden, and then left all the windows open. The smell still lingered.

It was after 1 a.m. when they fell into Tim's bed and were asleep like two spoons in a drawer within minutes. The two kittens tucked themselves into the folds around their feet. Neither of them could believe it when Tim's alarm went off at 6:00. 'Sorry,' he mumbled into her neck, 'staff meeting today.'

Rosemary Cottage still reeked when Mary got there. She opened all the doors and retreated with two days post and her morning coffee to the garden. The Records Office would provide suitable sanctuary today and the cottage could give up its smell in its own time.

The letter from her solicitor was no surprise. It was what she'd been expecting but it still made her angry. The new proposal was stupid and she wanted to tell Robert that to his face. But a phone call would only make her even angrier and make him intransigent as well. A reply by post wouldn't get to him until next week by the time it went through her solicitor – an e-mail would be a better option. Perhaps she could use Tim's computer.

As she dialled his mobile number, she hoped he was not having another bad day. He'd been through enough this week. The call was picked up by the answering service. She left a message: Tim, its Mary. Call me on my mobile when you have a minute. Nothing urgent. Then she rang the pest control people. They could come in the afternoon if that was OK. Goodbye to another day in the Records Office.

Somewhere near the end of her pile of post, her mobile rang.

'Hello my dear.' Tim smiled into the tiny telephone, as he walked by Susan's desk. She looked up at him and he saw her smile disappear.

'Tim! I'm dying to know what happened this morning and well, to ask you a favour. But first how is everything? Can you talk?'

'Hang on, I'm on my way to the staff room. It's just that in this open office, nothing, but nothing is private.' The little room was empty and he sat down at one of the tables. 'It was quite interesting here earlier. You would have been proud of me. He'd heard about the mix up yesterday – well we knew he would, didn't we? And he very much wanted to have a go. But I just kept saying that I had fixed it and there was no problem. The big cheeses at Telfords weren't that bothered – it was a wasted trip for them, but that's all and Susan charmed them into bits and fed them tea and biscuits while they waited so no real harm done.'

'So there was nothing that he could really yell at you for? Did you show him the diary printout to prove that it had been changed?'

'No, I figured I would just carry the can for this one and not put too much wind up him if you know what I mean?'

'Good. I think that was the right thing to do.'

'Now you need a favour?'

'Yes, can I use your e-mail? I got the anticipated noxious reply from Robert today and I'd like to hit him between the eyes before he has time to plot something else.'

''Course you can. It's in the little bedroom. Help yourself.'

The door opened and Susan's head appeared. He held up a finger to her. 'I've got to go, love, duty calls. Give me a bell when you get there and I'll coach you through how to log in.' He blew a kiss down the phone and rang off.

Susan's voice sounded strained. 'The architect from that restaurant project is on the phone. He needs a word.' Tim winked at her and her face crumpled. She ran in the direction of the ladies room. Tim stared after her wondering what he'd done.

Tim's computer sat, malevolent and glowing, on a desk in the small bedroom. Mary looked at it for several long minutes before she sat down in front of the screen. It towered over her, its large face judging. The desk chair was so low the keyboard was almost under her chin so she took a pillow from the single bed and put it on the chair.

With courage she pushed the mouse and the computer whirred into life breathing a sinister hum across her hands.

'I have used e-mail before,' she told it. '... so I'm not completely illiterate nor am I stupid. So we'll get along just fine, won't we?' She dialled Tim's mobile number with more courage than she felt.

'OK, I've woken it up and it is showing me a Windows screen. What do I do now?'

'There's an icon on the left of the screen – a little blue thing. Just click on that and the ISP will open up.'

'The what?' The machine went off to do what it had been asked to do and Tim continued, '...then just click on log-in. You won't need a password.'

'You might after what I'm about to say to my solicitor. Can you be sued for libel or is it slander in cyber space?' Tim's laughter sparkled around inside her head like champagne bubbles. It made her feel wonderful to hear his thorough and honest laugh. There had been precious little to laugh about in the last few days. 'At the top you can see something like 'write' or whatever...'

'Yes.'

'Good, click on that then put in the address – be careful to get it exactly right or it won't go.'

'OK, I've got it. Now, this will take me sometime because I come from the hunt and peck school of typewriting. So what do I do if it doesn't go?'

'I'm afraid you will have to re-type it.'

'Can I call again if I get really stuck?'

'Of course you can. I'm in the office this morning and out later, but I'll have the mobile with me.'

Tim was still chuckling at his desk when his internal phone rang. James' voice sobered him in an instant and commanded his presence in the glassed in office. He felt the muscles of his smile relax and the ones around his eyes and jaw tense instead.

It took Mary a full half hour to get the message onto the screen and was pleased that it looked so coherent. As she was reading it through for the last time, Tim's telephone rang. She got up to answer it then realised that if he'd wanted her, he'd call her mobile number, so she let it ring through to the answering service. Suddenly a woman's voice pleaded from the computer's speakers, 'Tim, I need to talk to you. Please call me, please.' Then words appeared on the screen. 'You have one message.'

20

Mary's mind became a solid block when she heard the tone of the message. *Get a grip. It could be Ann, or his mother. But it was a young woman. It's just an innocent telephone call. Why am I shocked?* She made herself breathe. *Come back to first principles. We agreed no claims on each other. Stop it Mary. Is it going wrong? What I'm feeling is wrong. Am I really strong enough to believe that?*

With half a mind she clicked on the Send button and a message in a box told her it had been sent. She straightened the keyboard, locked the house and walked home.

The Pest Control man drove his little van into Mary's drive about 4 o'clock, just as she was finishing weeding the tiny vegetable plot. She showed him where they had found the dead rats and he sprayed the area, recommending that she dispose of any open food in case the animals had been in the kitchen.

Then he looked around the outside of the house. 'Just trying to figure out how they got in,' he explained. 'There's no ivy or climbers for 'em to get up. Heard any noises in your attic?' Mary hadn't. 'It's possible they got up that big tree at the side of the house onto the roof. So if I were you I'd have a look at the roof t'see if there's any broken tiles or loose barge boards. But I don' know how they ended up under the floor. There weren't any nestin' material or anything.'

Tim arrived at Rosemary Cottage about 6 o'clock with a large bag of fish and chips under his arm. He could feel the tension across his shoulders and he didn't need Mary to ask if he'd had a bad day. It must have been clear from his face.

'James is at it again. Someone corrupted a quotation of mine – badly – on the computer and he's saying that it went out that way. It made it a very attractive quotation with high quality stock instead of the stuff they need.' He poured two very large glasses of wine. 'I knew I hadn't created the quote like that I just know it, but the file he showed me was a right mess. Anyway, he wasn't to know that I'd worked with the engineer over there and when I called him he didn't know a thing about it – the quote was exactly what they'd asked for.'

'But... but surely that's ...that's... unethical.'

Her disbelief made Tim laugh. 'Oh it's that all right. He's trying to sink me for some reason. He lied about the quotation. He's got someone who can manipulate the computer network to make me think I've screwed up. I don't think he's got the brains or the balls to do that part himself.'

He gathered the newspapers on the table into a pile and folded the local paper to put on top.

'It just seems so odd. I can't work out why.' Tim took the papers to the counter. 'Well, I'll be damned.' Mary looked around him at the lead story. 'We quoted for some work on this property. The developer is looking to restore, but there's been a huge break in. The place has been burned.' He scanned through the article. 'Police are suspicious. I remember it because it was local.' He replaced the paper and Mary brought the salt and pepper to the table.

'I think we have to try to find out why James wants to get rid of you – because to be blunt, it looks like that's what he wants. Maybe he's feeling threatened because you're a better designer than he is or you're getting near something – something he doesn't want you to know.'

Tim sobered for a minute. 'I can't think what. It must be serious for him to feel this sensitive about it. I'd better start reading the vacancies section again.' He took the paper packages out of the plastic bag and put them on the plates.

'What's more important though is that we've got to be sure that when – or if – you leave Conmac, he hasn't destroyed your reputation. He may try. Have you talked to your professional association?'

In that moment, the gravity of his situation became concrete. Conmac might be all over for him. His career might be all over.... He reached for Mary, folded her in his arms and held onto her. He put his face into her hair. 'Mary, I'm worried.'

She lifted his face with her hands and looked at him. 'Tim, I know how this feels. I really know. There's a great hole in the pit of your stomach and everything you are or ever were threatens to fall through it. It made me wonder if I was in the right profession. As it turned out, things unfolded in such a way that I had little choice. But I did have to ask myself if I would be prepared to start again.'

She leaned on him. He felt the warmth of her head on his chest through his shirt. 'Why didn't you start again?'

'My Head got to the staff room cabal and the union before I did and things were stacked pretty high against me. And with what else was going on in my life at the time, I guess I lost confidence. Or maybe I was just too tired to continue. I didn't have the strength any longer to face a whole staff room that didn't want me there. And now that I've looked at the profession from the outside, I see it for what it is – not a profession at all and I don't want to go back in.' Tim stroked her hair.

She put her head back on his chest. 'But it's not too late for you. If we can protect your reputation, you can go on to do something else. I am worried that James is going to do some serious damage.'

He kissed the top of her head. 'How did it end? For you I mean.'

'Well, I tried a little threat of my own in the end. I told the Head, Harold that I'd make the whole affair public, unless he agreed to let me go on some other grounds – early retirement due to ill health – anything, I didn't care. And that's how it ended.'

She was quiet for a few minutes. 'So you see, I do understand what it's like to see your career beginning to fall around your ankles. And when you identify yourself with what you are, like we do, it's like seeing a good chunk of yourself being shot away.'

He hugged her closer. 'I just admire you more and more every day.' He tipped up her chin and kissed her as if he meant it. 'I think you have just made me realise what I have to do.'

'What's that?'

'I've got to find out what this bastard's really up to. This isn't just a personality clash anymore. Whatever he's doing, it's not legal or moral. Other people could be involved – it could be damaging to the company, clients, the employees... Somehow I've got to find out what it is and then stop it. Trouble is, I haven't the faintest idea what it is.'

'Come on, this is getting cold.' Mary didn't mention the telephone message she'd overheard – she wanted them to be just as they were now, for a short while longer. She wanted to believe they'd be safe – for one more day...

The grey-skirted archivist greeted Mary by name and smiled with genuine pleasure as she signed in. 'Do you want the estate court records for Eaton Manor today, Mrs Mitchell?'

'How amazing that you remembered that. I haven't been in for awhile.'

The archivist smiled, flicked a red index binder from a long shelf with an exquisite fingernail and put it on the table beside Mary's pencil case. 'There were two kinds of court,' she explained, leaning on the table beside Mary, '...courts baron that administered transfers of land - and met now and again - or courts leet that dealt with day to day administrative matters like broken hedges, straying animals or grazing in the wrong part of the common or at the wrong time of the year, or for petty crimes. Just day-to-day matters. A jury was made up of men of the manor and these are usually listed at the beginning of the documents and they agreed the fines to be paid.'

According to a brief summary at the front of the index, the manorial courts were active in the 15th and 16th centuries but continued for some time after that although records became fewer into the 17th and 18th centuries. As she was finishing, the archivist slid some plastic covered documents off her arm and onto the table. 'I'm not sure what kind of thing you are looking for, but these are the some of the court records for Eaton Manor. They cover the 17th century.'

Mary thanked her and looked first at the records closest to 1670. There were very few. There was a jury list from 1658, an undated fragment of fines and payments for crimes brought before it and a sheet that listed the infringements of manorial rules in 1669. Being the date closest to the probable executions, Mary read it through. The name John Roberts appeared on the jury list and assumed some position of importance because he was the only one referred to as Mr. The archivist explained that this was an honorary title for the important men of the area. Perhaps he was the Lord of the Manor, or related to him.

'Mar 15, 1669 Alice Abbott against the lord's peace took, 1 smock price 8d, 1 towel price 3d the goods of John Butler,

'Thomas Cresman assaulted Richard Hopkin and struck him 6d,

'Richard Trent was summoned to pay to court and did not come therefore he is amerced 4d.

'May1670 John Roberts aggrieves Rose and Mary Flitch of unchristian acts and deeds, visiting the spirit of murrain and flux on one Jane Fench and others.' Mary clutched the edge of the table, just able to avoid a shout of discovery.

21

There is it was: John Roberts charging two girls with something approaching witchcraft. The story was unfolding at last. She tipped all the papers off her note pad and began to list all the bits she had in date order. There had to be a connection. If she'd found the charge, then there had to be a connection to the execution.

The link between this charge and the little map showing a place of execution was still very thin and she had to admit that most of it existed in her imagination. Proof? Was there any? Maybe it would always be a supposition.

She scanned the fragmentary remains of the court leet records but there was no further reference to the charge or its resolution. Not willing to let go of the precious information, she asked the grey-clad girl if it would be possible to have a photocopy of the record. The little stud sparkled in the girl's nose as she laid the plastic covered document on the glass and Mary took the copy back to her table.

Looking at it for several minutes she tried to put some rationale around the information. Why had John Roberts charged them with such a serious crime? Why was no outcome or fine recorded in the court leet records? He'd gone through with some kind of executions because later he was in the Assize Court for the deed. She was certain that it was Rose and Mary that he'd killed, but she couldn't prove it. Nor could she establish with any certainty, when in 1670 the executions had taken place. She asked for the execution map again and looked at it through a magnifying glass. The little drawings were very sweet – a tiny fragment of time and place, bringing in the harvest and hay making three and a half centuries ago. What had it been like at the time? But why were the little drawings there? They had little to do with the horrifying drawing beside them. A window opened in the off-side of her brain. Hay making and harvesting took place in July and August. This was a subtle and simplistic way of telling when the executions had taken place – two or three months after John Roberts' charge.

She narrowed her mind on John Roberts. What would make a man go to such lengths? She let her thoughts make their own way. Lust? He wanted one or both of the women and for some reason failed. Was that because he attempted something and was found out; something like a sexual assault, or a forced marriage? Or had he been found attempting to do so? What other motive could he have? He wanted something. Land? Revenge? But if he was lord of the manor couldn't he just take it from his tenants. They had agreements - but if he'd been determined enough... And where did John Cooper fit in?

The archivist had referred to land transfers earlier - the courts baron. Were there any records of this estate in these archives?

Mary wasn't sure what she wanted to look for and was almost afraid to search, in case the answer was negative, but she asked the archivist to search the index and see what there was. The girl stopped what she was doing at the desk and together they went to the index books. They searched the date files without success, but did locate an undated paper from the Eaton Manor estate that referred to John Roberts. They decided that it was worth a look and in due course a flimsy piece of fragile paper in a plastic sleeve arrived.

It was a fragment of a court baron and the list of jurors was at the top of the page beneath the elegant script that referred to the sitting. A section of the document had been destroyed – where the date would have been recorded. The list of jurors however again included John Roberts himself – which was odd Mary thought. If he were the lord of the manor why was he a juror – perhaps this was the father or the son. But the names John Cooper and William Fletch both were written beneath in the same elegant script.

Mary took a sharp intake of breath. This could only mean that John Cooper and William Fletch/Fletcher were tenants on the estate at some time.

The archivist walking past looked at Mary's smile. 'I think that you may have had some success.'

'I have indeed and this shows that two people I have been interested in were tenants on the estate at some time. It is quite significant, but doesn't quite tell me what I need to know.'

'What is it that you are looking for?' The archivist sat on the edge of the table.

'I want to find out – prove if I can - that the lord of the manor, or perhaps his son, attempted something quite horrible to these two people. It may have involved lust or land or any number of things that I can't even imagine.'

'Have you looked at the rent rolls? They might tell you what land the tenants or freeholders held and for how long.'

In due course, a long thin book with a peeling leather cover was put in front of her. It listed all the parcels of land on the estate, who farmed them and the rents paid. The dates were from 1602 to 1754. Not daring to rush, Mary started at the beginning and read each page. She first found William Flitcher in 1646. He had taken over a parcel of land called Hilderhill farmed to that time by a Thomas Crown. John Cooper appeared in

1666 at land called Haynehurst. It was listed next to Hilderhill and William Fletcher – perhaps they were adjacent properties.

She followed the land and its rental payments to 1670. Here both William Flitcher and John Cooper disappeared from the rent books. A note against Hilderhill and Haynehurst showed them to be in the possession of 'the lord'. So somehow, John Roberts had got control of the two farms. But if that were so why had he found it necessary to execute Rose and Mary? Mary recorded the dates. The rent listing that showed 'the lord' as occupier was dated March 15, 1670. She looked at her notes from the execution map. The date was 1670 and if her assumption was correct, it was July or August.

Mary leaned back and sighed. The dates of the execution and accusation were after John Roberts had obtained control of the land. It didn't make sense.

The archivist sat down beside her. 'Having trouble?'

'Yes, I've found the connection I need, but the dates don't make sense.' She showed the young woman what was wrong.

The archivist smiled. 'You may not know that the calendar of the day was askew from the one we use now. The year numbers changed on March 25, not January 1. The system wasn't changed until 1751. Therefore, August 1670 occurred on the old calendar before March 1670. March 1670 was, by our reckoning, 1671.'

Mary was speechless. The factual link was there – established at last. John Roberts – father or son she didn't know - had executed the young women and got the land he wanted. Somehow she thanked the young woman and finished the last few pages of the rent book. In 1672 William Fletcher appeared again, but on different property and he was referred to as William Sr. A note beside the entry said: 'Assigned in perpetuity'. Mary stuck a piece of paper in the book and closed it as though it were precious. She rested her hands on the broken cover and tried to feel the hate, lust, grief and resolution that were inside. The circle was almost complete.

She asked the girl if she might have copies of the two pages she needed and was startled to find that it was half past four. She had been there all day.

She put the copies into her case, gathered up her pencils and magnifying glass, put on her huge cardigan. On the way past the desk she stopped and thanked the young woman who had been so helpful.

As she put her case into her car, she realised that today the young woman had been wearing a little name badge. Mary was sure she'd never seen it before and then she almost fell into the car. The name on the badge was Rosemary!

In spite of her excitement over what she'd found, a little chill of worry followed Mary home that afternoon. She feared for Tim and the woman's voice on Tim's computer nagged. Whatever was to happen, she'd postpone it for tonight at least. Denial? Perhaps. But a voice nagged: for how much longer?

Tim arrived at Rosemary Cottage straight from work. The strain was clear on his face. He looked exhausted and there were lines on his forehead and visible tension in his neck muscles. He hugged her for a long time without speaking. Something else was wrong. She pulled his head onto her shoulder. 'Tell me,' she whispered. Her heart pounded and anxiety banged in her throat.

He leaned on the edge of the kitchen table and took both her hands. 'A quote I sent off on Tuesday didn't arrive by the deadline. We've missed a chance to be considered. I know when I sent it. We do it electronically and when things started to get funny, I began to make notes in my diary. But they didn't receive it. The hard copy was held up and didn't arrive on time either. James was ballistic. I thought he was going to have a stroke. He just went on and on – it was so embarrassing – the whole office knew he was mad and that it was me he was mad at.'

'Oh Tim. What have they done?'

'I wish to God I knew. If it's James doing this, it's cost him and the company a lot. Either he knew that the quote wasn't going to be accepted, or he's getting reckless. I just don't understand it.' He pulled her between his knees. 'I'm being set up to look incompetent and I don't know why.'

She hugged his head to her shoulder. 'I might be able to help.'

When she let him go, she pointed at a bottle of wine and pulled on some oven gloves. Tim looked at her in surprise.

'Don't look as if I have just offered to split the atom. I can't tell you yet; I need to see if I can make the right contacts first.'

'You intrigue me – sure you can't tell me?'

'No, not yet.'

Tim looked around the kitchen. It was warm, loved and lived in. He felt safe for the first time all day.

Later, on the library settle amongst the pillows, he slid his arm around her and put his face in her hair. It was soft and comfortable and God only knew how much he needed both right now.

'So I think that . . .' her voice was getting further and further away.

'Tim?' He woke with a start.

'I didn't fall asleep did I? Oh God, Mary, I am sorry, what were you saying'?

She kissed his arm across her shoulder. 'I was saying that you're out on your feet. Why don't you go home to bed'?

'Only if you will come too.'

'No, this is one time when you need a normal night's sleep in your own bed – and the world and his wife gives you permission to sleep in as long as you like. It's a long weekend and there's plenty of time for you to get a decent rest and for us to plan what we do about James.'

She pushed him out the door and into his car. 'I'll bring breakfast up about 10.'

Mary was up early and on a strict schedule. She set the bread maker to make dough that she shaped into rolls. While they were rising, she found a nice basket, ironed a pretty cloth to line it and assembled what she needed. The buns went into the Rayburn at 9:20, were done and cooling by 9:45 at which time she started a fresh pot of coffee and warmed the flask. At 5 to10 it was all packed into a small basket and she locked the cottage behind her.

There was a small van in Tim's drive when she got there. The name on it was one she did not recognise - a delivery of some sort. She pushed open the door to the extension and called out as she reached for the kitchen door. 'Tim. I've brought breakfast. I hope you're hungry.'

She banged the basket through the door and came face to face with a small young woman in a short dressing gown. Her hands were wrapped around a cup. She was pretty with short dark hair and bare feet. Tim appeared at the door from the living room. He had jeans on and nothing else. His hair was uncombed, he hadn't shaved and his face told a story she could not read.

22

'I'm so sorry,' Mary mumbled. Only her mouth functioned; logical thought was sucked away like smoke up a chimney. There was no feeling in her hands or feet.

The young woman smiled. She was beautiful. 'Tim? When did you arrange this? How wonderful.'

'Macie! No .' Tim's voice came to Mary as if from across a field.

But the young woman had taken the basket and was looking into it. 'Oh, isn't he a dear?' She smiled at Mary.

'Macie, it's not...'

'I'm hopeless at breakfasts,' she bubbled on. 'I'm not awake enough in the morning to even think about food. But when it looks like this... well, who can resist?'

Mary let her mouth work, although her brain was still somewhere else. 'I hope you enjoy it.' She turned to the door.

Tim's voice was high pitched and tight. 'Mary!' But she was gone.

Macie took the pretty cloth off the top of the basket. 'Oh Tim, look at this. There are hot rolls in here. And fresh coffee too. Oh she is a treasure. Where ever did you find her in the back woods of Herefordshire? You're a lot more civilised here than I thought.' She was unpacking the basket in delight.

'Macie.' Tim pushed past her and wrenched open the back door. He stopped when his bare feet hit the sharp stones of the drive. Mary was not to be seen. He ran back into the house. Macie looked at him in surprise. He took the stairs to the bedroom three at a time. Pushing numbers on the bedside telephone, he crawled on the floor looking for a something to put on his feet. Where the hell were his shoes?

Mary did not look back as she ran back to her cottage. Her body weighed so much that she felt like she was moving ankle deep in wet sand. She wanted to cry, but there was too much pain in her throat to let it pass.

Inside, the telephone rang. She couldn't answer it. Her message trailed from the machine. She knew he'd want to explain but whatever he could say, she didn't want it;

innocence, mistaken identity, a blunt ending to their relationship; she wanted to hear none of it. His panicked voice pleaded, 'Mary, for Gods sake! Mary, speak to me.' But she couldn't. She pulled a coat off the back of the door, grabbed car keys from the drawer and drove away. She saw a figure at the top of the lane beside Tim's house, but she turned the other way and did not look into the rear view mirror again.

Tim had pulled the telephone from the table trying to locate shoes, slippers – anything. It fell with a crash as he pleaded to her answer machine. Somehow he got the receiver back on the cradle, then running back down the stairs, he'd missed the bottom two, landed hard, and wrenched his foot. Macie stared at him in amazement. He knew his mouth was open and he was gulping air. He blinked – his eyes felt dry.

'Tim? Whatever is the matter?'

'I – I've some papers to give her.' He staggered to the back extension, rammed his bare feet into some Wellington boots and sprinted, limping, for the gate and into the lane, just to see Mary's car leave the drive. He braced his arms on the gatepost and put his head between his elbows until he was able to stop gulping and the throbbing in his ankle slowed. Then he went to face Macie.

She had laid the little round kitchen table – it looked pretty - and was pouring coffee when he came back in. 'This is wonderful,' she oozed. 'What did you say her name was? Mary?'

'Yes, Mary.' He leaned on the doorframe. His knees felt like they had disintegrated.

'Where does she live?'

'Next door,' he answered as he kicked off the boots. He brushed past her and went back upstairs. Macie's voice floated up after him. 'Don't be long or this'll be cold.'

He sat down on the side of the bed and put his head in his hands. Oh God how could things go so wrong in 15 seconds. He had to talk to her; he had to tell her it was all a mistake. He dialled her mobile number. It rang to the answer service. He left no message.

Ludlow's pretty Georgian town houses and tilting black and white buildings had charmed Mary before. Today she saw them but none of their delight. The beautiful shops held no attraction. The wine merchant's shop beckoned; she did not go in. In the large market square, she allowed herself to be jostled among the crowded and busy stalls, seeing but not recognising flower sellers, bric-a-brac, lace, vegetables, fish and cheese sellers. When the clock in the old butter market struck noon, she realised that she was back in her car and on the seat beside her were a large bread roll, a tomato and a bottle of still water.

She put the car in gear and drove north. Spring flowers competed for space on the verges, swathes of cow parsley nodded above the buttercups; ox eye daisies filled any space not used by something else and wild roses blinked pale pink blossoms here and there on the hedgerows. She turned to the west at Church Stretton and climbed the Long Mynd, parked at the top and got out.

A strong dry wind threw her against the car and woke her enough to tell her where she was. She took the big coat off the back seat, stuffed the roll, tomato and water into one of its voluminous pockets and slammed the car door. The bang gave her some satisfaction, and she turned and walked away; the wind made her struggle. It felt good. She walked and walked.

She stopped at the edge of a very steep drop, sat down in a shelter scooped out by the sheep and looked over the enormous valley in front of her. The sun shone, weak but warm and in the protection from the wind she turned her face to it, begging it for a cure.

She pulled her knees up to her chin, wrapped the coat around and put her head down. The pain in her throat could not be gulped away. She clawed at controlling the pain that should not be there. She lay back on the earth with the shaggy grass and heather folding over her and watched the sun begin to curve to the west.

Tim went back in to face Macie. But his power of speech and understanding had disappeared. He could not eat, but filled one cup after another with black coffee that he drank unsweetened.

'Tim?' Macie's voice interceded at last. 'You never drink coffee in the morning. And you never drink it black.'

There's a lot about me you don't know, he thought, filling the cup again. He had no feeling in his hands.

'Tim?' The sound of her was beginning to make him sweat. 'Please have something to eat.' She got up and pushed her hands up his bare chest. 'Please come and eat something.'

His knees felt weak and his head was very heavy. He let it rest on her shoulder. He wanted to cry, but nothing came. Her arms were warm around his neck; her honey-like perfume and her soft, sweet flesh felt comfortable and familiar. A sensation of something normal, uncomplicated, habitual and sane rolled over his mind like the mound of a feather filled duvet. He breathed into her neck. *There are no terrors here – just life as it used to be; simple, benign, no professional crises, no personal ones.* He felt the muscles in his shoulders tense and knew that his arms were going around her. But he saw the coffee cup in his hand. It was Mary's.

He straightened up and pushed her away. If she spoke he heard nothing. He threw the last of his coffee into the sink and went back upstairs to find a shirt. He tried Mary's mobile again. Then he dialled her at home. He left another message. He pleaded.

Macie was packing the basket with dirty crockery when he got back to the kitchen. He filled his coffee cup again with what was left in the flask and held it in front of him. He needed to keep something between them – to shield him. 'Macie,' he made his voice say, 'I need to talk to you.'

But she didn't want to listen; she wanted to do the talking. He understood why. She knew that what he was about to say was not what she wanted to hear. Not hearing it meant it was not real. *Just like old times*, he thought. She talked, but nothing went into his brain. 'Macie,' he interrupted at last. 'What <u>are</u> you talking about?'

'But darling, haven't you been listening?' She went on without waiting for an answer. 'I tried to tell you last night. I've given my notice at work and I'm going to move out here to be with you. I realize that you didn't like the city and I can live in the country if I know I'm with you. We can be very happy here. It needs a woman's touch of course.' She giggled, '…but it's quite sweet in its own way and so much bigger than the flat. I'll find some kind of work and there are sure to be one or two good schools for when we need them…'

A great claw twisted in his stomach. Her voice ran on and on. His head was beginning to rotate. He folded himself onto the kitchen step and he put his head between his knees. The blood rush blotted out sound, but when he lifted it again, she was still talking.

Clutching his stomach he got up and ran for the bathroom where he threw up. It was only coffee but it hurt.

'Tim?' He heard her shout into the extension. 'Are you all right?' He slammed the door shut. *Is this the only place in my life I can be alone?* 'I'm all right.'

He sat on the floor with his back on the cold tiled wall and pressed his fists into his stomach muscles. *How on earth am I going to get out of this one? Nicely, nicely and hurt her all over again. Or brute force over ignorance and hurt her anyway?*

With effort he started the shower. It blotted out sounds from the rest of the house. He pulled himself and the world into a tiny tepee of rushing water. But his stomach continued to heave and he continued to sweat.

When he came out she was dressed and sitting on the settee reading a magazine. She smiled like a Madonna. He went to his room, dressed, found his shoes still stuck in the legs of his work trousers and came back down. A small segment of his mind had convinced itself that none of this was real and that she would not be there. But as usual it was wrong. He did not sit down beside her. He did not want to touch her. Controlling his lust was no problem, but shaking her to small pieces would be harder to prevent.

When there was no emotion left in her, Mary raised her head from her knees and looked at the huge sky.

Why? Why hadn't he the guts to tell me last night? Why let me bring breakfast up for God's sake? He forgot? Why do I feel this way? Don't be ridiculous.

What's gone wrong –no, not with him, with me? I own these feelings! I own my own heart. If I blame him, the pain just goes on and on. Dear God how much pain am I still carrying around from the last time I blamed someone else for how I feel. It takes too long to let go of blame – I mustn't grasp it in the first place. But where the hell did this pain come from? It's a misunderstanding – he wouldn't have asked me to go with him last night….

I'll see him again – we live next door to each other – I doubt that one of us will move overnight. I know he'll come to me. To explain. Do I want to hear? I've got to have my own thoughts straight. My emotions controlled. My soul calm.

With all her strength, she threw the bread roll and tomato down the precipice.

Tim sat down on the edge of the chair opposite Macie. 'Sorry about that, something I ate I guess.' She patted his knee.

He drew breath and tried to make a start but she interrupted. 'Do you know that there are no curtains in that little room upstairs? I had to get dressed in yours. It's really not on you know.'

'Macie. There is no other living person for miles in any direction. No one will see you or care if they did.'

'Tim, that's cruel.'

Not half a cruel as its going to be, he thought.

'Macie.' She opened her mouth to speak, but he leaned forward and put his finger over her mouth. 'No it's my turn.

'This is not the place for you Macie. You are bright lights and one long round of parties. There are no PR companies here.' He tried to claw back a little control of the situation.

'That's OK darling, I'll look for something else. I don't mind what I do. And anyway I've handed in my resignation.'

'I think you have missed the point Macie. What you see when you look out of the window is what you get around here. There are no people, no parties, not even any big shopping centres so far as I know. There are no nightclubs and no street cafes. This is the countryside.'

'I don't mind, really I don't.' She folded the magazine cover back. 'We can have this place landscaped. It'll look quite pretty and I've looked on the map and Shrewsbury and Gloucester aren't that far away if we want a night out.'

He could feel the tiny sliver of control slipping away. 'Macie. Landscaping here consists of a once a week gardener and trailer loads of cow muck spread on the fields. Believe me it will stink for days.'

'Well, we can go away for a few weeks...'

He tried again. 'Macie, listen to me. If you've quit your job, then I suggest you call them and beg for it back because I know you very well and you won't like it here. We'd both be miserable.'

'Then come back to the city with me. Please.' *Now she'll try the 'please and plead' routine. I know this one.* He got up and handed her a tissue box.

'What is this for?'

'I know what happens now. You're going to cry. I've been here before, so before you start, take it. No, I have no intention of going back to the city. I like it here and I'm staying.' *Please God, let Mary be here too.*

But she started to cry anyway. He pushed the tissue box into her lap and went out to the back yard. He called Mary again. Still no reply. He left another message at the cottage.

As he stood there in desperation, Macie picked her way over the gravel drive as if it was made of broken bottles and onto the disorganised grass. She tried to put her arms around him, but he backed away. 'Listen Macie.' He pointed at the little van. 'I want you to put your things in there and drive away. Go home – to your parents or back to London – I don't care. This is not the place for you. I'm going out...' She drew breath but he rushed on before she could speak, 'No, I need to go alone and you have things to do. Leave the key under the big pot at the back door'.

As the sun began its descent toward the north-western hills, Mary checked her resolutions. She pulled in a ragged breath, *I've no right to any possessive feelings. No commitment, just friendship and as many laughs as we can fit in. I let my emotions assume too much. This is my fault. Just mine.*

Now – look at the worst part. Go on look at the piece you don't want to see. Someone else. Is Macie the 'someone else'? If we've no promises between us, he can find someone else if he wants to. That's the deal. But...' She put her head back down. She wasn't ready to look at the picture. It was too deep. It had a real face, a real smile, real hair – bad enough when it was just a concept, but when it was real... no... she couldn't look.

Tim flicked the electronic lock on his car and with a shower of gravel began a search for Mary. He felt impotent in looking for her. He didn't expect her to go to places where they'd been together – but except for those places, he didn't know where to look. He drove to Hereford and then to the Corvedale. There was no sign of her, but he had not expected there to be. He looked in the car park of Acton Scott Working Farm, but she wasn't there. He knew she wouldn't be. He drove back through Ludlow and Croftbury looking into every car like hers that he saw. He stopped at Rosemary Cottage again in case she had returned. The drive was empty and he was not surprised. The sun was close to setting when he turned into his own drive. He banged the steering wheel with his fist and swore in all the words in all the languages he knew. Then he lost it.

She was making toast when he went in.

'Macie, what the hell are you still doing here?' He shouted it at her. She said nothing but swayed as she turned around. She was very, very drunk and flung herself onto his chest, weeping. He grabbed her arms and threw them down at her sides. 'Whatever's in that toaster, it's burning!' He wanted to put her outside and leave her there.

The sun was almost gone by the time Mary lifted her head. She gathered the coat around her as tightly as she could, to keep her resolutions firm. Was she strong enough now to go home? Probably. Possibly. Was it where she wanted to go? There were kittens to look after. She had no idea where her car was.

She knew that she'd walked to the west, so if she kept what little of the sunset there was on her back, she might be going in the right direction.

She stumbled over stones partially buried in the ground; fell into holes the sheep had carved. Sharp heather plants clawed at her legs. Bracken caught at her ankles. The wind dropped and so did the temperature. She listened for the sound of human activity. There was none. The light was almost gone. She splashed into a large puddle of water. The shock of the cold water made her stop. She realised that it was a broken piece of pavement. She was on the roadway. Taking her keys from her pocket, she pressed the automatic locking pad as she walked. Then a short distance away, she saw a lone car and watched as its taillights flashed. Thank God. No matter how distraught she was, a night in a sheep hole in this beautiful, but barren place would punish only her and she was still too damn mad for that.

23

Mary put a black, blank mental barrier between her cottage and Tim's. She didn't let her mind through it. She concentrated everything on her garage door. In the low lights from her car, she unlocked it, threw enough boxes out of the way and got the car inside. She shut the door and locked it. The click in the lock sounded like a safety-catch on the day.

Inside the cottage the telephone blinked a message. With insane calmness she deleted his messages one after the other without listening to them. The snatches of his voice that she heard became more and more hysterical as they disappeared. Then she fed the kittens and sat in the dark in the library with the last wisps of sherry in the bottle. She wanted to be invisible.

The problem before her and its resolution became clearer as the darkness deepened. Tim wanted a relationship but not commitment; she didn't want dependence and anyway what happened was all a mistake. Their relationship was as insane as it was possible to be but there it was plain, simple and true. Her contract with her feelings was firm again and she felt stronger, calmer. She could face him in the morning and she could admit that she and she alone, had got it very wrong.

Macie was too drunk to make sense and too insensible to send home. He'd said all he could to make her understand. Whatever he said now would be the same arguments. He didn't love her and didn't want to share a life, a home or even a cup of tea with her. That was all that he could tell her; the truth. But she wasn't in any condition to hear. Maybe she already knew and being incapable was her way of distancing herself from it. He didn't have any chivalrous desire even to sober her up, so when she fell asleep on the settee, he threw a duvet over her and left her there.

For a long time he stood at the open bedroom window, listened to the silence and tried to claw some peace from the darkness. There was such beauty in the silver world of moonlight. Leaves glistened and sparkled in the air currents. A singular cow continued to graze among clusters of others tucked into the pasture grass; the ripping of grass almost the only sound on the night air. The warm tarmac glowed between dark hedges. The verges flickered with parsley and nodding grasses. Thousands of ox-eye daisies floated like numberless polka dots on a dark net skirt. A few birds communicated through the leaves of the trees and the moon made its silent progress across the sky. He stood there for a long time seeing, but not seeing.

What the hell's happened to me? OK, so apart from a crumbling job, life here is warm and comfortable. I don't want to give it up. I want it to stay like this but why is everything so fragile? Why so, so...

He thought about Mary, his heart lifted, and a smile came unbidden. But it was a bitter sweetness. He'd never felt so safe and natural in his life.

Then after a few seconds – just a few, tiny, microscopic seconds – it had all disappeared. The softness, the warmth - all right, admit it, the happiness has been sucked out. Like a tornado. It seemed like a lifetime ago.

I've got to fix it. I need what we had: together but not together. That suits me. I want a relationship, not commitment. I want what we had, simplistic though it was.

The sense of loss began somewhere near his knees and rose in a rush to slam into his chest. He clung to the window frame and hung on until the night was silent again.

Deep in his heart he listened for any sound that could be coming from Rosemary Cottage. There was none. He went back downstairs – Macie was where he left her – and walked down the lane to see if Mary had returned. The gates were still open as they had been all day and there was no sign of her car. Worry clamped a cold fist over his heart. Had something happened to her? Should he see if she was home anyway? She wouldn't thank him for waking her at this hour. They needed to talk but this would not be the time.

But he knocked on the door anyway. There was no reply; he expected none. She was a sensible person he comforted himself. She was safe – he just did not know where. Alone and under the starlight, he walked back up the lane - again.

With a blanket and two kittens on her knees Mary sat in the darkness – cold, tired, restless, stomach muscles tight. The dark was her friend – it came with relentless routine, and she could join it if she wanted to. They used to talk with each other in another lifetime and she told it her troubles then. Sometimes it responded and sometimes it made her make her own decisions. In the past year, she spent a lot of time in the dark. It reduced the multiplicity of life around her and let her dwell on one issue at a time. It shielded her from all those ancillary things that were there only to confuse and compound her thinking. She solved problems in the dark. It let her catch up to her feelings and put priorities in the right places. It healed her and she needed it to do so again.

She looked into the silvery blackness without focussing her eyes on anything in particular. She heard someone knocking on the door and she knew it was Tim. She also knew that, in spite of her resolution, she couldn't speak to him yet. She pulled the blanket over her chest and stared again into blank, black space for a long time.

Then together, both kittens bolted upright, ears flicking. One of them hissed.

A thin stream of smoke-like grey threads rose from the darkness and swung in the night air. It neither came nor went, it just was – swaying in space.

Breath caught in the back of Mary's mouth – not again, she cried, but no sound came from her choked throat. Please God, not again. Give me the strength to stay sane – don't let me fall now. Give me my sanity – take anything else, but leave me a sane mind. She clutched the arms of the chair with such force that her fingers hurt. Pain. Pain will keep this real – don't go away she pleaded to the hurt. She wanted to bite her lip, but her breath was coming so fast and hard, she couldn't close her mouth. The grey vision was taller, closer and wider now. With a huge gulp, she turned her head away and screamed.

At some time during the night Tim felt someone snuggling up to his back. Rising from a deep sleep, the cool flesh made his heart surface before the rest of him. Mary? Then he realised who it was, sat up and turned the light on. 'Macie, for God's sake go to bed.'

'Tim, please.' The dazzling light stung his eyes. Squinting he could see she was still drunk and about to cry again. But Tim was out of bed and pulling his jeans on. He tried to pull her out of the bed, but she clung to it, weeping. *If this weren't so disgusting, it would be comedy*, he thought. He left her there and sat under the duvet on the settee in the living room until daylight.

Wearing all he could find in the morning – his jeans and the robe from the back of the bathroom door, Tim waited in the kitchen.

Macie came downstairs as the coffee maker finished making its last slurping noises. She was wrapped in his duvet and not a lot else. 'It is cold in here.' She climbed onto a kitchen stool at the counter and pulled her bare feet off the floor. 'What time is it?' Her hair was sticking up in all directions. 'Ten past nine.' He might have found this waif just a tiny bit endearing in another lifetime. He poured her some coffee and pushed a box of paracetamol toward her.

'But darling, you know I don't drink coffee in the mornings.' He banged the cup down in front of her a bit more aggressively than he meant. It splashed on the counter top.

'Don't call me darling. Drink the coffee.' He sat down at the kitchen table and put his head in his hands. She did as she was told. By knitting what courage he had left, with the anger he was afraid to let loose, he spoke, 'Macie, come and sit down at the table.' She looked at him through foggy eyes. 'Please.' She trailed the duvet over to the table and pulled it around her, then stared out the window. 'Now listen to me. Look at me Macie. Are you listening?'

'Yes! I'm listening'.

'I left London, not just because I wanted a change, but because my whole life was wrong. I did not like the city. I no longer cared about my job and I am sad to say, that I no longer cared for you either. Macie, look at me.' He spoke each word as if it were a statement. 'I don't love you – I never did.'

Her eyes brimmed over. He pushed the tissue box at her and waited while she cried her heart out. 'How can you say that?' Her voice was murky through a clogged nose.

'Because it's true.' He tried to sound gentle. He tried to take her hands in his, but she drew them back into the duvet. 'It took me a long time to realise that there is more to life than living forever with someone I don't love. You are bright and cute and clever and it's a lovely morning. There's some nice city bloke waiting for you in London right now. Just go home and find him.'

The morning air outside Mary's bedroom was beautiful. Silent and calm. Above it the gentle curlew called in the bottom of the valley. Soft fragrance from the wildflowers in the hedgerow underneath the window floated up with the morning heat. Two kittens reminded her that their breakfast was late.

She'd felt worse, but circumstances then were exceptional. This time? Well this time, the pain in her heart was self-inflicted. She'd not forget her promise – he needed his space and time and she must never trespass on them again.

The pain in her head could be put right with a paracetemol but there was no such cure for her mind. Giving him the space and time he needed would now prevent her from telling him about her new fear; that she was losing her mind.

Alone and losing it. The black field of terror with the translucent sides and no end stretched away in front of her. She would have to deal with this by herself. Her part of the bargain was to take control of her own life, to learn to do things for herself. Pulling her dressing gown tighter around her, she addressed the kittens, '...but not today – today I will deal with one thing at a time.' That one thing had to be Tim. Today she had to let him go and let him go far enough that she would not be hurt when he found what he was looking for.

Dressed, she went outside to feel the sun, warm on her back. 'Come on kittens.' She coaxed them outside. 'Today you can discover trees.' She took some tools from the garden shed and started to weed the overgrown herb garden. She knew he would come.

Tim got Macie into the little van about mid day. There were tears and more tears until she at last drove away. He wrenched the big gates out of the tangled grass and weeds and barricaded the drive. Then he sat on his back step and relaxed his stomach muscles. They had been so tight for so long that it felt like he'd been struck by a very large man and a very large boxing glove.

Why was that so goddamn difficult? Why couldn't I just say that there was someone else? It would've been so much easier – but would it have been true? Was she still there for me? God I'm exhausted.

Inside, he washed every dish Macie had touched, put every wet tissue and scrap of magazine into the bin and put all the bed linen into the washing machine. He washed the counter tops. He jumped at every sound, expecting her to drive back into his life. He needed to get control – of himself, of the immediate world around him.

He washed Mary's flask, and her mugs, re-folded her pretty cloth and put it all with great care, back into the basket. He felt his stomach muscles tighten again. *I've got to face her. I've got to explain. I haven't the first idea what to say. Oh, I'll tell her what happened – will she believe me? All I can tell her is the complete and unvarnished truth – from start to finish.*

And what then? He didn't expect her just to laugh and life to go on as if nothing had happened. Because something had happened. A very large wedge of no consequence had been driven between them. How could he hope to repair the gulf? But the real question was, what was he prepared to commit to the repair? He had no answers. He just knew he had to try.

He found her sitting in the hammock the proper way: feet over the side, just touching the grass, swaying between the trees. Small garden tools were lying in the grass along with muddy shoes where she'd kicked them off. The two kittens were wobbling up the ropes of the hammock to the tree branches. She was wearing dirty jeans and sunglasses. He couldn't tell if she were asleep or watching him.

He sat down on the grass at her feet and put the basket beside him. 'Hello,' he whispered in case she really was asleep. 'Hello,' came the immediate reply.

He clutched his knees. 'I'm going to tell you what happened. I'm going to tell you every detail,' he began. She put up her hand to stop him, but he spoke interrupting the gesture. 'No, I have to do this. If you don't let me say this, I will lie here in this orchard until you do. I don't care if it is for days or weeks. I will eat whatever I can find and I'll wait for the apples if I have to. I'll piss on your compost pile, but I will stay here until you let me speak. What I will tell you is not an excuse, it is not a reason for anything, it is just history and I swear every word of it will be true. Then if you want, we can discuss what happens to us next.'

'Then I guess you had better begin.' She continued swishing the hammock with her toes on the grass.

'She arrived on Friday night, just as I got home. She'd left me a message on Thursday, but I ignored it. I'd no idea she'd come. That was a mistake. If I'd called her back I might have stopped her, but I didn't. She went to Birmingham by train and borrowed her father's van. They live there somewhere. She thought that she could just carry on as she left off with me. I was so tired; all I could do was show her the spare room and fall into bed. I am ashamed to say it... no I'm not.... I put a chair under the door knob so she couldn't get in.'

He thought he saw a flicker of a smile, but she said nothing. 'I'd just woken up when you arrived yesterday morning – not more than a couple of minutes. I barely knew what day it was. I wasn't capable of taking control of the situation.' He took a shaky breath. 'I thought I'd have her out of the place long before you arrived. That it would all be over.'

She still did not speak.

'I am sorry for the things that she said to you. I should never have let her get away with it.'

'That wasn't your fault.' There was a moment's pause but she said no more.

'She wanted to move back in with me. Said she'd quit her job, was prepared to get work here, landscape the place, look for good schools for the kids.' He saw another flicker of a smile and felt a rush of something he might have taken for forgiveness. 'I tried to describe what muck spreading was like and what night life in Croftbury amounted to, but Macie has selective hearing.'

He got up, lifted the black and white kitten clinging to the tree bark and put it in Mary's lap. She stoked it and it curled up to sleep.

'I was so worried about you that I went out to look for you. I told Macie to be gone by the time I got back, but she was still there and stone drunk besides. I just wanted to be alone to sort out things in my head – instead there she was and not capable of going anywhere. So I left her on the settee and went to bed. What I didn't do was put the chair back under the door handle, because at some god-awful hour of the night, I found her in my bed crawling all over me. She wasn't going to go back to her own room, so I spent the night on the settee.'

The tabby kitten was swinging from the edge of the hammock by its claws having mis-judged the distance from the ground. He unhooked it and put it on the grass. It climbed into his lap.

'This morning, I saw that I would have to just tell her the truth, which is what I should have done in the first place. I told her that I didn't love her, that I guess I never had and I had no intention of leaving the countryside, ever.' He thought he could hear her let out a long breath.

'She left about noon and I binned everything I could that she'd touched and washed the rest.'

There was a long silence. When Mary spoke she was so quiet, he had to lean towards her to hear.

'None of this matters, Tim.'

He felt panic rising from inside. 'What do you mean it doesn't matter?' His voice sounded angry in his own ears. 'I've hurt you and I want you to know that it was one stupid loose end I should have wrapped up long ago. Nothing more.'

'Tim, it doesn't matter. I've been doing a lot of thinking over these past two days. I have to admit that I was very shocked and hurt yesterday morning.' She pushed the sunglasses up on to the top of her head. Her eyes were puffed and tired. 'But I behaved like an adolescent. Comes from being around them too long I guess.' There was a faint smile. 'I should have stayed and listened to you yesterday morning. Instead I, well I read the situation completely wrong and I'm sorry.

'Then I needed some time too, to put myself straight. We have an agreement that we won't form any kind of a relationship that we don't feel comfortable with, and that we'll allow each other the space to be ourselves. You have to have the room to be who you are and if that means other relationships, then I have no right to condemn them.'

'But Mary.' His voice felt close to breaking. 'I have to be your friend and I need you to be mine. I need the calm and the fun that you put in my life. I need your help and I need you to understand me – like you do. No one has ever done that for me before.' He swallowed hard. 'I... I...'

'Then shall we try again - to be friends?' Her voice was very small.

He laid his head against her leg and she put her hand on his hair. They stayed like that for quite a long time.

24

On Monday they had a choice: stay home alone and feel miserable, or do something together and feel uncomfortable. They went up onto the ancient limestone escarpment of Wenlock Edge and tried to relax with each other.

From the gentle height of land, they looked down into the long green slopes of Corvedale and the other way, over the steep edge into Ape Dale. Strong thin stripes of new green cereal crops created contour lines in the brown soil. Mounded ridges of fine tilth were still bare of the potatoes planted underneath. Sheep, most still heavy with wool settled into the shade of the hedge or a few fine solitary oaks standing in the pastures. Lambs, no longer tiny, and with tight wool and black faces, watched as they passed. Oilseed rape fields blazed, the colour discordant for the fine English air. They talked, but it was the speech of strangers; feeling and testing for a topic that wouldn't offend either of them. It was hard work.

Then they dropped down through a narrow lane to the ancient town of Much Wenlock. In the abbey ruins full of majesty and mythology they sat on the fine grass, put their faces to the sun and let the peace of the wonderful old walls drift around them.

Tim looked at Mary as she sat leaning back on her arms, eyes shut, head tilted back in the summer air. Her straw bag lay on the grass beside her soft green skirt and her fluffy hair fell over the collar of a white sleeveless blouse. Little gold sandals lay beside her and she wiggled her toes on the short grass. He looked for what they had before and found that it was not there. The trust they had was damaged and the comfortable ability to touch was gone.

In its place, he felt something that he could only describe as brightness. He saw things more clearly; things like the few fine silver hairs that streaked through the loose curls by her ears and tiny lines at the sides of her eyes, the ones that deepened when she smiled. He saw softness in her throat and firmness on her shoulders. Her face was soft and her skin was beautiful, he wanted to touch it, but there were still tiny lines on her forehead and he knew he couldn't. Light sparkled from her earrings, and her fingers with smooth pink-varnished nails laid on the close cut grass. He couldn't understand what he felt - it had no proper name – it was just a clarity and a clearness, comfort and stillness.

'Tim?'

'Hmm?'

'I was just telling you about the torrid love affair I had with the Archbishop and you haven't heard a word.'

'I confess,' he laughed, 'I haven't heard a thing. I was thinking of something else altogether.'

She lay down on one elbow. 'Can I hear what it was?' Her voice was full of understanding for words he had not yet spoken and he knew that this was her way of recovering some of what they'd had – at least so that they could trust each other again.

'I was thinking about you and how I might feel if you weren't here. It was not a pretty thought.' He folded a tiny blade of grass. 'Things have changed between us and it scares me.' The blade of grass broke and he dropped it onto the lawn. 'I'm afraid of... well, I see in myself things that I've never noticed. I've never missed them because I've never known them before and I'm worried that they might be gone forever.'

She waited and he continued.

'I've never had a best friend before.'

She took his hand, held it in sympathy. She waited while Tim let it out in a rush: childhood as an army brat; life in more countries than many people ever see; private boarding schools; an older brother with his own agenda; no real friends and a fear of making any in case they or he were suddenly sent off somewhere else.

'Dad was ballistic when I told him I wanted to leave the army. He's never got over it. But...' He took a deep breath, '... I've been lucky. I've worked all over the place – here, abroad and I enjoyed it. But still no roots – no real relationships and no friends. Until now.' He crossed his feet in front of him. 'Looking at you made me realise that I've never had a real, true and good friend and I never knew that there was a hole in my life until I came near to losing it.' He looked at his ankles and pulled on his socks. 'I know we've slept together, but I thought that what we had, was more than just that – a lot more. I never, ever want to lose that – no matter what else happens between us ... or doesn't.'

Mary's voice sounded thick. 'What are friends for?'

For the rest of the afternoon, they talked, held hands and laughed. They didn't try too hard and they didn't pretend that nothing had changed. But what they did not discuss was the future. And in the lowering afternoon sun, Mary put her little car into gear and slipped it onto the ridge road of the Wenlock Edge. The light was soft and the air thick on the hillsides. The late afternoon covered them both with a peace that began to suppress the hurts they'd dealt each other.

In the fading light of early evening, he left her at her door with a gentle hug and a chaste kiss and was gone. She went inside and wept. He went home and did the same.

The bedroom of the cottage was hot. Mary woke while it was still very dark, feeling sticky with sweat. She got up, opened all the bedroom windows and flapped the duvet up and down to cool it, then got back into bed. She tried to see where yesterday had left her and where their relationship was now. It was almost the same impossible, crazy, idiotic relationship it had been, but it was different than it had been on Sunday. Had it matured or had it become more complicated? Sleep took the answer away from her.

Sometime later she woke again covered in sweat – but she wasn't hot – there was something wrong; she was panting in terror. She felt herself being pulled along by a force outside herself. Then somewhere in the darkness – her eyes would not focus to identify distance - Mary saw a small shape in the dullness of wet daylight. Strands of gauze streamed and snapped behind it as if it were a girl running – running for her life. The duvet ensnared her hands – she couldn't move them. Terror foamed up inside her from a source she could not identify. A feeling of insanity – out of control insanity - took over her. She wanted to scream again and again – but she could make no sound. Her limbs would not function – she was trapped in a theatre with a scene of terror playing out in front of her.

Wide eyes became visible on the face of the little shape of the girl. A feeling of panic gushed between Mary's eyes and a pain exploded in her head blackening everything. Suddenly she was pushed and knocked as a crowd of people, some with sticks, knives and hayforks, rushed around her. There was no sound. It was overtaken by a feeling from the cursing anger in the people in front of her and for the first time Mary could feel fear – real fear. This time it wasn't her own, but someone else's and she did not know whose. It had to be the girl's.

Then a horse tossed its head above the crowd and a large hat with a wide brim appeared above it. The arms, hands and cudgels waved and stabbed in the air while a face became visible under the hat. It was contorted with fury; its eyes wide and white. A mouth was shouting at the crowd, encouraging it, leading it, and inciting it. One long arm stabbed again and again in the direction of the frail figure, now being dragged away. The mob turned and rushed after it. The face above the horse changed to one of sinister satisfaction and disappeared after the crowd. She had seen the face before – it was that of the man who had murdered the young man.

In the distance, Mary saw two tiny figures swaying from a stout branch of a huge tree. In the dull daylight, they swayed, kicked, and jerked from the rope. Their hands were bound behind their backs and their feet were a few inches from the ground. The jerking and kicking went on a long time – the figures blended into one shape in Mary's mind then became two again. They swayed from their own struggles or from prods by the crowd that encircled them. No one came close except to strike them; no one offered aid nor tried to set them free. The scene took a long time to change and the horror seemed never ending, except that the jerking became less and the struggles fewer. It took such a long time.

The scene vanished without trace leaving a stunning pain in Mary's head. She wanted to cry from fear of what had happened, and fear that it was she who was being pursued into a situation she could not control, but she had no strength left. She began to shake. Oh God she needed help. This was more than she could do alone.

The cold plastic of the telephone surprised her. She didn't know how she got out of bed. She didn't know how she had been able to dial his number.

'Tim,' she sobbed when he answered. 'Tim, I need help.' The line went dead before she finished.

He found her on the floor of the kitchen, the telephone still in her hand and the duvet pulled so hard around her, he could barely find her in it. She was still weeping.

He hugged her and held her for a long time. At last, exhausted, she stopped, but clutched his T- shirt. He realised it was on backwards. She held on as if she could not get her fingers ever to unclench. Then she started to shake and with it she found her voice. She just said his name over and over.

'It's all right, I'm here.' It was all he could say and he said it again and again until she began to calm herself. He didn't know how long they stayed on the floor, but the sky become paler outside the window.

On the settee with brandy he forced her to drink, she told him everything she'd seen – not just tonight but also before. 'Tim, I'm desperate – about what I saw – was it real, was it imagination, was it a vision, a dream, a nightmare? I'm worried that I'm losing control.' She started to cry again, and he pulled her closer. 'I've tried so hard to make it on my own – I am afraid I'm losing it – everything.'

He kissed her hair and pushed his own worry about her mental state to the back of his mind. 'Mary. Listen to me.' She rested on him with his arms around her. 'You are as sane as anyone I have ever met. And with the amount of stress and upheaval you have been under in the last year, well things could begin to mount in your mind.'

'Tim,' she shouted. 'You think I'm losing it, don't you? Oh God, I am, I'm going mad. I know it.'

He stroked her hair and her face. 'No, I don't think you are at all. Now come here and rest.' He tucked the duvet around them both and she slept on his chest. He watched her and worried, but could not let his mind accept.

When they woke a few hours later, the sun was beginning to light the living room. As she moved, he hugged her to him, 'Are you all right?'

'Yes, I think so. I feel quite normal, thank goodness, and the pain is gone.' She yawned. 'But I don't know what I'd have done if you hadn't been there.'

'Thank God you called. Scared me though.'

'Tim, I don't think I have ever been so frightened in my life. I just don't know what's happening to me. Thank you for coming and listening to me – and for being there. I needed you.' She rubbed the corner of the duvet over her face.

He slid up on the settee. 'Are you sure you are all right now? I'll stay with you today if you want me to.'

'No you don't need to do that. I feel as if it was all a dream, or that it happened to someone else, even though I know that it didn't. I'll be fine.' But her mouth felt dry.

'Morning, boss. Nice weekend?' asked Bryn from a perch on the corner of Susan's desk.

'It had its moments. Did you want me for something?' A look passed from Bryn to Susan and she raised one eyebrow.

'Nope, just visiting.' Bryn slid off the desk and ducked behind his own screen divider.

Tim dropped his brief case on his desk and snapped it open then pushed the 'on' switch on his computer. 'Anything urgent this morning, Susan?'

'No – a nice slow start for a change.' She handed him his post. The trade paper was on top and the banner headline made everything around him disappear. *Major fire at Renovation Property.'* This wasn't the one he and Mary had looked at, but the similarities were striking. He turned on his terminal and brought up the spreadsheet he'd made from his notes. He hit the print key for wide paper, went to the big office printer and read the article while he waited for it to print.

When it finished, he snatched the stack of paper from the machine and dropped it with a smack onto his desk. He looked at the companies he'd visited, the ones he hadn't, the ones where they had won contracts and the ones they hadn't Then he compared the details on the print out with the article. He searched Google for the properties on each of the files where there had been renovations and looked up who had prepared the quotations.

Howard and James had prepared most of the quotes, but that's as it should be. They were made before he had been hired.

He found that Conmac had taken on design and build contracts for a company called Etherstone and Partners - several of them. There seemed to have been no competition for the contracts. No quotations or estimates on the plans were on file. He recalled that most of the sites he had visited where work was still on going, and he had not been made welcome, belonged to Etherstone. Co-incidence?

He also noticed that many of the unsuccessful quotations were for renovation work in large redundant properties, most rural and all unoccupied. He went to Google again. The fate of the properties was a surprise. Several had been burned and others robbed. No wonder the work had never gone ahead. There was no property for the work to take place in.

25

The evening air was very still when Tim closed Mary's gate behind him. Something caught his eye at the top of the orchard. She was waving from the top of an apple tree. 'What in God's name are you doing up there?'

'Getting some old netting down. Be there in a minute.' As she came up to him, she rubbed her hands down her jeans and pulled a dirty t-shirt straight. She had a smudge down her nose. 'It's a lot easier going up than coming back down I can tell you. But come in. Before I forget, my car's making strange noises. Do you know anyone...?'

'There's a garage near Conmac. I'll call them see if they can fit you in and drive it in for you.'

'That's kind of you.'

'I've brought you Davidson, my history of architecture book. I found it and it reminded me that you wanted to find out when the cottage was built.' Tim put the book on Mary's kitchen table while she washed her hands. 'This might give you some clues.' He patted the book's hard cover.

'Thanks. I'll have a good look at it tomorrow and thanks for calling me today.' She drew a chilled bottle of wine from the fridge and without asking, pulled the cork.

'I needed to know you were OK.' He looked at her, searching for the cracks but there were none – the lines on her forehead had disappeared.

She poured into two large glasses on the table. 'Well, don't worry. I've been fine.' She pushed one over to him. 'At this rate, I shall have to consider opening an account at the wine merchants. '

'We might qualify for a bulk discount.' He sat down at the table. 'I thought this might interest you too.' He pushed the engineering paper towards her.

She folded her legs under her as she sat down. 'This isn't the same one that's in the local paper is it?' She scanned the article and pulled the neck of her t-shirt over her nose and wiped her face.

'And Conmac quoted for this one as well.'

'Isn't it a bit too co-incidental?'

He swirled the wine in the glass and breathed in the aroma. 'I am beginning to think so. But I've got some more digging to do.'

'Is there anything I can do to help you find out?'

He brightened. 'I think you have quite enough to do already, what with Davidson here and those bags of sand outside. Is that bucket the lime putty?'

'Yes, delivered today. I lose confidence whenever I look at it, so I have decided that it will keep for a few more days, while I read the literature one more time.' She got up to retrieve some papers from the kitchen dresser. 'But I didn't get to tell you on Friday night...,' his heart slipped sideways – *oh God, Friday night*, '...what I had discovered at the Records Office. I looked at the Estate Records.'

'Why those?'

'Well, they were about the only thing that I hadn't already looked at and as the archivist explained to me – remind me to tell you something interesting about her by the way – most of the land was owned by the landed gentry. So there are things like rate and rent books, maps, sale particulars, that sort of thing. But also there are records of local courts.'

She flipped over pages of her notes. 'But look here.' She pointed to the copy of the court leet report. 'It says that in 1670 a John Roberts tried to charge Rose and Mary Flitch with some unchristian offences of some kind. John Roberts seems to be the lord of the manor or perhaps his son.'

'Amazing, but I thought the name of the women was Fletcher?'

'I don't think that literacy was all that wonderful at the time, so I expect the clerk just wrote what he heard. There seem to be several spellings.' He filled their wine glasses again while she rushed on.

'And then, I found these two entries.' She pushed the other photocopy towards him. 'John Roberts did get hold of the two farms, after the two girls died, but this entry shows that their father William – it says William Sr - was given other land – it says in perpetuity.'

Tim looked at the pale copies of the fine writing. 'Incredible. That all but proves it, but we still don't really know if this is where it all happened, do we?'

'Almost, because of the maps and transfer details, but this more or less proves that he did manage to have them executed.' She felt the blood draining from her face and felt again the terror she felt last night and the vision of the two figures swaying, swaying... 'Because he was tried at the Assizes for their murder.' She began to shake and gripped the edge of the table as hard as she could.

'But he was acquitted wasn't he? I suspect that he was just a dirty old man who wanted his wicked way with two girls.'

Somehow, she made her voice sound normal. 'It's possible, but I think that that would have been easy enough for him to achieve that if he'd wanted — I just felt that there had to be more to it.'

'I'll bet John Roberts wanted the land.'

'That's what I thought. The archivist was really helpful and suggested I look at the rent rolls — and there I found that William Fletcher and somebody called John Cooper were tenants of the estate and it told me the name of their holdings and the size and all sorts of things. I followed their payments of rent until 1670 — then the land of both of them had reverted to the 'lord'.' The shaking stopped.

'But you said that he did get their land — he had to compensate one of them...'

'Yes, but the dates were confusing. John Roberts got control of the land in March 1670, but the two girls weren't executed until July or August 1670. It didn't make sense for him to have gotten the land before he went to all the risk of murdering them. If he already had the land, why bother?'

'Now I am confused.'

'Well, so was I until the archivist came back and explained that at the time, the year numbers changed at the end of March, so July and August 1670 occurred before March 1670. March 1670 is by modern numbering 1671.'

Tim pulled a pencil out of his shirt pocket and drew little lines on the back of an envelope putting dates on them. 'So instead of January being the date for the year to change, it happened in March? I see, I see. So the bastard did it.'

'I'm quite sure of it.'

'But what about the archivist — you said there was something interesting about her?'

'She was so helpful and seemed to be steering me in the right direction all along. It's almost as if she knew what I needed to find and what I had to look at. But on Friday, for the first time, she had a name tag on and her name was Rosemary.'

He looked at her in some disbelief. 'Honest.' She held up her hand to swear the truth.

He finished the last wine at the bottom of his glass and got up. 'Well, I can't compete with any of that and the only reading I have is a stack of quotations to see if any other company is suspicious. So now that I've finished your wine, I'll go. I'll let you know what happens tomorrow.' *I need to see you tomorrow – I need to see you everyday.* 'Promise you'll call me if you need me.'

She followed him to the door. He turned and took her face in both his hands to kiss her. Her skin was warm, moist and soft. He wiped the smudge from her nose. 'I will.' *Please ask me to stay, please.* He bent over, held her close and kissed her again. 'Good night.' His voice felt tight. *What was he doing? What on earth was he doing?*

As he went up the lane he remembered the first time he'd walked up this hill in the dark. He recalled the aching bruise on his back and how he had marvelled at the night around him. He also remembered the sickness he'd felt with the vision of what he'd done to Macie, but that feeling was gone. Even though he'd sent her away in tears he knew it was the right thing to do for both of them and he felt no remorse. In doing so, he'd almost lost Mary, but tonight he felt that perhaps she might still be there for him. Was she always going to be there for him? If she was, then he had to admit that he had to give something. But what?

Mary pushed up the green canvas umbrella against the sun and opened Tim's book on the garden table.

She looked up timber framed cottages and began to read and make notes. Close timber framing dated from the 15th century but was taken over by box timber framing in the 17th century when timber was in shorter supply. Well, she wasn't surprised to find that the cottage was not built before 1600. If the details from the Records Office were to be believed she might expect the cottage to date from 1675.

When bricks became widely used certain patterns became fashionable. English Bond seemed to be the first regular pattern of brickwork used – coming into use in the middle of the 16th century. It consisted of a double thickness of bricks in which one row was laid end to end, and then the next row was laid across. This made a row of long sides, called stretchers in the book, and a row of ends, called headers, visible in the finished wall. Davidson also went on to say that this arrangement was used until overtaken by other patterns at about the end of the 17th century.

Mary wrote the dates on a blank sheet of paper. *No particular pattern: until 1560 English bond: between 1560 and say 1720. Flemish bond after 1700.* However Davidson went on to say that it took 50 or more years for this kind of sophistication to make its way from London to the north and west. OK then, she crossed out the dates and wrote 1610 and 1770.

She looked at the bricks in the front wall of the cottage. There was no pattern between the timbers at all. Was it built therefore before any pattern was established – about 1610 - or was it built before anyone cared about such sophistication? It could mean that it was built by unsophisticated hands. It was becoming confusing.

Under the irregular pattern of bricks, the thick foundation of stones interested her. Davidson said that people used whatever material they had at hand. Stones existed everywhere around here and would have reduced the amount of timber and number of bricks needed. Or perhaps the cottage was rebuilt on an earlier foundation. It was still very confusing.

Turning back to Davidson she opened the index at the back. The words 'long house' caught her eye. She found the page and read: '*At the beginning of the 17th century, it was considered that a minimum requirement for domestic housing in rural areas should be a single span structure. The measurement was therefore one pole by two; the pole being the medieval measurement of 16 feet as established by the stall room for a yoke of 4 plough of oxen. The internal span was the primary dimension being 16 feet, while the length was measured externally. Most long houses were therefore 16 x 30 on the inside; the other two feet were taken up by the thickness of the gable ends. This style was most in use in the northwest during 17th century only.*'

She found a foot ruler in her desk and carefully laid it out end over end on the living room carpet.

Tim sat down in the canvas chair. 'Well don't keep me waiting? What was so exciting that you just had to tell me?'

By early evening the heat was beginning to slacken when the sun slipped behind the orchard. But the air was still sticky and thick beneath the trees. Mary sat at the garden table and tried to avoid having any contact with anything, least of all her own skin.

She pushed her notes and Davidson towards him and smiled, lips turned with mischief. 'Your book is wonderful, and even with its lovely diagrams I still don't know what a mortise and tenon joint is. But - I think I've found an approximate date for the cottage without it.'

'Wonderful. What is it? Will it fit in with the executions?'

'One thing at a time dear boy. Give me my moment. An English bond brick pattern would tell me that the cottage was probably built before 1750 and probably after 1610. The timber framing indicates sometime after 1600, which still leaves quite a long gap and could be well wide of the 1675 date that we are looking for. But the <u>absence</u> of any brick pattern and the stone foundation which I assume are the earliest, suggest some time early in that period rather than later.'

She rushed on. 'Then...' she flipped open Davidson to reveal the definition of the long house, '...I found this'. She turned the book around and he read the little paragraph about long houses. 'It says they were built in the 17th century and, given that it took a generation or two to reach this part of the country, well... That's why I asked if you had a long tape.'

He snatched a yellow electronic measure from the table, reset it from metric to Imperial and she followed him inside. His measurements confirmed hers. 'Fifteen foot 10 inches by 30 feet.' He was triumphant. 'I think you've cracked it. It fits with the history – sometime up to about the latter half of the 17th century. We know there was no cottage here in 1670 when the executions took place. This could be the very cottage that what's'isname built after they died.'

'William Fletcher. I wish I could find out if that's what really happened to the girls. Were they really hanged here and if so, why? I just feel that there is a piece of the mystery I'm still missing, but I don't know what it is.'

They went back outside. The sun was beginning to go down behind the trees. The air was still again but it remained hot. Mary slipped off her sandals and wiggled her toes in the grass. 'But what about your mystery? Did you get anywhere with the contractors?'

'Yes and no. I've found that the same company appears again and again in the new builds. So, while James was out of the office, I looked up the companies to see if I could find who the directors are.'

She raised her eyebrows.

'Sadly, nothing that I could find, but...'

He pulled some papers from his shirt pocket. 'This is the instruction from Royston Contracting to quote for some racking and it's signed, there at the bottom.' He unfolded a cheque. 'And this is for my travel expenses last month. Don't ask me why they don't just pay it into my account, but look at the signature.'

'It's the same!'

'Yes and I happen to know that the one on the cheque is the FD of Conmac.'

Mary leaned back. 'I'm completely confused. So Conmac and this Royston are owned or managed or something, but one or some of the same people...'

'And,' Tim looked triumphant and terrified at the same time. 'I found that the only company to have been approached to do these contracts was Etherstone and they were arranged by Howard.'

'How does this contracting business work then?'

'When we manage a project from start to finish, there will be a lot of other specialist contractors involved – things like the electrics or water and drainage systems or the roadways and cladding. Now normally we arrange for the sub contracting ourselves, but in these cases, it seems like everything has been handed over to Etherstones and they've done the sub contracting.'

'Is that unusual?'

'It just seems to be a waste when we could do it ourselves. But it seems like that's what Howard and James have decided.'

'Is it just because they were short of expertise before you arrived?'

Tim leaned back in his chair. 'I have no idea.'

'Tim, I have to admit I'm getting worried about this. Is there a connection between this contractor and Howard – you said he's been jumpy? But if he – and there may be others involved, others like James - if they suspect you're finding ...'

'I know. I've got to give Howard the impression that I've found nothing so I'm moving on to other things.'

'Tim. This could get dangerous.'

They faced each other and Tim took and held a deep breath. 'I've no idea what I'm up against here.' He looked up into the trees. 'Come and sit with me in the orchard. The bats are flying.'

They sat against a ragged damson tree and watched the little animals as they hunted through the leaves and branches. Mary could see the tension in his jaw. Wonders of nature aside, he was worried. She leaned against him and he put his arm around her. His face relaxed.

His lips whispered over hers like petals of silk. The caress softened the ache in her heart. Her resolve disappeared like smoke. They made love in the grass as the last apple blossoms fell and the bats flew overhead. But still they did not talk about their future.

26

Mary confronted the bucket of lime putty and the bags of sand with a sinking heart.

'It's clear that equipment beyond two bare hands is required here.' She spoke aloud, but with confidence evaporating as she said it. She knew she needed the builders' merchants - the gloom of the dusty warehouse – long stacks of unidentifiable building supplies stretching into the distance and piles of stone, bags of sand, stacks of wheelbarrows – the very idea shrivelled her enthusiasm.

With a deep breath, she prepared herself for the barely-suppressed snickers, sideways looks and rude comments that she knew women get from male domains like garages and builders' yards. The 'this-isn't-a-job-for-a-nice-little-lady-like-you' looks. They'd know that she didn't have a clue what she was doing. She looked at the stone wall again. *Come on girl, this ain't getting it done.*

With her list in her jeans pocket – *leave the handbag at home* - she leaned on the tall counter of the builders' yard office. It was difficult to be casual and put her elbow on the counter when it reached almost to her neck. A lad old enough to have been out of school about a week and who now figured he knew everything there was to know about building, asked if he could help her. *And here was I hoping for a nice sympathetic little old man*. She pulled the list out of her pocket.

There was no way of concealing the fact that she knew nothing at all about wall plaster. 'I'm planning to do some plastering,' she began, 'and I need some help to get what I need'.

'Of course Madam. Would you care to come with me?' He led her down an aisle around boxes of tiles and bags of nails. 'This is what you need.' He held out a little box of polyfiller.

'No.' Mary swallowed to stop the squeak of uncertainty at the bottom of her voice; 'I've a big job to do and I already have the materials. I need the equipment.' She unfolded her list again and looked up to find that another lad had joined them. 'I need a hawk and a float and . . .' She caught the look that passed between them, somewhere about a foot over her head. It was the look that has passed between males since Adam was a lad. It was the one that said: humour her, then we'll have a good laugh. In that second, she lost it. She rammed the list into her pocket; her face stretched over jaws jammed together. 'I think it would be better if I spoke to the manager. *If* you don't mind.'

He was the nice little old man that she had been hoping to find and she left feeling smug, with her hawk, trowel and float, her goggles and safety gloves, a huge sheet of plastic and some large soft brushes. *Damn it but I hate these places.* She slammed the boot lid of the car. It was just as well that she didn't see the look that passed among the three men watching from inside.

Mary looked like a bundle. The legs of her bib and brace over sized overalls were rolled up; a long sleeved shirt did its best to escape from the gaps and a scarf squashed her hair flat to her head. By bracing her back on the wall and her boots on the piano, she moved it a few feet and did the same to the last few boxes. When the plastic was laid out on the floor she looked at the hole in the wall. They had established that it had been built and not hacked out later so it was too precious to fill with rubble and plaster over. It deserved to be left. From the garage she located a few pieces of thin wood that would serve as lath and she pinned them to the frame timbers. She debated whether or not to put the message back, but decided that now the secret was in the open, the document deserved to be free.

Mary lined up her tools on the plastic, and went outside. Grabbing the ears of a bag of sand, she realised with the first heave that some of the tactics available to men – those involving muscles specifically - were not available to her. Taking an old washing up bowl to the sand and putty, she measured 3 parts sand and I part putty with her float into it and chopped it together. It still looked like sand, but now sand with bright white lumps in it. The float wasn't mixing it very well and she wondered if it needed water. It was obvious it wasn't going to stick on the wall in this condition.

She rammed her sleeves up over her elbows, pulled up her gloves and worked the lumps of putty into the sand with her hands, a bit like making pastry. The more she mixed, the wetter it all became. This was odd. Was it supposed to happen? She looked again at the old book. It said, '…knock it up. Then, when fat…,' so that was no help.

Soon, the sandy mixture began to look like smooth gooey plaster she remembered seeing somewhere and she dragged the bowl over the carpet to the wall. Scooping a small amount out with her trowel she brought the little pile of plaster to the wall. It lay on top of the trowel and it would have been obvious to a three year old that there was no way it was going on the wall from that position. She poked it onto the stones with her fingers, held it on with her glove for a moment and let go, expecting it to come away. It didn't. It sat there in a brown mound. She used the bottom of the trowel to smooth it. It looked quite nice. She tried several trowel loads.

There has to be an easier way. The stuff is caustic, surely they haven't been putting it on with their hands all these years, and anyway what are the hawk and the float for?

She made a cup of coffee and read the chapter in the little book again. Trowels were better for pointing and mortaring – whatever they were – she'd come to that later if she needed to. Floats were for plastering. Then there was a picture of a hawk mounded with plaster. OK so that would stop her from bending to the bowl when she got to the top of the wall. And – now this was useful – use the float upside down and let the plaster slide off it to knock it up. Knocking it up seemed to be words for mixing the stuff. Now she was getting somewhere.

There was a loud smack from the living room. She rushed back to find that her plaster was crumbling and dropping off the wall onto the plastic. *Great, just bloody great.* She looked at the book again. Although it didn't say so in so many words, it seemed to imply that the plaster needed to be more worked and the surface wet, so she went back to the bowl and scooped the clod up with the float, let it fall back into the bowl. Again and again. It soon began to look smoother and started to look sticky and glisten like, well, like fat. This was encouraging.

She wet the wall and tried again. This time she managed a larger section. Using the float was awkward, but she found if she flung the plaster at the wall from the float, she had time to grab it and push it on before it fell off again. She felt in control for the first time since she opened the bucket of putty.

When the washing up bowl was empty, Mary buttered a roll and squashed some cheese in it. Eating it as she walked around the garden, she wished Robert could see her now. *Take that you bastard.* There had been so much happening to her that she hadn't nagged Joanne to see if Robert had responded to her e-mail.

Pulling her gloves on she went back into the living room, to see the plaster sagging into wrinkles like those on the belly of a sumo wrestler. In slow motion her plaster slid down the wall and oozed onto the plastic. 'No,' she shouted and tried to push it back on with her hands. But it fell around her, great gobs of soft brown plaster. Hot tears stung the back of her nose.

'No damn it. Don't you dare! I am not going to give those two cretins in the builders yard any tiny chance to say that they were right – even if they never find out.'

This would be the moment that Tim walks in, she thought swallowing the bitterness in her throat. *He'll laugh until he's sick and then he'll fix everything. Because that's what men do. No bloody way. I'm going to do this myself or live with the damn wall the way it is.* She gathered up the plaster, slopped it back into the bowl and read the book again.

The big brush, heavy with water put some reality into her anger. She smashed the brush against the wall again and again and then dragged some short steps onto the plastic. Cutting and turning the plaster with the float again, she dropped a good lump onto the hawk. It was heavy and she clutched it against her chest and wobbled up the steps to stop it sliding off. This time she began at the top, pushing the plaster hard onto the stones and smoothing it upwards to the ceiling. She worked a section below and then another below that.

She scraped the remaining plaster back into the bowl, put down the hawk and float, made a cup of coffee, sat on the living room floor and waited. Nothing happened.

Then with more water on the wall, more sand and lime putty into the bowl, more cutting and turning with the float, another mound on the hawk she plastered another section of wall. She made no attempt to keep it smooth, but concentrated instead on pushing it hard into the stones.

She hurt in places that had no reason to hurt by the time she was finished. Her overalls had as much plaster on them as the wall, but what she had pushed on to the stones stayed there. Looking at the rough plastered wall, her tiredness was insignificant compared to her jubilation. But now what? The instructions talked about it needing to dry slowly or it would turn to powder and fall off again. She snatched up the book again. The plaster had to be kept damp until it no longer dented under a knuckle, but could still be marked by a fingernail. This could be anything from two or three days to two or three weeks. WEEKS? Then the second and third coats could be applied. SECOND and THIRD coats? What had she started? She flung water at the wall with one of the big brushes and pinned a sheet of plastic to a roof beam to cover it all.

Then she ran a very hot tub with an extra gloop of bath foam.

27

'I am so impressed that..., well I'm speechless.' Tim looked behind the plastic again. 'Are you sure you haven't done this before?' He felt as proud as if he'd done it himself.

'Well, my muscles will tell you I haven't.'

'You look like the cat that swallowed the canary.' He pulled her into a hug.

'I'm pleased with myself. It wasn't quite as easy as it sounded in the book. But what about you? Come and talk to me in the kitchen while I finish this bit of ironing.'

'I'm afraid I had to do real work today. Howard was quite normal – but God he does look like a worried man.' He turned a kitchen chair around and straddled it. 'And I arranged a site visit for Bryn, Derek, Susan and myself tomorrow but James found out and refused to let me take Susan.'

'Is it any of his business?'

'None whatsoever, but he made such a big deal about it that – coward that I am – I told her to phone in sick tomorrow morning and to meet us in town and we'd take her anyway. I'll probably get us all sacked for it. James is behaving like a complete adolescent and I can't blame his age for it.'

'Well, I've been thinking like an adolescent too this week.'

He lifted one eyebrow.

'Seriously. Do you fancy a trip to Birmingham?'

'Why?'

She unplugged the iron and folded a t-shirt on the ironing board. 'I think we are seriously lacking in information. We don't know who, for example is doing these things in your computer. It seems to be a planned attack on you personally or at least on your abilities.'

Tim put his chin on the back of the chair. 'Someone is trying to make me look incompetent.'

'But there are employment laws and I suppose you have a human relations department?'

Tim nodded and banged his chin on the chair. 'I was given a permanent contract at the start, so they can't use any probationary period excuse.'

'Now, because I have a simple mind,' Mary put the iron on the counter, 'and I can only think in one plane at a time, I have to ask myself why? Why are they doing this? Is it connected to something else that you've done, seen, uncovered that they didn't want you to find.' She collapsed the ironing board.

Tim put his forehead on his hands. He felt faint. 'How on earth can we find out? Maybe I should just resign.'

'If you resign, there will always be a professional shadow. I think we need to find out more and act first before something else happens to you.' She stood against the chair and took his hands. They were pale and cold.

'Now, I've been making some inquiries among all those bright young students of mine, the ones with a keen interest in computers.'

'I think I know where this is leading, but carry on.' He squeezed her fingers.

'Well, someone is able to change things in your computer system to damage your work. So I think it's time we found someone to have a look around and see if there's anything of interest - maybe even to leave something behind, if you know what I mean.'

'You are a dangerous woman to know.' He pulled towards him. 'But you're right and I made a decision today; no matter what happens, I can't stay at Conmac. Even if by some miracle, I manage to come out of this on top, I've lost my affection for the place and I think the odds of beating them – and God knows how many there are – aren't all that great. I've got to be ready to move.'

She wrapped her arms around his head. 'Then we've got to get you out of there before they ruin you. That's what's really worrying me. I know what it's like to lose your professional enthusiasm. We've got to think about your future.'

Later on the little settee, while he held on to her in the quiet he realised that she had fallen asleep.

He kissed her hair and held onto her for a few more minutes. *Dear God, I've almost lost her once. When I look at her, I see the friendship we had still there – stronger now but different. I admire her. She amazes me. I'd trust her with my life. She doesn't judge me. I can tell her anything. I've been alone all my life and if I lost her, I'd lose more than just a friend.*

The scale of that loss hit him harder than he expected but he let his mind wander into the probable outcome – a cosy domestic scene of life together, bumping into each other in the kitchen where he was now used to being alone. In the living room, with her piles of papers and books where he preferred things tidied and put away; in the bedroom where.... He drew back from the permanence of another commitment. He couldn't face it – not yet. But how long could it go on like this?

Mary let Tim put her to bed. She was asleep before the two kittens that nested at the bottom.

Mary woke alone in moonlight streaming through the window. Getting up to pull the curtains, she realised how beautiful moonlight was. It put a silver whiteness on everything in the room; it dusted the vase of flowers on the chest of drawers and the furnishings were soft grey. She pushed open the window. Outside, the grass sparkled with silver dew, black branches were speckled with grey lichen and the new leaves shivered in the night air. The half moon glided in silence over the pasture. Cattle and sheep made small grey mounds in the fields and a lamb called for its mother. Birds were still, except for the occasional fluttering in the foliage. Cool air drifted past her and settled around her ankles. *Why are we sunshine people, when there is such beauty at night?*

She jumped when she heard the kittens hiss and spit. 'Hey, you two.' She turned to find two little creatures - fur standing in clumpy spikes, tails up and twice their normal tiny size. They were both staring at something. Mary looked into the darkness to see what it was. But there was nothing. She got back into bed. 'Come on, you.' She reached out to smooth the fur on Rosie's back, but the little tabby turned, hissed at her and ran off. Marie followed.

Mary looked after them in surprise. She reached to pull the duvet over her, and saw a murky shape in the corner where the two kittens had been staring. The little shape was only a foot or so high and had no real form. It hung in space like a wisp of smoke and as she watched it drifted up, elongating until it created a triangular shape about five feet high.

Softness and silence floated from it and her instinctive alarm evaporated like thoughts in sleep. Instead the shape fascinated her. It advanced a few feet into the room and stopped. Details began to form. The smoke thickened and thinned into fabric folds and facial features. Mary saw a young woman being created. She wore a long skirt; a plain bodice with long sleeves. There was a shawl around her shoulders, a collar under her chin and a bonnet on her head. She floated a few inches above the floor and did not seem to have any feet. Mary saw a pretty face, with small features and bright eyes. She was too enchanted to speak.

The feature drifted wider and began to divide like a binary cell. Mary could hear the rustling sound she had heard before - the waves on a pebble beach. She sat up on her knees. The widened form created another young woman identical to the first. The sound modulated again and Mary could see the mouth on one of the women move and began to understand what she was saying.

'I be Rose.' The girl from behind spoke in a smaller voice, 'And I be Mary'.

Mary grabbed a handful of the duvet and yanked it towards her. She tried to speak herself, but could make no sound until she cleared her dry throat. 'Sisters?' was all she could manage.

'Aye,' whispered Rose. 'We be sisters.' Mary slipped behind as if content that Rose should speak for her.

'Why are you here?' What she had found in the country archives was beginning to make sense. She had to know for sure what had happened to them. Two sisters, Mary and Rose, baptised on the same day, buried on the same day; their father the first owner of her cottage if what she knew was correct – just like the archives hinted and the message in the wall heralded.

'To tell ye.'

'Tell me what?'

'He killed us y'see.'

'I know,' Mary felt a huge lump in her throat. They were beautiful and innocent. She struggled for the name from the County Records – her mind like mist. 'It was John Roberts wasn't it? But why?'

'Aye, it were Mr Roberts.' Rose appeared to look to her sister and something passed between them that Mary could not understand. The rustling sound rose and Mary wanted to grab it to keep it still so she could hear.

Rose continued. 'This 'ere house has always bin lived in by Marys from our family an' they all knew what he done. You be the first Mary who weren't ours.'

'And I didn't know until I found the letter hidden in my wall and looked for you.' The grey colours deepened and the two shapes almost vanished into the dark wall shadows. Then the forms strengthened again as if resolution gave them courage.

Rose looked at her sister again and Mary spoke this time. 'John Cooper, he be my betrothed, but Mr Roberts, he wants Rose 'ere. John, he tries to save us. He speaks to Mr Roberts but...'

'John in your message... and in the records...'

'Aye.' Rose continued the story. 'Mr Roberts, he wants the land y'see. The land our father farms – it be good land. But Da' has agreement y'see.'

'And that means that John Roberts couldn't just take it back.'

Rose went on as if Mary hadn't spoken. 'Mr Roberts, he wants me see and 'e takes...' Her voice faded.

'I think I know what you mean.'

'So 'e sets agin us, tells folk we be witches, cause we talks to our animals and uses herbs and flowers an' such.'

Mary felt near to tears. Injustice stung her throat and she found it hard to speak. 'So he roused the people and they...?'

'Aye... he led them here.'

Mary spoke from behind her sister. 'An' he takes our Da's land and John Cooper's land.'

'And John Cooper?' Mary had to know if what she had seen were true.

'He be wi' me now. Mr Roberts, he did ' im too, after us...but you saw...' The little shape slid back behind her sister.

Mary needed to be sure she had the story right. 'So John Roberts was charged with – with what he did to you – but he was found not guilty.'

'Aye.'

'Was John Roberts a young man...?' Mary needed to know.

'It were Mr Roberts, the son...' There was a crackling silence.

'But he had to compensate your father with this land...'

'No it be Mr Roberts Senior who give the land.'

'...and he built this house. And he named it for both of you.' Mary was clutching the duvet so tightly her fingers hurt.

Tears were stinging the skin on Mary's face. 'Why are you telling me this?'

'You be a good person Mary Mitchell an' you live 'ere now. Y' needs t' know tha' it not be over.'

'What?' Mary's mouth suddenly felt dry and cold.

'There still be Roberts 'ere who wants this land.' The girls began to recede into the distance.

'Wait,' called Mary, but as they disappeared all she could say was, 'come back'. Her voice drifted into the darkness. 'Who is...?

The calmness around her was universal. These visions, sightings, she didn't know what to call them, had been given to her to explain – so that she would know what had happened here. They were a gift and a warning. It was over now – the legacy could go on. The girls had trusted her enough to tell her and she had to be sure the trust would be honoured.

Maybe she wasn't mad – just a bit sensitive – psychic perhaps – dear God she needed to believe that it were so. Through whatever connection they had to her or whatever gift she possessed, they could be free now, knowing that the cottage would stay safe. No Roberts was going to get it from her.

Mary wasn't sure if she slept again that night, or if she just sat waiting for the sunrise. A calmness and a cloak of understanding seemed to have covered her and separated her from the reality of time. When it slid from her, she saw that it was almost 7 in the morning. There was no sign of the kittens.

Wrapped in a long warm housecoat and thick socks, she ran her fingers through her tangled hair and went downstairs, still wondering what she'd really seen. Into the living room, she stopped in surprise. There was a large lump on her settee covered in a heavy blanket, with two kittens nested in the folds. It had dark curls across its forehead and one arm dangled onto the floor. She sat down on the edge beside him.

'Tim. It's nearly 7.' He opened wonderful dark eyes, smiled at her and pulled her down on top of him.

'So what?' he mumbled over her shoulder.

She sat up and rubbed her hands over the stubble on his chin. 'What on earth are you doing here? And why didn't you come to bed? This settee is disgusting and uncomfortable.'

'Tell me about it.' He rolled onto his back. 'I wanted to be here so I'd know if you were ... well needed me.' She smiled at him, as if he were a silly child. 'Well, you didn't expect me to just leave you here did you?' He yawned and pushed back the blanket. 'God but my clothes feel slept in and I think I've just been run over by a tank.'

She didn't mention what she had seen. It was so private and so tender and sad that she wanted to encase it in her own mind, before she shared it, even with Tim. She hadn't needed him this time.

'Come on, I've got work to do and if I'm right you still have a job to go to — something clandestine with your secretary...'

28

On Saturday morning Birmingham was like any large city in late spring. Boy racers with sunroofs open and music banging; women with prams and carrier bags; people with papers and plants. Commerce and business had moved from the trading rooms and offices to the storefronts and pavements. Street cafés and coffee shops would be busy all day and well into the evening. There were buskers on the canal side and entertainers in the plazas. It was alive, chic and the sun shone.

Where there was less chic and a little less sunshine, Mary and Tim waited in a café. The street was narrow, with litter in the gutters. Broken cars leaned here and there on the pavements and children on skateboards preformed dangerous flights from home made ramps on the street. Babies cried and dogs barked and narrow brick houses paraded in perfect rhythm down row after row. Corner shops, newsagents and cafés like this one made occasional stamps of indifference on the Victorian uniformity.

They took a chance on the coffee and it arrived very dark and very black. It was clear it was not meant to be drunk that way, but the milk looked very untidy.

'What are we doing here?' Tim spoke under the loud music that buzzed and banged out of bad speakers mounted on high wall brackets.

'This is not far from where I used to teach – although the school wasn't quite this ragged I admit. A young man called Jason Lockley was a student of mine.' She tested the coffee, shuddered as it went down. 'He has a stratospheric IQ, but uses it these days for questionable purposes.'

'How did you find him again?'

'I made a call to a friend of mine at the school who got his telephone number from the files. I am afraid I told her I might have a job available rather than some 'freelance work' as it were.'

'You're too honest.' He looked around at the variety of tables, some covered with cracked Formica, others with place mats of various patterns. The chairs were all different and groups of large young men in baggy black jeans seemed to be propped up by young women in tight ones. 'I feel like a colour sergeant in a lingerie factory.' The air was thick with foul language. Mary laughed at him.

'They are just young people. Terrifying to look at, but very harmless. Unless of course you get on the wrong side of them.' She laughed again as he looked at her in surprise.

He whispered hoarsely over the music. 'And just how to I avoid doing that? I look like the embodiment of the establishment. For Gods sake I look like a cop.'

She smiled at him again. 'Relax.'

A small young man dressed like the others came up to their table. 'Mrs Mitchell?' Mary smiled with obvious pleasure and Tim stood up. 'Jason. How nice to see you again. Please do sit down. This is my friend Tim Spencer.'

Tim shook hands as normally as he could. 'Can we get you something?'

'Yeah – tea please.' Jason pulled his large dark jeans up and dragged a wobbly chair over. He put its back against the table and straddled it; his hands on the top. His short hair was gelled into perpendicular spikes and a large silver stud hung through one eyebrow. His black roll neck shirt seemed unreal in the summer heat. He looked uncomfortable but not from the temperature. Tim went to get the tea. He heard Mary trying to put Jason at his ease.

'Please call me Mary. I haven't come to see you as an old teacher of yours. I've come to ask for your help so I'm very glad to have found you.'

Jason seemed surprised and was silent until Tim put the tea in front of him. He put two spoonfuls of sugar into the cup and stirred it. 'Help, like what?'

'Well, we need some computer advice and I've been told that you are the best.'

Jason sipped his tea. 'Don't you want some big guy from the city or somethink?'

'Not this time. We want something done and we don't want anyone to know about it if you know what I mean.' She waited.

'Is it big?'

'The system or the job?'

Jason shrugged giving nothing away.

Tim felt as uncomfortable as Jason looked. 'The system is a company network – about 45 or 50 stations – the usual stuff, office, accounts, CAD/CAM – a few years old I'd guess. I need to find something in it, if I can.'

'That's a big job.'

'Can you tell us what you'd do to help us?' Mary winced as she took another sip of the coffee.

Jason stirred his tea. 'I wouldna thought that this was the sort of thing for you, Miss.'

Mary smiled. 'I'm afraid I am rather involved in this. You see, some people where Tim works are doing something that we think is illegal and at the same time putting some of Tim's work at risk.'

'What kinda work is that then?

'Structural engineering.'

'So you ain't a cop then?'

Tim looked at Mary and they laughed, 'No, but I was sure I looked like one, sitting in this café.'

Jason smiled then. 'I might be able to help you then. Whatcha lookin' for? In the system like.'

'I have had several pieces of my work corrupted so that what went out was not what I had created. Some sections of my diary were changed without my knowing. I need to know who's doing it and why – if there is any way of finding out.'

Mary continued. 'We think we know who is involved but of course we can't find proof. What we don't know is how we can get the information. We will, of course make sure that you are not – what shall I say – out of pocket.'

Jason thought for a few minutes. 'I can have a look around and let y'know. If'n I can find out who it is, will ya want me to do anythin' fer ya?

Tim felt like a man facing Armageddon. 'Get me the information first OK? But if you can find anything about a company called Etherstone while you're there I'd be grateful.'

Jason took a deep drink of tea. 'What's your company and the e-mail address?'

Tim patted his pockets, 'I've got a business card ...'

'Just tell me, I'll remember and your phone number – and y'r e-mail at home.'

Tim gave him all the numbers and addresses.

Mary smiled wanly at Jason. 'How long will this take, do you think? We're afraid Tim may be running out of time and we don't want to be found out.'

Jason grinned and finished his tea. 'I'll have a look tonight and let y'know.' They nodded weakly. 'Bye sir, miss.' He got up, smiled and left.

The cacophony continued around them. Tim looked at his evil cup of coffee. 'Get me out of here.'

Tim lay on his stomach in his deep grass. With his chin on his stacked fists, he could just see over the top into the afternoon sun. Mary's two kittens made moving trails as they stalked each other through it. 'I must mow this. I thought once a month would do, but something tells me I was wrong.'

'Leave it any longer and grown adults will be lost in it for weeks.' Mary wiggled around and put her head on his back. 'Why don't you call Phil?'

'I did, but he said he had enough work now and didn't have time. So I'm on my own it seems.' He rolled over, and put his fingers in her hair.

'He's been strange the last few weeks.' She twisted her shirt straight and pushed it into the tight waist of her jeans.

'He's strange to start with by all accounts.'

They lay in the peace of the sun for a few minutes – Tim looked down at her head. *God, but you are beautiful.* The wind ruffled her wavy curls. Tim's mouth curved in a satisfied smile.

'Tim?'

'Mmm?'

'I saw something Thursday night – in the middle of the night.'

He sat up with a jerk, bouncing her head. 'Again? Why didn't you call me?'

'I didn't know you were downstairs and anyway this was different. I've been thinking about it and I'm beginning to understand it.' She sat up and crossed her legs, Indian fashion.

His eyes narrowed and he felt frown lines his forehead as she told him about Rose and Mary. 'This wasn't anything like the others. It was calm and beautiful and so, so sad.'

'But they didn't tell you anything that you didn't already know or suspect, did they? What am I saying? Is it possible that it was in your head?' He ran his fingers down the hair at the side of her face. 'Remember I'm a hard nosed engineer with zero intuition – no sensitivity at all.' He leaned back on his elbow. How was he going to help her with this when he had no idea what she was talking about or what it meant?

She laughed. 'I don't believe you have no sensitivity, but no, what I saw wasn't in my head. The kittens were well aware of it too.' Her voice had a new quality of tranquillity. She smiled at him.

He picked up her hand and kissed it, her fingers were calm and cool. 'Truly?' He had to believe her, but he knew he couldn't do it – not completely.

'Please just trust me and if I ever wake you up - screaming in the night again – well just hug me and in the morning you can take me to whatever padded room you like and throw away the key.'

'I still worry about you. I don't understand psychology - or the paranormal - give me the creeps.'

'I'd have expected no less from you,' she teased. 'But it's what these two said that interests me. It was like a warning; that it wasn't over; that there are still Roberts around who want the land back. We didn't know that.'

'If that's so.'

'I don't know of anybody around called Roberts, but I'll ask at the next Garden Club meeting. Maybe someone knows.' She pulled the heads off several dandelions and tossed them onto his hair. 'But, I've also been thinking about our situation.'

His stomach lurched. *Why do I assume she'll say it's all over?*

'What you're facing is like a modern witch hunt. It happens all the time. It doesn't end in execution these days, but it still destroys people. Only now it's called bullying.'

Tim was silent for a long time.

'There's something in what you say,' he admitted at last. Then after another pause, he drew a circle on her arm with a blade of grass. 'When this is all over, do you think I could start a new career as a ghost buster?'

She tumbled him into the grass.

29

'Why don't you use the dishwasher?' Tim asked picking up a tea towel. Mary lowered a stack of breakfast dishes into a mound of suds in Tim's shiny stainless steel sink.

'Your kitchen is so tidy – I just like to stand in it.'

'Well, I'm about to mess it up again because I need more coffee. I never drank coffee in the mornings until I met you.' He flung the tea towel over his shoulder.

'That should be a note of caution. Lord knows what else I can do to you if I can destroy your morning cuppa.'

He kissed her head as he reached to open a cupboard door over her head. He took out a silver package. 'I thought we could look on the net today and see if we can find any information about those damaged buildings. He filled the coffee pot with water. 'I know roughly where they were so if we can locate a local or regional newspaper site, we might find something.'

One of the sites on Tim's list was not mentioned in press reports. The internet pages of the regional papers were basic and offered very little information. Even when Tim put in the probable dates, the screen just blinked and returned to the home page.

'Here, put in the next site on the search engine, I'll get the coffee.' Mary typed in the next location and trying to remember what Tim had done, pressed the search button. The Google screen flashed as Tim returned.

'Anything?' He handed her a cup.

'Well this might be interesting. It has the same name as the property...'

The screen cleared and the headline told them just about all they needed to know. 'Historic House Gutted.'

'According to my notes, either Howard or James, did a site survey of all these projects, but no quotations were ever made.'

As they tried one more property, the phone rang. Mary took the coffee cup out of Tim's hands. 'I doubt it's for me.'

'Mr Spencer? Jason.'

'Yes Jason...'

Jason wasn't interested in small talk. 'Had a look last night. System's quite easy to crack. I looked at your use of the system – for your work like – and I saw that someone else in the system was accessing your stuff.'

Tim's mouth was dry. He tried to ask who it was, but Jason carried on. 'Also, someone is tracking your access to other stuff.'

'What do you mean 'tracking'?'

'Well, following like. Wherever you went in the system or whatever you opened, a record was made of it.'

'Do you know who?'

'Not yet. But that company you wanted me to look at?

'Etherstone'

'Yeah, well they work for another company called Royston. They gets their orders from there.' Tim couldn't speak. 'Mr Spencer? Are you still there?'

'Yes Jason. I'm here.' Tim's voice was a squeak.

'What do y'want me to do now?

Tim took a deep breath. 'Can you find out everything you can about Royston please?'

Jason rang back before they had time to speculate about the odd connection between the two companies.

'The name you gave me, Royston, is gone from the main system.'

Tim's felt disappointment begin somewhere in his bowels.

'...but it was there – it's been deleted.'

'I think I knew that.'

'Well, I found it again in the accounts. A bit harder to crack into. Sort of like a separate company – with its own accounts and stuff – you know, payments in and out that sort of stuff. But hidden.'

'Yes!' Tim rammed his fist in the air.

'Money in comes from all sorts of places, most of them Europe. Money out goes to numbers and not names. I might be able to find out who the numbers are if the money goes to bank accounts 'n stuff but banks is big stuff. A lot of it goes to Etherstone's.'

'You've found what we need Jason. Don't go into the accounts just yet. I may need you to do something later, but can you leave it with me for now?'

Mary hugged her coffee cup to her chest while he told her.

'So, Royston is selling something abroad and paying people for something.'

Tim got up and began walking up and down the little bedroom. 'What are they selling?'

'And who is getting the money?'

'One of them is Etherstones.'

He sat down on the little bed, pulled a pillow across his knees and put his elbows on it. 'James and Howard get information about renovations and invite themselves onto the site on the pretext of providing a quote. They must use some other ruse than steel, because not all of these renovations need any. So, they have a look around – promise a quote will be in the post – and then what – burn the place down? It doesn't make sense.'

'Insurance? No. Investigators would notice things like that.' Mary answered her own question.

'I think they need something quicker.' He swung his fists up and down onto the pillow. 'I think this is money laundering – big time. Using Etherstones as a public front keeps things looking somewhat legitimate.'

'But where does the money come from and why did they suddenly start attacking you and your work?'

'Because if someone is tracking me through the system, they will have known that I was looking for Royston some weeks ago. That will have worried them, because Royston should have not been there. They knew I'd keep looking and uncover more than I should have. They also knew that they couldn't just get rid of me because there was no cause, so...'

'We need to have some insurance of our own.' Tim looked up at her. 'Well if they get really nervous about you...' She left the rest unsaid. 'We need something planted – in the computer system I mean – that will uncover what they are doing even if we aren't sure what it all is.'

'I need to talk to Jason again don't I? And then I have to keep a straight face until he gets it done.'

'You don't have to do this.'

'Oh, but I do Mary, I do. I've got to stop being such a bloody coward and <u>do</u> it and then I've got to find out who's doing all this to me. It can only be Andy.'

Mary pulled the visor over her face and pulled on the start rope. The little chainsaw snapped into life. She engaged the trigger to start the chain and coarse sawdust poured in a shower onto the ground as branch after branch fell from the dry brush. A huge pile of broken branches hidden by stinging nettles and dock was reduced to a tidy pile of small logs and twigs for the fire.

A woodpile is a satisfying sight. It meant warmth and security when everything around them was turmoil. Them. She tried to stop herself from thinking about them as 'them'. Every day she had to stop thoughts that were beginning to seem normal and strengthen her resolve again. Loving him was too dangerous. The litany ran itself through the logical side of her brain again and again. He was too good looking – he could have any woman he chose. What chance did a 40-something, overweight, out of work schoolteacher with junk in her hair have? Precious little. Important to keep that in mind – at the front of her mind. Very important. And she was more than happy to admit that she wasn't ready for another committed relationship. Look what had happened the last time – commitment – love if that's what it was – just dribbled away until its thread was too thin. Then there was the problem of careers. For people like them, having a career is a part of who they are. Tim was gifted – he needed the challenge of a career that demanded his gifts. Small chance of that happening in rural Herefordshire. Her career was over and she'd move onto something else – or nothing, but Tim... No he needed his freedom – to live where he wanted to, to work as he needed to and to love in his own way. But it was fun while it lasted.

The little saw revved in her hands and as she engaged the chain again, she saw a movement at the bottom of the garden. It was Tim. He looked grey. She shut off the saw, ripped off the visor and ear protectors, dropped them on the ground and rushed down the garden. 'Are you all right?'

'Where on earth did you get the chainsaw?'

He panted with shock and she was embarrassed. 'Borrowed it from Harry. This dead wood was such a mess I couldn't stand it any longer. But I didn't hear you arrive.' He brushed bits of twig and sawdust from her hair and she gave him a long hug. He was trembling but his breathing steadied.

'Scared the life out of me.'

'Sorry,' she smiled. 'Bad day?'

'I've had better.' She held him as they walked back to the house. He told her about James throwing his drawings back at him – drawings that were neither correct nor competent.

'Whoever he is, he can do what he likes – I don't know how to stop him.' He folded himself into one of her outdoor chairs and put his elbows on the table. 'The drawings are write-protected and I've changed the password so many times, I've almost forgotten what the current one is. But I know I can't beat them on this so long as they're tracking me.'

Mary rubbed his shoulders. 'We don't have to go through with this. We can just walk away.'

He pressed his palms on to the table, fingers wide. 'No. No, I can't – not now. I just need Jason to come up with the goods.'

In the dark, Mary reached for Tim's hand. 'I hope you can get some sleep – I wish there was something I could do.'

She heard him smile. 'You already have.'

'I mean...'

'I know. Just talk to me about something else.'

'OK then. Let me ask you something. You surprised me when you came home early. I'd meant to have the brush cleared before you got here. But you looked, well...I don't know...scared or something...'

The bed linen rustled as he turned on his side. 'You terrify me.' His fingers fluttered down her arm, laying down the fine hairs that rose under his touch. He smelled warm and moist.

'Terrify? It was just a chainsaw...' She tucked her head down beside his shoulder.

He laughed – a soft honest laugh. 'You had all the safety tackle; it was a very small chain saw; I presume Harry showed you how to use it. There was nothing for me to be terrified about, but I was.'

'Why?' She looked into his face in the darkness.

'Yes. I'm scared of all the things that you can do that I can't and never will.' He moved closer to her. 'Come here.' She put her cheek on his chest. 'I've found you up trees, buried in the garage, mud and compost to the knees, covered in plaster, lost under a chain saw helmet and having tete-a-tetes with people who've been dead for 350 years. I'll have to be content living in a state of intimidation.'

The morning weather girl on the radio in Mary's car predicted reducing temperatures for the rest of the week. Unseasonable, she remarked, but not unusual.

Tim's mind drifted in simultaneous directions and with thoughts elsewhere, he came up to the roundabout far too fast. He braked hard as the rear end of a stationary red estate loomed in front of him. Swearing at himself and the world at large, he grabbed for the papers and his case on the seat beside him. A ring binder shot forward and hit the radio panel. Flailing for the papers on the floor, he heard a horn behind him and realized that the way in front was now clear. Ramming the car into gear he accelerated onto the by-pass. The radio was now tuned to some gold station and bleating some ancient rock and roll.

'You are the only song I ever want to sing

The music that gives my heart its wings,

The magic that makes my soul take flight

Don't ever leave me......'

Who writes this drivel anyway? He accelerated and took his foot off only when he got to heavier traffic beginning the long grind up Dinmore Hill.

'... letters I've meant to write,

things I've meant to say,

things like 'I love you.''

For a moment he was back in a college disco remembering the tune.

'...times I've wanted to hold you

thousands of times a day

times when I love you.'

Those were the days when he thought he was in love with every girl in the common room, pretty or not.

'I'd give my life to be near you, ...'

He hadn't been as much in love as much as in lust and he'd gone from being a boy to being a man without much in between, events driven by immature emotion alone.

'......to touch you, to see you smile.'

But 'in love'?

'I need you beside me.....'

Mary. Yes he needed her, now, more than ever.

'.... The colour of her hair...'

Without remembering anything of Dinmore Hill or the main road into the city, he found himself turning into Hereford. For Christ's sake, this music makes sense!

'Tell me where the magic comes from when I see you,

Tell me where the sunshine goes to when you leave...'

He parked the car in front of Conmac's mosaic front, piled the mess of papers on his arm, kicked the car door shut with his foot, trying to pull himself away from the realisation. I can't cope with this today. He left the keys with Clive and told him that a garage would collect the car this morning and bring it back later.

Tim sorted the crushed and mixed up papers with everything in his in-tray. He made three piles: one for new designs and queries; another for material related to on going work and the third for everything else. He knew there was no point in dealing with new projects if it was all about to fall down so he put the pile back into the in-tray. There was little point in concentrating on work in progress either, but Derek and Bryn had already begun work on some of them. They might survive the maelstrom that was about to hit, and if they did, it might all be of some use to them. He dropped the third pile on top of the first and put the tray back into his bottom drawer as Susan handed him the morning post and e-mails. At that moment James walked past. He looked at no one; his face tense. Tim's palms felt moist on the papers.

'...I need to see you smile...'

I'm cracking up!

At about mid morning, the music in his brain had been diverted by legitimate work until the low grumble of activity from the Transport Office down the stairs at the back of the building was overtaken by shouting and screaming. Tim and several others bolted for the stairs.

One of the company's lorries loaded with steel had crashed on the M1 ramming a bridge abutment, killing the driver. The Transport Office was in chaos and the rest of the company stopped work in disbelief.

Tim made yet another coffee and put his feet up on his waste paper basket. What to do now? Everyone waited for information – real or inspired it didn't matter. As the afternoon wore on, the Transport Office went into shock and several people went home unable to carry on. The only good thing about it was that it diverted attention from him.

As things quieted, he looked around the clean but disorganised office. It was pretty ordinary in spite of the noise coming up the back stairs. The job he'd been asked to do had been challenging to begin with, but it had little to do with what he'd been trained to do. He liked the clean office – but he also liked the dirt and noise. He took his feet out of the bin. He needed to get back to real engineering. The chaos downstairs put everyone and everything around him into a grey focus. None of it was important any more.

30

'Shit.' Tim banged the car door shut and dropped his briefcase on the car park pavement. The smile that another comfortable night and that funny radio station put on his face yesterday vanished. Papers, plans and notes slid in a slippery stream across his feet. He stamped on them to stop the wind taking them into the next county, crammed them back in and slammed the lid. *Another shitty day at the office. I've got to get out of here. Jason, for God's sake hurry up.* Clouds with dark heavy bottoms collided in the low sky and reflected in the car window as he opened the back door again for his hard hat. He couldn't remember if he had a site visit today or not. He threw it back in. So what? Even if he did, he didn't need the thing in the office. He smiled at the extension of the thought and walked up the stairs not trusting his legs to take them two at a time.

In his eyes everyone in the office looked different. Most of them were unfortunate foot soldiers about to be caught in something that they had no knowledge of and no control over. For them he hesitated to do what he knew would have to be done. The hard work for now was to maintain the farce until Jason gave him the means to undo it all. But perhaps the accident had changed things. Maybe that's why it all looked so different. Death does that – it makes the world look different.

Mary pulled the plaster-covered overalls on and went outside for a bucket of mixed plaster. The cold wind shot though her sweatshirt as Phil drove in through the gate.

'Nasty isn't it?' he shouted over the noise in the trees. He was wearing a clean shirt and what looked like new trousers. 'What're you doin'?' He sounded surprised.

'I'm putting the second coat on the wall...'

An unusual expression rested uneasily on his face. She felt as if perhaps she had forgotten to dress. '...the one I plastered...' He walked over to her and stood uncomfortably close. She stepped backwards, but he followed. '...last week...'

He cleared his throat, 'Mary, I've got to say – I think you are a very nice person and we've got to know each other quite well these last few months.'

Where is this leading, thought Mary. *Should I panic?* His voice continued. Mary could only stare at his chest. 'Well, will you marry me?' He reached out to touch her. But she recoiled into the doorframe.

'Phil?' Her voice squawked and he stopped and looked at her in amazement. 'Phil.' She struggled for the right words with a brain that contained few functioning parts. 'Phil, that is the sweetest thing that anyone has ever said to me,' her voice was dry, '...and I'm..,I'm... I'm surprised ... I guess.'

'Well, you can think it over if you want. You deserve some time.'

'No, it's not that Phil, its well . . . ' *Come on girl*, the few brain cells that still functioned shouted at her – *stop him, sharp, and quick.* 'Well, to be honest, I'm seeing someone else.'

'Well.' His cheeks puffed out in surprise. 'I am sorry then...' His face flushed with anger and he walked back to his car. Mary grabbed the door frame and watched him drive out.

Tim had trouble finding his mobile amid the chaos of his briefcase when it rang about mid-day.

'Everything all right?' he asked when he read the number.

'Well, sort of... no trouble with the plastering, but you'll never guess what happened to me this morning.'

'Well, I hope you said no.' His voice was louder than he meant it to be when she told him.

'Of course I did, I'm not ready for that again. But I just had to tell you.' They both laughed uncomfortable little laughs.

When she rang off he put his forehead on his desk. Why do I feel like I've just been punched in the stomach? All I needed now is an ulcer or something. And what the hell do I do if there ever is someone else in Mary's life? This can't go on. It's no good for either of us. He pulled his jacket from the back of his chair.

As he got one arm in the sleeve, Howard walked past his desk. Staring straight ahead, he seemed to see nothing around him. 'Howard?' The poor man looked startled. 'Is there any more information about Frank? There was only rumour yesterday.'

Howard's hairline seemed to close over his eyebrows and he rubbed his hands on his jacket pockets. 'No, I... I haven't heard anything.' The skin on his face looked thin.

'Howard? Are you OK?' Tim looked around for a chair to sit him in.

'Yeah.' He looked around the office as if he wasn't sure where he was – everyone was at lunch. 'It'll bugger up Saturday night,' he whispered rolling his eyes at the ceiling.

Tim grabbed his arm. 'What did you say?'

Howard's eyes were still wide, as if he'd just been woken from a deep sleep and was surprised to find he was still in the same century. 'Nothing, nothing.' He jerked his arm away and went back to his office.

Tim put his other arm into his jacket and shrugged it onto his shoulder. Out in the wind he walked up and down the car park until all he could feel was cold. His breathing was high and fast. Take some control. It's all heading for chaos. What the hell did Howard mean? The wind threw a handful of sand and dirt in his face. Mary? Did he want another long-term relationship? Yes or no? Did she? Come on, think about it. Litter scuttled across the tarmac and over his feet. Relationships were a trap. He was never himself. He stepped up on the kerbstone at the edge of the car park and turned his back to the wind. What they had was great. But was it enough? For him? For her? He turned up his collar. Anything else would mean commitment. That's what's wrong isn't it? He'd have to commit himself and he couldn't do it. He couldn't cope with her delicate mind. He looked at his inadequacy and saw the truth.

At the far edge of the car park beside the big entrance gates, he leaned on the brick pier. He didn't want to hurt her, but shit. If he was going to do it, he had to do it now. Could he? He had to. Tonight he had to tell her and then he'd go. No first he'd hug her, then he'd go.

Tim saw the flashing blue lights reflecting from the bottom of dark late afternoon clouds before he reached the brow of the hill. But from the top the strobes filled the roadway, gate and Mary's garden. The wind had died, but the air was cold and thick with the menace of rain.

He shoved the car into the hedge, skidded to a stop among all the vehicles and ran to her gateway. A thin layer of smoke seeped out of the garden and into the lane. The sharp smell caught in his panting throat and the cold cut into his heaving lungs. A clump of wasted white smoke slid over the orchard grass and whips of steam rose from the cottage roof around two fire fighters emptying limp hoses onto the tiles.

Through the crashing spikes of blue, he saw a small figure on a wheeled stretcher being folded into an ambulance. His eyes widened in shock. A policeman in a large high viz vest stopped him. 'Excuse me sir. Who are you?'

Tim found some kind of a voice, 'Tim Spencer – neighbour –.' He gestured up the road, 'and – ah – friend. What's happened? Is she hurt?' His voice rose. His throat tightened again.

'Don't know yet. Seems like she fell off the roof trying to put out a fire in the chimney. Farmer, there, he called for help when he saw the smoke.'

Tim saw Harry talking to another policeman. His face was ashen even in the dusky light and blue strobes around them.

'Harry?' Tim called, 'What happened?' Dragging leaden legs, he tried to move. The ambulance doors slammed shut and it began to drive away. Without waiting for a reply, Tim made his stunned limbs run for his car.

Tim sat at the end of the row of hard chrome chairs covered with cracked leather in the A&E corridor. In a small rural hospital, it was quiet at this time of day. Playground injuries had been patched up and sent home; the drunken ones had yet to come in. It remained quiet for a long time – there seemed to be no one at all in this part of the building.

At the other end of the long corridor he could hear muffled coughs and low conversation in the general wards. Somewhere a telephone rang and was mutely answered. It got darker and darker outside the big glass doors and a light rain began to fall. In the darkness the other end of the corridor became quiet. Tim thought for a long time – about nothing in particular but about many things in general.

He was unable to make his thoughts coalesce around anything firm. He remembered the little figure on the stretcher but was unable to make emotional contact – she needed him this time and he couldn't reach her. Harry at the gate – shaken and worried. He wondered where the kittens were. Mary's mental panic over losing everything – how close did this come? Maybe she really was psychic. He'd pushed that thought around in his mind for the past few days. But that was a step too far for him to go. Then she'd needed his help, but it had turned out that she was in control all the time although she didn't know it. Would she still need him? Where and when did one ask for help, but stay emancipated?

His foot had gone to sleep. He stood up to push his toes into the floor when doors behind him opened and a medical figure appeared. 'I'm Doctor Rogers – did you come in with Mrs Mitchell?'

'Yes, I'm her nearest neighbour – she lives alone you see and has no family here...' He found he was rambling.

'She was knocked out from the fall, so we will keep her in over night to be sure there is no concussion. She's got a few nasty bruises, but nothing's broken. She is quiet and asleep now, but you can go in and sit with her for a while if you like.'

Tim nodded numbly. 'Will she be all right?'

'We think so, but she'll be uncomfortable for a few days. If there's no further development over night she can go home tomorrow. Is there anyone who can look after her when she gets there?'

'I will, of course.'

The doctor smiled. 'Then I am sure we can work something out.' Tim followed the doctor into a room with four beds, three of them empty. Equipment with electronic read outs glowed green in the low light.

A small shape all but disappeared under a smooth net blanket in the last bed. Her hair was in disarray on the pillow and a large bruise was beginning to form on one cheek. There were scratches on her forehead and a large dressing on one arm below the hospital gown. He felt weak and completely and utterly useless. Someone brought him a chair. He watched her light breathing – and tried to imagine her on the roof trying to put out a chimney fire by herself.

A little smile crossed his mind. His life had been quiet, predictable, boring until one evening he'd slipped on the tiles at the back of his house. Nothing but nothing had been quiet, predictable or boring from that moment on. In that instant his life had become one wild ride.

But he could stop it if he wanted to. In the hours of the night he dipped into his past as if it had all happened to someone else. He laid one ghost after another to rest; Alison who had left him one day and never told him why; Macie who had wanted from him what he couldn't give; his mother who wanted him to settle down; his father who was disappointed. In the dark hours, he tried to forgive them all and he forgave himself. Then he started his life again.

Tim looked at the small figure in the bed in front of him. His thoughts focussed dimly. Could he do it now? Tell her? He watched her slow, natural breathing. And then the fog in his mind cleared. She was all he wanted; to look after, even if she said she didn't want him to. He wanted to laugh and dance, cry and sing with her – only her. Above all he wanted to stay with her for the rest of his life. He had almost lost her twice and God does not give hints forever. Now, please God, he would not lose her again. A huge lump of emotion rose in his throat.

'I love you.' It was only a whisper but it was from his heart. Then he lowered his head onto the bed beside her and silently wept.

'You scared the hell out of me.' She heard Tim whisper when she woke up enough to remember where she was. His hand shook as he smoothed the hair off her forehead.

'Only about half as much as I scared myself. God, but I hurt everywhere.'

'The doctor says you are a bit roughed up, and knocked yourself out, but there's nothing serious.'

'Wish it felt like it. What time is it?'

'Just after six o'clock, why?'

'No particular reason. I presume that's morning?' She tried to sit up against the pillows. 'Jeez, but my head hurts.'

'I'm not surprised. Do you want me to call someone?'

'No. Don't go away, please.' She felt him pick up her hand. His was warm. He kissed her fingers. She shut her eyes and slept again and when she woke an hour later he still held her hand and watched her.

'Shouldn't you be going to work?'

'Not bloody likely!'

'But what if things happen and you aren't there . . . I don't think I'm making much sense.'

'You are incredible.' A nurse came in then and showed Tim the door. They would make Mary more comfortable, she heard her say and the doctor would like to check things, but would he call back after lunch. She might be ready to go home by then. She saw his face through the glass door as the nurse pulled the curtains around the bed.

'Your husband's lovely isn't he?' Mary opened her mouth to speak. 'He was here all the time you know – refused to leave. Spent all night in that horrible chair. He's going to be as stiff as you are bruised today.'

Tim called Susan when he got home and said he wouldn't be in. He told her what had happened and asked her to let Margaret know. Maybe, just maybe James and the others would find a shred of truth in it and not jump to the conclusion that he was out somewhere drilling holes in the bottom of their rotten boat. If he could just maintain some sense of ordinariness for a few more days – just until he heard from Jason.

He showered and changed and checked his messages. His mother had called again. Jennifer was having her projects remarked, but she wasn't sure of the details. That teacher was cutting up rough about it and what was wrong with Macie? She couldn't get a sensible word out of the girl.

He drove down to Mary's where he checked the house. There were some broken tiles on the roof and some damaged flowers in the tubs. The garden hose and a bucket lay on the path. There were some water stains on the wall upstairs and a lingering smell of smoke, but little other damage. He'd crawl up into the roof space later and check. He found some clothes that didn't smell and put them in a bag.

Then he went through papers stacked on Mary's desk and located her address book. He called someone named Kelley, hoping it would be the right one and explained that Mary had had a fall, but was all right. As he put the kittens into his car he wondered why he'd bothered to phone. It was obvious that Kelley was more relieved that she didn't have to drop everything and rush to Herefordshire than that Mary was unhurt. He tipped the kittens into his kitchen, fed them and threw an assortment of pillows and blankets into the back seat.

Back in Croftbury he found a visitors parking space in front of a new pale brick building with two huge roll up doors and a main entrance behind clean block paving. The sign on the door as he opened it said Hereford and Worcester Fire Brigade. The officer on duty hadn't attended the fire at Mary's but was helpful. He was sorry that there was little information yet. It seemed like a straightforward chimney fire. It happens from time to time in older properties when the chimneys haven't been swept he explained. It was a very cold day and she'd just made a fire. He checked the call log and said that the call had come in at 5.16 p.m. from a woman and that the appliances had responded, arriving within...

Tim stopped him. 'A woman made the call?' The officer checked the log sheet again and nodded. 'There's no record here of her name though.'

Tim thanked him and left.

He went to the estate agents, and then stopped at the library to look at the roll of electors and the yellow pages where he found the name of a chimney sweep. Then he went to the police station and the florists. At a few minutes to one he arrived back at the hospital and handed over the bag of clothes to a nurse.

The same hard cracked leather chairs lined the corridor. He sat in one and thought for a long time.

Mary appeared on the arm of a nurse, in the things he'd brought and smiled at the sight of him. 'I hope the clothes are all right,' he mumbled as he handed her the flowers. 'I should have asked what you wanted.'

'They are just fine.' She hugged his arm and he bent down to kiss her.

The nurses beamed at them both as they left. 'Ain't love grand?' sighed one.

31

Rosemary Cottage sat serene and undisturbed. The gravel drive showed no marks from the huge vehicles and the cottage looked unassaulted. Overnight rain had softened the damage in the garden planters and washed the step. Weak afternoon sun put a soft shine back on the black timbers.

'It looks like nothing has happened – at all.' Mary sounded amazed. 'I mean after all that – I feel cheated.' The kittens scattered across the grass when Tim opened the car door for her.

He held out his hand. 'Do you need me to help you?' He saw her eyes under joined-up eyebrows. 'Well I'm learning to ask. Lord knows I'll never doubt you're capable.'

She took his arm. 'I am feeling almost normal, thank you. I say almost, so don't stop fussing just yet.'

He tried to pack her into a pillow-padded chair but she insisted on arranging the flowers and making coffee, claiming the hospital stuff unfit for human consumption. He un-strapped the folding ladders from the roof of the car and climbed into a pair overalls. He checked Mary's lime plaster and sprayed it with water again. Then ramming his hard hat on his head, he clanked the ladders up the stairs and heaved himself into the roof space with his big torch.

'What's it look like?' Mary's voice followed him through the hatch.

'OK so far.' His boots bumped from joist to joist. The torch beam swished through the void and his voice echoed back to her. 'The chimney's OK and the roof timbers aren't damaged. Fire must have been just in the chimney itself or outside on the roof.' He put his head through the hole. 'There is a bit of daylight showing where the slates have come off and heaven only knows what has happened to the bats, but the roof is sound.'

He lowered himself to the ladders. 'I'll fix the slates for you and I'm not going to ask if you want to do it. And we've still got to get some insulation up there before winter. Now is that coffee ready or what?' He replaced the loft hatch, folded up the ladders and thumped them downstairs again. Still in overalls and hard hat, he opened the back door and collided with a man, almost as tall as he, with wavy grey hair and a sagging face. Before Tim could speak, the man's brusque voice demanded, 'Who are you? What are you doing here?'

At the same moment, Mary spun around, the glass coffee pot banged down on the counter top. 'Robert!'

Robert glared at Tim. 'You going out or what?'

Tim tried to speak. 'I'm ... '

Robert pulled Tim and the ladders past and went in. 'Thanks, I'll look after things from here.'

As the door closed in Tim's face, he heard Mary shouting, 'Robert!'

Tim stood on the step in shock, the aluminium steps digging into his shoulder.

Mary's voice came to him over what seemed a long distance. 'It's OK. Tim, I'll call...'

With a rib cage that felt empty, he carried the ladders back to his car. A huge black Mercedes was parked beside it. What the hell did he do now? Was that Robert as in ex-husband Robert? No question. Was she safe with him? Who knew? Shaking, he tied the ladders on the roof and listened. All was quiet.

Somehow - he had no recollection of doing it - he found he'd driven home. Not for the first time, he asked what the hell did he do now?

Mary had some things to clear up with Robert. He knew about them. Robert was a bombastic person but would she be safe if things weren't sorted out to his satisfaction? She had never said that he was violent and she must have dealt with his anger before. Had he come because he was concerned? Did he still love her? The bottom fell out of Tim's stomach again. He felt ill.

He ripped open the studs on the front of the overalls and threw them in the corner of the extension, then put his head under the bathtub tap. The shock of the cold water drove the breath from his lungs.

He could still let her go. He hadn't told her yet that he loved her. Thoughts swirled in a panic. He wouldn't make her choose. He felt the muscles in his chest crunch. If he wanted to – or needed to – he could let her go. He could save himself from being too hurt – he could pretend to himself that his first realisation was correct – that another relationship was all wrong. He could make it his fault – his decision to break it off. He could – he might have to.

Robert looked at Mary. 'Don't look so shocked. And who the hell was that?'

Mary found some of her voice under the frothing mound of rage that surfed over her. 'Robert, what the bloody hell are you doing here? How dare you barge into my house like this?' Tears tore the rest of her words from her throat.

He opened his arms to hug her, but she backed away. His voice became softer. 'Sorry, - still bruised are you? Kelley called and told me that you'd had an accident – falling off a roof or something stupid.'

Mary felt the mound of anger ripping up to her chest. 'Robert... '

'Don't you think that this has gone far enough now? You've proved your point.'

'What point? What are you talking about?'

He walked toward her and she backed into the living room. 'You've bought a house by yourself, you've moved in and done a few things to the place, I'll bet, so now...' He stopped as he saw the plastic sheeting. 'What are you trying to do here?' He looked underneath and roared with laughter. 'You?' He pointed at it.

'Don't touch it.' Mary almost shouted at him. 'And what do you mean "trying to do"? How dare you?'

He grabbed her elbow, but she yanked it away. 'Now don't be like that.' His patronising tone made her want to grind her teeth. She could hear her own heart pounding in her ears but something made her stay calm. She pushed the frothy mound of anger aside, but it stayed in broken lumps around her.

She inhaled as much as her sore ribs would allow. 'Robert, sit down.' She pointed to a settee and waited until he did so. She sat in the other. The thought that he might touch her made her flesh itch.

Before she could speak, he went on as if she had not intervened. 'Look sweetheart, don't you think this is enough? We all appreciate what you've tried to do and we admire you for it.' He looked at her with a smile one would reserve for a child caught doing something cute. 'I'll bet you've had a bit of fun too. But I think it's time you finished this experiment of yours and came back where you belong. Country living isn't for you. I mean what happens if it snows or something?' He looked around the living room. 'I suppose you can always call that young fellow, what was his name? Tim? But things are going to get harder here and you'll regret it I know you will.'

'Robert you just don't get it, do you? I don't want to give it up. I like it here. '

He didn't seem to have heard. 'God this settee is uncomfortable. Whatever made you buy these? I know you like it here, but it's not safe; it's not you is it sweetheart? There's a bit more than the family back garden here to look after out there and you can't do that alone.' Her voice spewed out in protest, but he talked over it. 'You aren't the country type and this old house - I mean how can you pretend that you can manage this by yourself? It'll need all sorts of things doing to it. My God, just painting it is going to be a job. What would happen to you if there was something serious? Besides Kelley's having this baby and she needs you back and I need you back.'

The emotional field in front of Mary cleared. Now she understood. She could take no more and stood up. 'Come with me.'

She took him out the back door and around to the front of the cottage. 'Do you see this cottage?'

'Of course. Now sweethea...' But she interrupted this time.

'It may be old, it may need repairs, but it's mine. I bought it myself, furnished it myself. I am repairing it myself and I am looking after it myself. I will not give it up. No don't interrupt me. I have got to say this and you have got to understand it.

'I am sorry if you have lost your lady friend. I know that Kelley is having a baby and of course I will help her. But you're both grown up people. I am also a grown up person now – I wasn't until you left – but by doing that, you gave me the last – and the only - great gift of your life. You gave me my independence and I will never give that up again.'

She rushed on before he could interrupt and put her off her stride. 'I negotiated a divorce from you, and a settlement on the house and a legal agreement on the business. And I did it all by myself. Now if you decide you want to re-negotiate that, I'll fight you all the way. I got a copy of your company accounts on Monday, so I know things aren't as bad as you say they are. And you've got a lot more to lose than I do. Because, except for this house, I've got nothing to lose. And I will make sure that I never lose this.' She had no idea how she'd do it, but right now it didn't matter.

She spread her arms wide. 'This is what I want. Not you, not a phoney, shiny, dusted life style in Solihull, where even the newspapers are tidy and folded, and where no one knows the people they've lived beside for 10 years. I want friends I can count on and who know who I am. Work in this house means I'll no longer be just some teacher with a field of vision this wide like all the others.' She pinched her fingers together. He opened his mouth to speak.

'Don't interrupt, Robert because I am not finished.' She pushed one finger on his chest. 'I am not the person you knew. I cannot and will not go back to anything, least of all to you.' She paused and in his shocked silence she drew a long painful breath and pointed at the gate. 'Now, get out of here.'

Tim lay on the cold kitchen floor tiles. He felt that if he moved he'd throw up. If he couldn't control his body there wasn't much hope he'd be able to get a grip on the rest of his life. His brains refused to merge any sensible thoughts. He didn't know she was kneeling beside him, until she spoke.

'Tim.' He sat up too fast; the blood rushed from his head and black spots flickered in front of his face. She clutched his arms. 'Tim? Are you all right?'

He wrapped his arms around her. 'No.' His voice had sand in it. 'Are you?'

'Tim, I've done something I should have done months ago.' His stomach heaved again. 'I've put into words what I want and what I don't want.'

He found he couldn't speak. If he had a voice, he could tell her – he could.

'I've sent Robert away and told him that I don't want him near me again. He tried very hard to make me feel "the poor little woman" just like he used to. This time, for the first time ever, I told him that I didn't need him. I could do things for myself and...,' she looked up at Tim's ashen face, '...I can Tim. I can do just about anything.' There were tears in her eyes and he felt them stab the back of his as well, but he waited. She had to say this. 'I don't need anyone else to run my life...' He felt the sting in his heart. '...but I do need...' Then she cried. They both cried.

He gathered her into his arms again. 'My darling.' The words came over and over until she was quiet on his chest again.

'I love you.' His breath blew the words into her hair. He wiped the tears from her face with his cuff. 'I love you with all my heart. I want to be with you forever.' She covered her mouth with her hands and he heard great gulps behind them but he couldn't stop. 'You make me feel important even when I'm stupid; you make me laugh. You don't need me to be the strong one; you can look after yourself. But, I, me, I need you.'

She wiped her face with her arm, but seemed incapable of speech.

'From the first moment I set eyes on you, my life has been one amazing roller coaster ride and I never want to get off. I haven't laughed or cried so much in my whole life.' He stroked her bruised face. 'My God, you can scheme better than anybody I know. You aren't afraid of the black arts or the Birmingham underworld.' He touched her hair. 'I can't begin to list the things that you can do that I would be terrified even to start. I want to spend the rest of my life with you. I love you with all my heart.'

Tears were dripping from her chin. 'Tim, don't do this. Please don't do this.' His eyes widened – he felt the hole opening in front of him again.

'Tim look at me; I'm seven years older than you.'

He smiled and the hole receded, 'Mmm?'

'I'm over weight, look. Fat thighs.' She slapped her hips.

His smile widened, 'And...'

'I'm not what you would call beautiful or svelte or ...'

'So?'

'You need someone slim, glamorous and gorgeous ...' She wiped her nose on her sleeve.

He felt his grin broad by now.

'We've only known each other a month...'

'Six weeks, less one day.'

'I'm unemployed and in all likelihood, unemployable.'

'Now that could be a problem.'

' I'm...you're not being serious.'

'Are you healthy?'

'Yes, why?'

'And you've got all your own teeth?'

'What?'

'Well, I guess you'll do.'

'Tim.' She swatted at his head, but he caught her arm. Then he put a finger over her lips and his voice cracked. 'You are all I want. Ever. You are beautiful. I... Please - please - don't say you don't want anyone else in your life.'

'Tim,' she whispered into his wet shirtfront. 'Tim, I love you. I've loved you from the first time I saw you.' She giggled. 'How could I help it – all wet and shiny – and that pink towel, well...I didn't stand a chance did I?'

He tipped her chin up, 'Will you marry me?'

Her smile brightened the growing darkness around them. 'Not yet Tim, not yet – I need to test this ability of mine to make decisions and you need to feel what this commitment you've made is really like. But when and if, the time is right ...'

He could feel his smile getting wider and wider until he wanted to laugh out loud; he wrapped her into his arms and tucked her head under his chin. 'I'll take that as a yes, then, but maybe not this week.'

'Yes, I think you can.'

When Mary woke in the morning, she was on her own side of the bed and she found Tim propped on one elbow looking at her. 'What?' Her voice was husky with sleep. 'Am I that fascinating with my hair everywhere and mascara down to my chin?'

He laughed and touched the bruise on her face. 'No, I've got to wake up before you because I'm terrified that you might not be here – or worse that there isn't an impression in the bed to show that you were ever here.'

She yawned, 'I'll always be here, I promise.'

He tucked the duvet cover around her. 'When I looked at you in the hospital, I counted all the things I'd lose if you weren't there: friendship; comfort: understanding, you know how I feel; you never judge; you amaze me and I admire you for all the things you can do.' He folded his pillow under his arm. 'I feel such a sense of wonder when I am with you. All of that and all of the things I haven't even discovered about you – well I realised that they added up to love. I just didn't know what it was.'

She pulled herself over to him. 'Love also is about taking risks.' She ran her hand across his chest. 'It makes you vulnerable. You've allowed me to see into your past and you've shared real emotional pain with me. Those are not easy things to do. I think this is a side of you that even you didn't know about.'

Tim put his lips on her forehead. 'Mary, I couldn't go on living knowing that you were only ever in my imagination. I will always need to convince myself that you are real.'

'Then,' she whispered, 'let's promise that we'll enjoy every minute we have together; if it's four days or four hundred years. Let's be sure that we love each other every second we have.'

He lay down beside her again, with their noses touching. 'I don't want a day to go by when I don't see you or touch you. There is a joy around you that I've never felt in my life and I never want to be away from it.'

'And I thought that I was the one with the words in this relationship. Please don't ever stop telling me how you feel.'

He rolled over onto her and kissed her. 'First I will bring you breakfast in bed – no excuses.' He kissed her again. 'So, how do you like your toast?'

32

'Tim. I don't need looking after. Please go to work. I'll be fine.'

He took the cats' bowls and put them in the sink. 'And leave you when I don't have to – not a chance.'

'But what about ....'

He opened the door to let the kittens in. 'They'll be weeks sorting out that road crash and I'm no nearer to working out what's going on anyway. Besides it's Friday and I still need Jason's little bomb.' The kittens looked up at them. 'And who's going to feed these two?'

Mary re-folded the newspaper and leaned against the kitchen dresser as Tim came in with the post.

The sight of him made her smile. 'Everything all right up there?'

'Yeah, but I missed the bin men again.'

'That was Wednesday...'

'And as usual I forgot.' He separated the small pile of letters. 'Yours... and mine.' He sat down at the kitchen table and flipped through his. His brows were low over his eyes and his jaw was tense.

Mary stood behind him and put her chin on his head, letting her hands slip down over his chest. 'I feel terrible for you – moving into your new house and working at Conmac should have been the end of pain for you, not the start.'

Tim put his arms around her and hugged her into the back of the chair. 'Believe me this is still the better option.' The eyebrows unlocked and the jaw relaxed.

He leaned his head back onto her. 'I've just remembered something.'

'What?'

'Something Howard said on Wednesday. I don't know if it's significant or just the ramblings of a man about to go over the edge.'

'What did he say?'

Tim rubbed her arms. 'He said something about buggering up Saturday night.'

'Odd.'

He chuckled. 'I'd forgotten it with everything that's happened since then. But he also had 'Leeds' written in his diary on Saturday. I saw it when I was in his office.'

'Leeds? Can he mean Royston? But there was nothing at the address you found.'

'Let's try Google Earth.'

'Those buildings all seem to be empty – but maybe they aren't. Maybe there is something there.' He breathed faster; excitement rising. He stared at the screen.

'Tim, Howard knows you've been interested in Royston – is it a trap?'

'Then there must be something there to trap me in. There's got to be something there.'

She hugged him looking over his shoulder. 'Tim, I know what you're thinking and I'm not sure I like it. I haven't got a brave bone in my body and...'

He laughed. 'Not a brave bone.... This from a woman who ...'

'All right, all right. But this is different. This could be dangerous.' She laid her head on his – feeling him chuckle.

'Then we will just have to be very, very careful.'

She saw the truth in his face. 'This means creeping around in a deserted part of a city we know nothing about <u>and</u> in the dark doesn't it.'

He pulled her onto his knee. 'Sweetheart. You told me that I didn't have to do something if I felt I couldn't. The same applies to you.'

'And let you go on your own?'

It was still cold on Saturday but dry, and the high late afternoon clouds were driven to the east by the wind. Tim looked into the boot of his car and Mary leaned in beside him. 'What do we need all this for? Coats, big torch, binoculars, rope ...'

'Well, you never know and I still haven't loaded the rubber dingy and the parachutes.'

'Tell me you're joking.' The wind was cold and getting stronger. She pulled her sweatshirt tighter around her.

'OK, we'll leave the dingy and chutes. But a flask of something hot would be good.'

She handed him a carrier bag with a small smile of triumph. 'Soup and coffee.'

He kissed her forehead and shut the boot lid. 'Let's go.'

Dull evening light alone did not account for the greyness in this part of Leeds. Dark ranks of warehouses hunched under low grey clouds. Nothing glowed anywhere. Dirt and torn carrier bags flapped through the gutters and swirled in abandoned doorways and broken windows. Tim drove across the end of Harvard Street. Everything was closed, deserted.

Tim parked on at the top of a street a short distance away. It too was lined with gloomy warehouses.

He took a second car key from the seat console and gave it to Mary. 'Put this as deep into your pocket as you can so you don't lose it. If we get separated and you get back here before me, you can get in.'

Mary gasped in surprise. 'What gives you the idea that I might not be with you every step of the way?'

'Darling, we don't know what's going to happen. So if we get separated and you get here before I do, lock yourself in, get down in the back and cover yourself up with the blanket. Or just get the hell of here.'

'But how do I find you? I won't go without you and if you get back here first and I'm lost out there somewhere...?' She was trying very hard not to become hysterical at the prospect of being lost alone forever in the warehouse district of Leeds - car or not.

'Got your mobile with you?' He patted her belt. 'Good, we can communicate, no matter what.'

Mary didn't feel convinced that there weren't a few unforeseen difficulties with this. A gust of wind raked her hair as they got out.

'Now, give me your jacket.'

'I'll freeze.'

'You'll also be seen and heard in that – noisy fabric and bright orange as well. Don't worry, we'll keep warm somehow.' He put it in the boot and taking the binoculars, closed the lid. 'I've seen a path on the map that comes out on Harvard Street a little way up from the scrap yard. We can watch from there.'

The path was little used and the entrance almost covered with bushes and nettles. Before they went in, Tim asked, 'Now, can you find your way back to the car from here?'

Mary's teeth clattered together as she nodded. 'Yes, I think so.'

'Good. Don't lose track of where it is. Come on.' He grabbed her hand. The little used path was a thin line of broken tarmac and cinders, closed in by high blank brick walls. The edges were thick with weeds and saplings; bottles, cans and crisp packets were caught in the thick growth. They walked almost to the end. Tim stopped and knelt down in a thin patch of dead grass with his back to the wall. Mary did the same. 'Wait here. I'll have a quick look.' He took the binoculars and at the end, lay in the weeds. In a few minutes he was back. 'There's no activity anywhere on the street. We'll have to wait.' They found a section of wall where they could penetrate ivy, dock and dead grass and waited under a sycamore sapling. There they sheltered from the cold.

Every half hour or so, Tim went out to look for signs of activity. There was none. No one used the path. No one used the street. They tried to keep warm and keep quiet. At about 11 o'clock Tim handed Mary the binoculars and she went to the corner. Still there was nothing to be seen anywhere. When she got back she whispered, 'I think we've been mislead – I don't think anything's going to happen.'

The sky was dark with cloud, but they could still see shadows from the buildings and vegetation. 'No, I think they'll wait until it's very dark" He put his arms around her and rubbed her back to warm her up. 'I think we've got a long night ahead of us.' Mary sat down in the leafy nest, leaned on the wall and stretched out her cramped legs.

Sometime later, she felt Tim squeezing her arm. Startled, she realised she had fallen asleep. She struggled to hear him. 'There's something happening.' In silence, he moved back to the end of the path and lying on the ground, parted the grass for the binoculars. Then he beckoned her to come forward. The light collecting binoculars allowed her to see more than she thought possible. There were silent wisps of movement – something drifted behind a large pile of rubber tyres. A dark figure glided along the fence and with a faint dull rolling sound, pushed open a wire gate.

She handed the binoculars back to Tim and pointed at the gate. He studied the activity for a few minutes and then motioned her back from the corner. 'They're expecting something. We've got to find a way to see what's going on.' He tugged on her sweatshirt. Over tin cans, broken bottles and stinging nettles they left the silent figures behind and returned to the car.

Huddling together they made a V with their bodies and Tim took out the street map and a tiny torch that he put in his mouth. 'Right,' he mumbled, 'if we go down to the street at the other end, we can try to get behind them.'

From a tin box in the boot, Tim took out two sticks of what looked like theatrical makeup. 'Cam cream,' he explained and spread the dark colour in streaks and blobs across her face and hands, then on his own and onto her light coloured trainers.

'Where did you get this stuff?'

'Left over from Haydn's birthday party a couple of years ago. I was in charge of making a dozen hysterical 12 year old boys look like combat soldiers.'

Cold air clutched them as they walked to the cross street. It too was encased in factory walls. Breathing in tense gulps they stopped where it met Harvard Street, five hundred yards up from the scrap yard and its moving shadows. He whispered in her ear. 'Run across the street and down the wall until you find a doorway you can get into. Be quiet and quick. Wait there.'

At his whispered 'go' she crossed to the long dark line of the building and 10 yards along to a disused doorway. Stepping on a drinks can, she cursed at the noise, slid into the gap, her breath coming off the top of her lungs. Her heart pounded so hard in her ears she almost didn't hear Tim slide in beside her. The bricks of the dark building were cold and dry and ended at another wire fence. There was no way to get behind the yard.

'We need to go through the building.'

'What?'

Instead of replying, he pulled her along by her sleeve back to the doorway where they'd started. 'If we can get in, we might be able to get to the other end and look into the yard from the building.'

'But what if they're inside.'

'Then we need to be careful and very, very quiet.'

'Tim, I don't think this is even legal.'

She saw his teeth flash in a smile. 'Don't think that matters much.'

The boarding over the doorway was screwed to the frame from the inside. 'No squatters at least.' Without tools, the boarding would not yield without a substantial amount of noisy brute force. Tim checked the large window next to it. It too was secure and boarded, but then, 'Aha.' He breathed rather than spoke, 'top window's broken and no boarding.' He pulled his sweatshirt off and wrapped it around one arm and hand. In seconds, he was up and through the little opening. Mary watched him disappear- the vacant space he'd occupied filled with the horror of abandonment.

'Tim?' She whispered in panic.

'Here.' She saw a corner of the boarding move and a piece of pipe came through. 'Lever the corner loose while I push. Quiet as you can.'

In seconds she too was inside and heard him pull his shirt back on. She leaned on the wall, reluctant to venture any further. 'Tim. What on earth are we doing?'

'This building's empty and I can't hear any noise from them. So they must be in the next building. I've got to find out for sure and see what's going on. You'll be safe here.'

'Oh no! Not alone and on my own I'm not.'

The cavernous space seemed to be echoing extravagantly to their whispered conversation.

'Remember, you don't have to do this.'

Mary pushed herself off the wall. 'If something's going to happen to you, it's going to happen to me too.' She did not feel even a tiny bit as brave as she sounded.

He pulled her head onto his chest. She could tell he was breathing hard. 'I want to get up to a top floor and try to see into the yard at the other end. There're two floors above this one and they'll use the lower floors first. If we can get up higher, we'll look for a way across and get closer.' He patted her cheek. 'These old buildings are often joined together.' He sounded breathless. 'We need to find some stairs.' He gave her a trembling hug. 'Ready?'

'Ready.'

'Hold onto the back of my shirt.' She slid her other hand along the wall.

Tim felt the floor before each step. It was hard and smooth. The air was still and dry. The smell of dust hung in pockets. They found a corner and continued down the back wall. Although he could see some resolution in the dark, the blackness was nearly total. Then his hand felt a gap and what seemed to be a pair of doors. He ran his hands over them. There was a pair of large bracket handles but no lock. He pushed. One door swung open on oil filled sockets. Looking back, he oriented himself with grey crack of light from the broken window.

The door led into a stairwell and they began to climb – one silent step at a time – their trainers disturbing only dust. They stopped to listen at each landing. All around them was the silence of a building sleeping a sleep of years. At the top floor, Tim opened the swing door a crack and listened again. Then wider so he could see inside. They entered and crouched in front of the doors. The only sound was their breathing which seemed far too loud. It was brighter here – not all the windows were boarded and city glow gave some faint reflected light.

The huge space was empty, but for bits of broken timber and empty sacks. In the grey gloom Tim found a hole in the dividing wall and handed loose bricks and blocks of concrete to Mary who laid them along the wall. When it was clear, he disappeared part way into the hole. Then stopped, wiggled out again and signalled her to follow him.

Mary's heart rattled in her ears as she wiggled through. A cavernous space lay in front of them. The street frontage had several ghost-like, gaping windows. At the end opposite them was another window. If her geography were correct, it would look down on the scrap yard. Tim pulled on her sleeve. They felt the wall to the front corner. Half way down the long back wall was a dark shadow – more swing doors. They walked past them to the window.

Sitting on the floor with their backs to the wall they heard a throbbing sound outside. Tim looked over the sill, scanned the yard and then pulled on her sleeve. She looked out to see a large lorry and trailer reversing into the yard. A man was directing the driver back to the building.

Tim tugged on her sleeve again. Returning to the door, they opened it and crept down to the next floor. Tim lay on the floor and opened one swing door a crack. 'Bloody hell!'

33

Tim lifted his arm and Mary looked underneath. The entire floor was covered with piles of what looked like stones or tiles, mounds of lumpy tarpaulins, carved balustrading, garden ornaments, water tanks. She could see hundreds of misshapen sacks and against the sidewall, a tilting row of telephone boxes.

She looked at him – not understanding what she was seeing. 'Salvage,' he whispered. 'They rob out the properties and then burn them or bomb them to the ground. Put the money into construction projects with Etherestones who sells them on. This is one hell of a big operation. How many people does it take to clean out one of those big old houses in one night? Come on.'

'We're not going in!' He was already through the door. She followed – ears and eyes straining for anything not of their making.

Step by silent step, they worked their way around boxes, sinks, piles of doors and slates, to the window into the yard. There was a large open stairwell to the ground floor in the far corner. Faint noises were rising through the hole. They squatted behind a stack of sash windows and looked over the sill.

The lorry stopped in the yard and when the engine shut down the silence rang in their ears. They watched two men pushing up the curtain sides of the trailer. With a whine, an electric lift truck came into view from underneath them with several large stone garden fountains or ornaments tied onto a pallet with heavy rope. Tim and Mary slid down on the floor again.

'They're beginning to load. That's a continental trailer. They're going to take the stuff out of the country.'

'Now what?'

'I've got to find out where it's going and what they are loading – and who's doing it.'

They shot a quick glance over the sill. The electric lift truck disappeared inside again – and the two men leaned on trailer. One lit a cigarette for the other and then for himself. As the light flared, Tim drew breath. 'Richard Davies.'

'Who?'

'Transport manager at Conmac.'

The men relaxed and as the lift truck noise diminished in the warehouse, their voices were clearer. The second man exhaled a stream of smoke. '....about Frank.'

'Yeah, well . . .'

'He was a good driver – been through it all had Frank. We hauled a lotta loads Frank 'n me.' He seemed to nod in the direction of the warehouse. ''Specially for this lot.'

'Yeah..... poor bastard.'

'Wife, kids and all.' The man took a savage drag on the cigarette. 'And for what – doubt that this lot'll see'em OK.' His voice thickened. 'What d' they care? They know we can't say anything.'

'Have a care Colin.'

But Colin was warming to his subject now – his voice rose. 'They can pay us what they damn well like and we've gotta do it, don't we? No pension when we're gone. And all for a stupid accident ....'

Richard dropped his voice and grabbed the front of Colin's t-shirt. Tim and Mary strained to hear. 'Wake up Colin; it was no accident. So I'd watch my mouth if I were you. All it takes is a little tinkering with the mechanics you asshole – it could be you next. They won't give you a second chance.' Richard ground his cigarette into the tarmac. 'Don't ever forget what they've got on you – ever. 'Cause they won't.' He walked away.

Mary grabbed Tim's arm and they stared at each other. Mary leaned into the sash windows. 'Tim, I don't like this.' The wooden frames ground against each other. He rammed his hand over her mouth. Richard's voice came from half way up the stairs. 'Al? You up here?' Tim and Mary did not breathe. 'Let's get it loaded, Colin's got to be out of here in an hour.' There was a long pause and a voice from somewhere else called. Richard went back down the stairs.

Mary held onto Tim's shirt as if she'd never let go. Then a whisper startled her. It was hers. 'Call the police, Tim.'

'They won't get the big guys and this lot'll be out of here as soon as they hear a whisper. We've got to stop them from moving.'

A clump of panic clogged her throat. 'You can't just stand in front of them and yell 'stop', Tim...' her voice was beginning to rise. He pulled her close. '... these people play for keeps.'

'Sh shhh. I know. So I've got to be a bit more creative.'

210

'Creative. Tim. What...'

His fingers dug into her shoulders. 'I'm going to disable the trailer. If I do anything to the tractor, they'll just get another and be away in an hour. But if I stop the trailer, they'll have to unload it, move it and transfer to another.'

'Tim. What if they see you?'

He spoke into her hair. 'I'll go to the other stairs and get around the back of the trailer. They're loading from this side and it looks like there's only Richard, the driver and the loader. Stay here and keep watch.'

'What am I supposed to do? Lean out the window if I see something and yell,' yoo hoo'?'

She was amazed to see him smile. 'I'll put my phone on vibrate.' He took it off his belt and put it in a shirt pocket under his sweatshirt. 'Dial my number into yours, and hit the call button if it looks like they're getting too close.' At the sound of the lift truck again, they looked out the window and saw Colin and Richard in the trailer with coils of rope, about to receive a huge stone fire surround on a pallet. 'If they catch me, call the police and get back to the car.' He kissed her and before she could speak, he was gone into the darkness.

The swing doors whispered closed behind him. She peered over the window sill again. A few minutes later she saw a dark movement between some stone columns and the wall. It had to be Tim. The two men were tying the stone down through rings in the floor of the trailer.

Tim felt the rough surface of the leaning stone columns on his back. He waited. The whine of the lift truck changed as it turned. When he heard it echo inside the building, he ran to the shelter of the double trailer tyres and stopped again. There were grunts and occasional words inches away behind the closed curtain side. He ran for the front tyres and again stopped to listen. A voice called from inside the building. Richard replied, 'Three altogether.' Then aside to Colin: 'Wish he'd get a move on – we're running out of time.'

The lift truck returned with something heavy. Tim felt it bump the side of the trailer as he reached for the handle of the cab. While the trailer was still rocking he opened the door, pushed himself onto the floor and pulled the door to.

A green light glowed from a dashboard dial. On the seat lay a greasy clipboard, partially covered by a sandwich box and a leather jacket. He pulled the clipboard out and flipped through the papers, released the delivery note and manifest, folded them and pushed them into his shirt pocket. The lift truck motor whined and he felt the trailer rock as it dropped the next load. He opened the door and slid out as he heard the door latch on the other side click. Out on the ground, he pushed the door to as Colin called, 'Got some coffee in the cab, want some?'

The answer must have been in the affirmative, because the cab door opened. Tim leaned against the warm tyre, breathing through his mouth. If Colin got up to the seat, he may well notice that papers were missing from the clipboard. There was a rustling and the cab rocked again. The door shut with a soft slam. Tim let out a long breath.

He watched Colin's feet disappear back up into the trailer and the tyres of the lift truck appear. It stopped. Tim ducked under the back of the trailer and taking a stout knife from his belt, began to cut through the airlines as the next load hit the trailer deck.

Mary stared into the darkness and saw the little light flash in the cab. She was hypnotised to the spot. As she wiped the sweat from her eyes, she heard someone coming up the steps. Her heart beat so hard in her ears that she heard nothing more. She slid down to the floor and pressed herself behind a line of lumpy sacks of parquet flooring. A torchlight whisked across the sacks above her. It got closer to where she lay holding her breath. The sacks sheltering her moved as someone looked inside. The light shone over top of her. The white terror in her eyes would give her hiding place away if he looked. She wanted to close her eyes but they were dry and stuck open. At the end of the line of sacks, he walked back down the line stopping at each sack. She heard the squeak of a marker pen and smelled the sharp sting of the ink. Then he went back down the stairs. Mary took deep breaths and with feeble strength she crawled back to the window. Tim had vanished.

The three men now sat on the trailer and legs dangling when a fourth man walked towards them. He was neat and clean; even his shoes showed no sign of dust.

Tim stopped sawing on the airlines when the loading ceased. If he moved the trailer at all, they'd feel it. He listened to their mumbled conversation and then it stopped. From his squatting position under the trailer he saw a pair of very shiny shoes appear. *James. Gotcha.* The whine of the lift truck covered their conversation.

Tim cut through the second line when the next load bounced the trailer. The lift truck reversed into the warehouse and Tim ran to the corner of the building and turned to the backstairs.

Mary's saw a movement at the back of the trailer. Tim? Should she wait at the window or meet him at the stairs so they could get out of here? She took one more look. The man with the shiny shoes had disappeared. The other two were dragging something into position on the trailer. Then she felt a squeeze on her arm and almost shrieked in shock.

Tim gave her a thumbs-up and beckoned her to follow him to the stairs. As they made their way through the salvage, they heard someone running up the open stairs. Between a stack of slates and a pair of stone sinks there was nowhere to hide.

' Hey! There's someone here.' There was a clatter as at least one body fell on the stairs. Someone else was running up the bottom steps. 'Colin, get that rig out of here.' Richard yelled. Torches flashed up the stairs and into the roof space.

At the sound of the shout, Tim and Mary ran through the swing doors – not caring about the noise they made. Up the stairs.

Richard's voice reached them in chunks. '...find out who .... for Christ's sake... everybody up here.... Stop them.' The truck's engine coughed into life. A door slammed.

They heard at least two people crashing over the salvage. Stonework and metal crashed onto the floor. Men shouted. Feet pounded on the stairs. Someone smashed the doors open.

A cracking explosion of sound ricocheted through the cavernous space. A thousand tiny fragments of concrete erupted in front of them. Mary saw Tim dive into the hole in the wall. She threw herself on the floor in front of it. He caught her hands and pulled her the rest of the way, skidding her on her shoulder. Even before she was on her feet, they were running for the back stairs.

'Oh God. It's a gun!' Mary heard herself scream. Grabbing a loose timber from the floor as he ran, Tim hit the other swing doors with his shoulder, knocking someone off his feet as they smashed the door into him. Down the stairs. Through the doors at the bottom. Tim rammed the timber through the handles. 'Run.' He yelled.

Mary ran ahead of him toward the loose boarding. He caught up to her, grabbed her shirt, threw her at the boarding and crashed it with his shoulder at the same time. Their combined impact drove one half of it from its housing and they fell through it, landing among the tin cans and crisp packets outside.

Someone was breaking the doors open behind them.

Clawing at Mary's sweatshirt, Tim pulled her to her feet and dragged her down the street. They ran for the corner, turned and ran for the next. They turned corner after corner but could still hear shouts and feet pounding behind them. As long as the men behind had lungs to breathe, the chase would follow the noise they made. Mary knew her ability would be gone before Tim's or the ones gaining on them. Her chest was on fire and her throat raw, but still she ran. 'Shit.' The little lane Tim turned into ended in a low brick wall – there appeared to be nothing on the other side of it.

'Over the wall,' he gasped pulling Mary against the bricks and dragging her to the top. There they teetered. The other side was black, inky, wet and full of abandoned shopping trolleys and rubber tyres. 'Canal.' Mary turned to go back. But Tim grabbed her again. 'No,' he grunted, 'into the water. Don't swallow anything.' He jumped down to the steep bank, pulling Mary off her feet. He slid feet first, she head first, slipping like otters into the water. Mary lost contact with Tim, but touched the bottom and spluttering broke the surface. 'Here,' she heard him gasp. He grabbed her again and towed her towards a discharge pipe at the corner of the canal-side building. It bent in a curved right angle to send its frothy effluent straight down into the water. He pulled her against him and flattened them both against the building and the pipe. He did not need to tell her to be silent. The foaming discharge splashed down their backs disguising their heaving breaths.

A bright torch slit the rubbish-strewn darkness and drew rainbow patterns in the oily skims on the surface. The discharge rippled the water and their wake drifted into the reed along the edges.

They clung to each other and to the pipe. When the torch and the voices disappeared, they leaned on each other in the weeds, weak with exhaustion and waited. Then Tim drifted them both down the canal until they could climb out.

Mary lay on her stomach on a broken wooden wharf just conscious of Tim splashing onto the boards beside her before he disappeared again. Lying there wrapped in total exhaustion, she no longer cared whether she was going to be caught or not. She let the rough boards suck her wet clothes into the dry surface and hoped she would be sucked away with them. When the planks bounced she knew he was back.

'I said we should've brought the dingy.'

'I hate you right now,' she croaked, 'I really do.'

He squeezed her wet hair and the fetid water ran down her cheek. 'How much?'

'Enough to divorce you even before I've married you.'

'Oh good, I like an emotional woman.'

She tried to lift her arm to hit him, but it was stuck to the wooden boards.

'Bastard.'

He rolled her over and sat her up against him. 'Does your phone work?' He found it and tried. 'Neither does mine. Come on, up you get.' He lifted her to her feet with unreasonable ease. 'We aren't home and dry yet.'

'No shit.' Sarcasm made her voice rise. She was amazed to hear him chuckle.

'Where are we?' wheezed Mary in a whisper. Water streamed from her clothes and pooled around her feet. Her hair stuck in disgusting clumps to her head.

'I haven't the faintest idea. The map book is back in the car, but my instinct says that Richard and the rest are that way.' He pointed behind her into the darkness of the warehouses. 'So if we go the other way and swing around until we can get back to the car...' He negotiated her past used hypodermic needles, broken bottles, plastic bags and aerosol cans and through a piece of broken fencing.

'Remind me not to do anything *really* dangerous with you. I doubt if I could cope.'

He pulled her against him. Water ran onto the pavement around them. 'God, but life's exciting around you. Come on – just a couple of more miles.'

'What?'

'I'll hold you up.'

'They'll be miles away by now,' she panted.

'Maybe. But I'd rather not have to explain to some cruising police car why I've been in the canal at this time of night with all my clothes on.'

She looked back as they walked. Two long lines of large wet footprints and trails of running water wandered their uncertain way down the street behind them. The sky was beginning to grow a little lighter, but she had no idea where she was. She clung to Tim's hand and concentrated on the mechanics of putting one foot in front of the other. Water squeezed between her toes and out of the insoles of her shoes. It ran down her arms and legs and dripped off her hair. She knew she smelled disgusting if the aroma wafting back from Tim was to be believed.

After half an hour, the trail of water and wet footprints were sporadic and Mary began to feel cold. At the corner of another brick-built warehouse, Tim pulled her into the wall looked around the corner. 'Almost there,' he whispered and with what energy she had left, they sprinted across the street and down a long broken pavement. At the car, he opened the door and pushed her in.

Five minutes later, he drove behind a parade of shop and stopped in a loading bay.

'Come on – out of the wet things.'

Tim pulled off the rest of her wet clothes and tucked a big coat around her, helped her back into the car and put the blanket over her. She felt very cold – too cold.

34

The grey dawn air was still and damp when Tim left the phone box. He was wearing only a thick jacket and body parts that in the normal course of daily life didn't experience fresh air were receiving a full blast this morning. He hurried back to the car.

'What did they say?' Mary asked. Even her voice was shivering.

'That they'd already had a report of a break in – bastards've got their story straight'

'Sssso, we sstill have to find out wwho's behind it.' She began to shiver harder now. He touched her cheek.

'James was there; I saw his expensive shoes.' Her skin felt cold. 'Come on. Home.' When they got there Tim put her into a hot bath, fed her something warm and put her to bed. Then he had a long conversation with Jason.

When Mary opened her eyes a slit, Tim was sitting in a chair beside the bed, head back, asleep. He woke with a snort when he heard her move. She stretched one arm at a time and winced where it hurt. Tim brushed her hair back from her face. 'My darling. I haven't looked after you at all.'

She opened one eye. 'No one asked you to.'

'But I didn't mean to bruise you up anymore. I was supposed to help heal the first lot.' He kissed her forehead. 'I've let you get shot at, hurled you over piles of stone lintels, dragged you through concrete walls, thrown you at boarded windows, made you run for miles and then slung you into a canal. Not the romance of the decade is it?'

Mary opened the other eye. 'Wouldn't have missed it for the world.'

'That's not what you said before.'

'Well, I was annoyed then.'

He knelt on the floor beside her and kissed her cheek. She closed her eyes again. But for a quirk of fate, I might have missed you altogether. It frightens me to death just to think about it.

In the lawn chairs, under the big umbrella on the front lawn they listened to the light Sunday afternoon rain dance on the nylon. Mary drew her legs up onto her chair under a blanket, 'Do you think Richard recognised you?'

'He didn't use my name and we had paint all over us. I don't think the torch caught us.'

She saw exhaustion and worry in dark lines on his face. 'But what will happen tomorrow – if he knows I mean. Oh Tim, this could be bad. We went through all that and didn't stop them at all.'

He put his hand over hers on the arm of his chair. 'I spoke to Jason this morning and told him that I needed a few more things.'

'Like what?'

'It's starting to make sense. James was there, I'm sure of it and we have good reason to suspect Howard; Jason said that the second set of accounts in Royston's name is bigger than Conmac's, so that implicates Geoffrey Allen, the finance man, not to mention the order I found that he'd signed. The fact that it's antique and architectural salvage they're stealing and shipping abroad means that the Chairman, Ian Dennison must be in it too. His business is international antiques. So there's quite a list now with Richard, Colin, and Al, whoever he is, never mind the dozens it would take to gut a big house and get it moved in one night. Plus the guys that destroy the place.'

'What will they do now?'

'Well the big boys will either be planning a huge escape if they haven't gone already or they'll take a chance that we were just squatters and sit it out. The truck was hired – said so on the cab – but it'll be gone.'

'But if they recognised you?' Mary hugged his arm.

'Then they'll be gone and we'll have missed getting them.'

'But they murdered that driver.'

'Frank was a regular driver for Conmac and Colin seemed to know him – maybe he'll talk. And if Roystson's accounts show payments being made to them, the police will have something to question them about.'

'Colin didn't sound very satisfied.'

'Just what I'm thinking. So I need to widen the net. We've got to identify all those connections between Conmac and Royston – that means both sets of accounts - then the methods; the shipping, transport and delivery details. Richard will have done all that in the transport department.'

He put his head on her shoulder and sighed raggedly. 'I've asked Jason to work out a plan to send all that stuff to the police and Inland Revenue. It should be enough for someone to ask questions.'

'And if he can't do it or it doesn't work?' She cupped his chin with her hand and put her lips in his warm, familiar curls. 'These people are capable of murder!'

'I've still got the manifest and delivery orders from the truck – that tells where the load was going. If the computer trick doesn't work...'

Mary was almost invisible in his puffy duvet – a tiny figure, curled up, relaxed and safe in sleep. Tim opened the window. The wonderful warbling bird song floated up the valley; one rising phrase after another ending in a long sigh of sound.

He woke her by wafting coffee steam under her nose.

'How many do I owe you now?' She rubbed one eye.

'How many what?'

'Coffees in bed.'

'At least a life time's worth. Hang onto your cup, I'm getting back in.'

'Do you know,' she sighed and relaxed back into the pillows, mug in hand, 'that until I met you, no one had ever brought me coffee in bed?'

'That is sad.'

'I'll rephrase that - sounds like I've been in bed with hundreds.'

'God, but Robert was a swine, wasn't he?'

'I let myself be hurt. I should have grown up a long time ago.'

'Thank God you did.' The bird song came in the open window again. 'What is that bird? I've heard it ever since I got here and it's wonderful.' They listened for it again.

'It's a curlew. Magical isn't it?'

The song came again. 'Just one of several magical things around here, I think.' He put his coffee on the table beside the bed and propped on one elbow looked at her.

'Will the needing you ever stop? I mean will I ever find that I've grown used to you? Will this wanting to touch you and feel you next to me ever end?' He pulled a fluffy curl out straight and let it spring back to her ear.

'I don't know.'

He drew his index finger over the soft V at the bottom of her throat. 'But does the terror go away – the fear that it might just end and the yearning be gone. I've got such a black hollow in my stomach; the one that's waiting to explode and swamp me with being alone again.'

'Then let's make sure that the needing is always there.'

He laid his hand on her stomach. 'What, like now?' He drew his fingers upwards over her warm flesh.

She put her cup down and kissed his shoulder, 'Yes, like now.'

'Have you a plan for today?' She handed him his tie.

He caressed her fingers. 'I'll take Jason's little bomb - wish I understood it - and pray that it works. Then I'll make whatever escape I can.'

'Tell me again what it is supposed to do. I know I read Jason's e-mail last night and we put all that stuff onto a stick, but I don't understand it.'

Tim stuck the end of his tie through the knot and pulled it down. 'I'm not sure I do either, but it seems to work a bit like a virus. It'll e-mail all the Conmac and Royston accounts, Royston's delivery notes and manifests to the police and Inland Revenue.'

Mary pulled up her jeans. 'I wish I could lose some weight – jeans just keep getting smaller. But what will prevent James from stopping the whole thing if he suspects what's happening.'

'Don't lose too much – I want to love every bit of you.' He winked and turned back to the mirror. 'Jason says he's put a sort of lock on it. No one will be able to access the process without quite a bit of time and skill – but don't ask me how it works.' He folded his collar down. 'It's on a stick that I can come away with – that protects Jason.'

'What if someone sees you doing it – or it's tracked to you.'

'I'll use the staff room computer; anyone can use it.'

She put her arms around him. 'Can I come and sit in the car park with the engine running or something?'

'I'd love nothing better, but I don't have the faintest idea when I can get to do it. I don't intend to wait all day.'

'And if Richard or James did see you? What then?'

'Well I'll either be home very early or in jail myself.'

A huge lump filled Mary's mouth. 'Oh Tim, I'm going to go mad today waiting.'

'You need something to keep you busy. Isn't there another wall or something that you can take down?' He sat on the bed and put on his shoes.

'No, but there are some roof tiles I could put back.'

'Don't you dare...Here...' He reached under the bed. 'I've got something for you just in case.' He handed her a hard hat with 'MITCH' stencilled on the front.

Tim signed in and walked upstairs making a severe attempt to appear normal. Susan was thrilled to see him. 'Tim. Tell us everything. We are all dying to know what happened.' A ripple of shock ran over his stomach – she couldn't know – how could she?

Bryn put his head over Susan's screen. 'Is Mary all right? Did she really fall off the roof and what was she doing up there?'

Tim shook in relief - of course it was Wednesday that he'd last been at work. 'Well incredible as it sounds, she was fighting a chimney fire more or less with her bare hands.' Recovering his centre of gravity, he elaborated on the details they already had. There was no reason why he couldn't make her into a super human being. In his mind she was. Several other heads appeared and so he told the story again.

Then James appeared; tension clear on his face. All conversation stopped. Tim waited for the axe to fall. God alone knew what his face was saying.

'Sorry to hear about ...I'm glad that she's all right now.'

'Thanks,' was all Tim could say before his knees gave way and he grabbed for his chair. James attempted a smile, but it was not a success and he walked puppet-like toward the stairs to the transport department, his tiny smile replaced by a black frown. Shouting and bad tempers floated up the stairs. There was no need to go down to find out just how tense things were down there. The others drifted back to work.

Tim dragged his attention back to his own space and looking to the staff room for his opportunity, saw a grey shape wobble into his line of vision. It was Howard. It was hard to tell if he was drunk or sober. He looked unsteady; his hair was limp on his head and it wasn't clear if he'd shaved. He walked toward his office, clutching the dividing screens as he went. Something, almost but not quite compassion, made Tim follow him.

'Howard?' Howard put his briefcase on his desk and opened it upside down. Everything in it slid across his keyboard. He didn't notice.

'Howard?' Tim spoke again and Howard looked up in surprise. He opened his mouth, but no sound came out. In retarded jerks, he sat down, but missed the seat and his body pleated onto the floor. Tim grabbed for him and got him back into the chair. Howard's skin was wet and clammy.

'Tim. It's all finished.'

'What Howard?'

'It's all over. It's over.'

'Come on Howard – into the meeting room.' Tim shouldered Howard into a standing position and levered him the few steps behind the screens into the glassed in room. He pushed Howard into a chair and a glass of water into his hands.

'All right Howard, what's wrong.' Tim knew what was coming.

'The bastards. I've had enough. I'll lose everything – my girls, my house – all of it.'

'Why Howard? Why were you involved?'

'Miriam and the girls – I needed money – her father gave her everything – I couldn't - so he let me in and then said he'd …stop the money. Richard too …he had us all …'

Tim rapped on the glass at one of the office girls and sent her off to call a taxi. The last person he or any of them needed around just now was Howard. The very last person who needed to see Howard, was James.

'Howard, go home. There's a taxi coming. Go home and talk to your family. Tell them everything and ask them to help you. It'll be OK.'

Poor sap, he thought as he handed Howard over to Clive the security guard. *Poor sodding sap.*

He was angry now. James had blackmailed Howard, Richard and how many others. Sure they didn't have to go along with it, but when you don't have something to hide, it's easy to say.

He didn't care who saw him now. Pulling Jason's stick out of his jacket pocket, he went to the staff room computer and shoved it into the port. With Jason's notes beside him, he typed in the start code. The computer began to make whiny whirring noises. It seemed to go on forever. He shut the screen off and looked through the glass in the door.

Office life unfolded in jerks in front of him – incredibly normal – incredibly stupid – like an animated cartoon. His ears had stopped hearing. He realised that the hard drive had gone silent. He flicked the screen on. The message made his heart stop. A firewall restriction had stopped the loading.

Shit. A goddamn firewall. Jason, you idiot! Maybe it was just this terminal. Jason would have looked into the central system not each terminal. Don't blame him. He wanted to take the stupid little stick out and run. Instead he leaned on the table and forced himself to take three deep breaths. Courage. Mary had said courage. What the hell was courage anyway? All he could feel was anger. Anger with her for being simplistic. Anger with himself for being such a wimp. Grow up.

He yanked out the stick and shut off the screen. Anger bubbled in his throat as, in isolated determination, he headed for the stairs. He didn't care who got in his way. Across the floor of estimators, designers and CAD/CAM terminals, he raged into Andy's space. Andy got up with the faint beginnings of a smile until he saw Tim's face. 'Into the gents,' commanded Tim. Inside the door, he grabbed the front of Andy's shirt. 'I want you to disable the firewall system. You have thirty seconds after which I will break every bone in your face. Do we understand each other?'

Andy clawed at Tim's hand on his shirt. 'He made me, Tim.' Andy coughed as Tim banged him against the side of a toilet cubicle. 'You fucking bastard. My drawings – my diary – the quotations.'

Andy's voice rose, 'I had to.'

'I don't bloody care. Right now you're going to disable the firewall. If you don't I'll let James tell the world what he's got on you. If you do, James will be the one doing the explaining. Got that?' Andy, on tiptoe, tried to ease the tension on his throat. He nodded and Tim let go.

'Which terminal do you want disabled?' Andy's voice was hoarse as he sat in his chair again.

'Yours.' Tim handed Andy the stick and start code and sat on the corner of the desk. He watched Andy's face until the computer was doing what was asked and the stick and code back in his pocket. 'Now then.' He leaned forward and whispered, 'A little programme is going to start sending e-mails in a minute. It's been designed so that it can't be stopped.' He had no idea if it was true. 'So unless you really want to have that heart to heart with James, you'll let it get on with it. If it gets stopped again, you and I are going to be having another chat in the toilets. OK?' Andy nodded and swallowed.

'Thanks.' Tim patted Andy's back and left. Anger of a new kind drifted behind him, foaming at his heels all the way to James' office.

Mary watched Tim drive away. The car vanishing in the distance sucked her strength away in its wake. The emptiness was more than just a vacancy; it was a fully formed vacuum.

At Rosemary Cottage she fed the kittens and looked around. She gathered coffee cups and put them in the sink, then walked into the sitting room and put the newspaper into a pile. Nothing was real, nothing had any purpose. Standing at her little desk, she looked out the window. Somehow she had to get through today. She picked up the historic package and went upstairs. Leaving the parchment on the bedside table, she took her dressing gown and went to the shower.

Wet but refreshed and rubbing her hair with a towel, she walked back to the bedroom, wishing that the phone would ring. The bedroom was still, dark and quiet – a small closet of peace.

Opening the curtains restored the room to reality. It also revealed an old man leaning on the fence.

35

Tim didn't acknowledge Margaret; he didn't knock. He slammed the door shut and leaned across James' desk, stared down at him and began to shout.

'You bastard. Do you have any idea what you've done?

James shoved his chair back. Once on his feet, he was for a second at eye level with Tim. 'Who the hell do you think you are? Coming in here – what's the matter with you?'

Tim reached for James' throat, 'Don't you dare play games with me. I know what you've done. Did they all give in quietly or did you have to get rough? You greedy bastard.' He managed to stop his hand.

James face was red. 'Hang on a minute. What are you on about? I...'

'What am I...? You fucking bastard. You've got Howard on his knees, Richard chasing his own ass, Andy in fear of God knows what and my career almost in shreds. Talk.' Tim leaned forward across the desk again.

James held up one hand. 'OK, OK. I know some of it.'

'Jesus, you can't even admit... Do you mean to tell me you don't know what's going on around here?' Tim felt his voice rising again.

'No, I don't. I knew that it had something to do with Royston, and that Howard was involved but that's all.'

'Then what the hell was all that messing around with my files about?' Tim was still angry.

James sat back down in his big chair. He looked small in it. 'I knew the minute I met you that you were the best design engineer I'd ever seen – and I've been in this business a lot of years. When I saw your stuff - style, flair – I've never seen anything so perfect.'

Tim stared at him. James stared back. 'I knew that if you got close to Royston; if you got caught up in it or if they got to you, you'd be finished. I had to get you out.'

'That is the biggest load of crap I've ever heard. You were under orders.'

James didn't reply.

'You really are a lying bastard aren't you? You're in this up to your neck. You weren't trying to save me at all. This is just about money. You had to get me out before I did something to bring down your house of cards.'

James lips were white. 'Royston should never have been in the computer system for you to find... the paper files should have been destroyed.'

'Well, you're about to go down the pan along with all the rest. Let me see your feet.'

'My what?'

'Your feet.' James stuck out one foot. It was a small foot. It wasn't the one Tim had seen under the trailer.

The old man was still there when Mary went out the back door. He had moved to the gate and had his elbows on the top rail. He wore a dull white shirt under a dark jacket, dark trousers pushed into tall black leather boots. A large hat with a very bent brim was pulled down to shade his eyes.

'Can I help you?' Mary asked walking to the gate. She did not know the man, but wondered just why he would be assessing her house albeit from the roadside.

He slowly looked up and seemed to see her at last. He withdrew a very short grey pipe from his mouth and touched his hat brim. 'Mornin'.' He resumed watching the house.

'Is there something I can do for you – do you need directions, or...'

'Ach, no missus. I just like to come here now and again – to remember like.'

'Really?' Mary propped one elbow on the top rail of the gate, staking a proprietorial right to it. 'Do you know Rosemary Cottage?'

'Aye. For a long time.'

'Do you live nearby?'

He looked into the bowl of his pipe. 'Not anymore, but I used to live up the road.' He nodded in the direction of Tim's house and beyond. 'My young'uns used to play in the meadow here when they were little.' He reached in his jacket pocket and took out a small knife. 'They played in the grass and climbed the trees, picked the flowers like all little girls.'

'How lovely. Are they grown up now and moved away?'

He used the knife to scrape the inside of the bowl of the pipe. 'No, they's both dead now.'

Mary's heart lurched sideways. Something very cold brushed past. 'Oh. I am so sorry.'

'I was just rememberin' them and their mother...' His voice seemed to get weak and fail. 'She was...was...'

'Is she still with you?'

He seemed to recover and checked the inside of the pipe bowl. 'No, she married someone else.'

Mary looked at him in surprise. He had blue eyes and looked at her as if surprised that she didn't know. He held the pipe bowl between his palms. 'See, we weren't married ...and we could never marry...it just weren't possible. So we agreed on a good man and he took care of her... and my girls.' He upended the bowl of the pipe and tapped it on the top of the gatepost before sticking the stem back in his mouth.

Mary stared at the post in disbelief.

In a state of shock he didn't feel could be real, Tim went back to his desk. Before he could sit down, Clive and another security guard appeared in front of him.

Shit. Now what? James, you bastard...

'Mr Spencer?' asked the bigger of the two big men. Tim stared at him. 'I've been asked by the Chairman, Mr Dennison to see you off the premises sir.' *This guy has to be ex-military.* Tim sucked a smile of black humour off his face. *So it was Dennison. James was the man on the ground, but Dennison ran things.*

'But why?' Tim looked behind them and saw Susan.

'Don't know, Ma'am. Jus' doing what we been asked to do.'

Clive spoke then. 'I expect Mr Dennison will explain in due course sir. Now will you collect your personal things?' *Keep eye contact. Make them concentrate on me. Don't argue – don't get angry. Keep it easy.*

'Tim? Tim?' Susan was saying feebly. *Stay calm, you want out anyway. Don't argue. Don't make a scene or demand an explanation. This way whatever happens the action was theirs not yours. In court it'll...*

With deliberate care, he lifted his briefcase onto his desk.

'May we just look in there, sir?' They found only a few trade papers and the internal staff directory that for some reason they put back in the lid. They stepped back and waited. Tim picked up a trade magazine with a hand he could only just control, and shoved it in. Then the steel pencil and ruler. He put a disk copy of the client addresses on top. 'I'll just take that sir.' A big hand took the disk away. So they'd been told to be sure he didn't take away any trade secrets. He almost laughed - if only they knew. He snapped the case shut.

Tim picked up the brief case, took his hard hat out of the in-tray and turned to leave. Susan was standing by her desk; her face was grey; she looked as if she were about to faint. 'It'll be all right,' was all he had time to say. The heavies were leaning on him. He pulled his jacket off the rack.

The military court martial close-order parade took them down the stairs and into reception. They invited him to sign out, relieved him of his pass and handed him a large brown envelope. 'Mr Dennison asked me to give you this.' Somehow he took it. They walked with him to his car, asked, with efficient politeness to see in his boot and waited like a pair of heavy bookends until he drove to the gate. He waited while a police car drove in and then pulled out onto the main road.

He stopped in the first lay-by he came to until he stopped shaking and could open the envelope. It was a contract, from the company solicitors, already signed by Ian Dennison in which Conmac would pay him substantial damages in lieu of notice if he left the company without comment. He pressed the stick in his shirt pocket to his chest, laughed until he cried, then reached for his phone.

Mary looked from the top of the gatepost to the man's lined face and back again. 'Did you have other children?' she asked, her voice shaking.

He put the little knife back in his pocket. 'Aye, I had a lad.' He pulled a small leather draw-sting bag from his pocket and opened it. 'He took over the farm ... but he wanted more...more land, see...and he wanted my girls...' He shook his head with the gesture of universal suffering and injustice. 'He were all evil... just evil.' He withdrew a pinch of tobacco from the bag and pressed it into the bowl of the pipe with dark, bent fingers; fingers that trembled. 'Aye, some things in life be too painful to dwell on be'n't they?'

Mary heard her telephone ring. She knew she had to answer it. 'Will you come back and talk to me again, Mr Roberts?' she asked. The man nodded and touched his hat. There were tears in his eyes; tears from a secret that he carried, but one that she too knew.

The truth – jealousy in a son who felt less loved; took land as he wanted and murdered to cover incest and coercion – was worse that any of the records could show. No wonder the girls had come to her. But who was still a danger to her?

'I'm still shaking.' Mary stared into the flames of the living room fire snapping in the darkness. 'I can't believe that it might be all over at last and I just want to get incredibly drunk.'

Tim pulled her head onto his shoulder. 'Well not without me. I hope for everybody's sake it was exciting when the police arrived.' He kissed the top of her head. 'But tell me about John Roberts. How did you know who it was?'

'Well, I didn't at first. It was when he tapped the ash from his pipe onto the gatepost and there was nothing there – no ash, no bits of tobacco, nothing - that something from the other side of my brain began to ask questions. I'd seen the smoke from the pipe, so I knew it had been lit...'

'But the woman, why marry her off if...'

'Oh he loved her, but I think he felt it was just too dangerous for her to be pregnant and not married and he felt an obligation to his children. So he found her a good man and got her safely married before they were born. The girls took Fletcher's name but John Robert's son must have felt that he didn't have the love he deserved from his father – or maybe he was just greedy for farmland and power of his own. Anyway he raped one of the girls and when he found out who they were he had them murdered and it solved all his problems.'

'But the court gave their father this land – a certain kind of justice I guess.'

'It may have been John Robert's way of smoothing justice.' She grinned. 'So are you prepared to admit that I might be just a tiny bit psychic?'

He kissed her neck. 'Not until I meet John Roberts in the flesh – well you know what I mean.' *Not if he could help it.*

She lifted her chin for a proper kiss, but with a jerk, he tightened his arm around her and whispered, 'Someone's outside the window. No, don't look. Where are your torches?'

'At the back door'

He nuzzled her hair. 'As soon as I give the word, grab a torch, go right out the door. I'll go the other way. '

229

'I hope whoever it is hurries up, my neck is getting sore.'

He relaxed his arm. 'Sorry – just don't look to the window.'

She continued to stare straight at him. 'Who is it?'

'Don't know... Now!'

They dashed for the door. Tim was out first. A dark shape disappeared around the garden wall. 'Here,' she shouted. Tim slid on the gravel from the other side of the cottage.

'This way,' he yelled and leapt over the wall, Mary following as best she could. The object slipped around the end of the trees and into the field beyond. 'I said I wasn't going to do this again,' Mary called to Tim's back. The shadow hurtled to the edge of the field – into the shadows of the next hedge line, then disappeared. Then the moon lit the field for a second. The figure was half way across running up the slope. The light disappeared and with it the shape. Then a silver flash. 'He's gone over the gate.'

Tim's long legs got him across the field ahead of Mary and he vaulted the gate. They raced after the dark figure. Then it disappeared with a cry. Tim disappeared behind it and a few seconds later, so did Mary. All three landed in a wet ditch. The shape, now formed of flesh and bone, was gasping for breath, as were Tim and Mary. 'Not again,' gulped Mary, 'you promised.'

Tim gasped, 'Did I?' The figure began to fight back. 'All right you son of a bitch, don't move.' He straddled the figure, holding it to the ground. 'Now who are you? Mary, have you still got your torch? I lost mine.' She shone the beam on one end of the shape in the ditch and located what looked like a head. It was wrapped in a dark scarf. Tim unravelled it.

'Harry!' Mary dropped the torch.

'Well, well,' Tim's voice was thick with sarcasm, as he retrieved the torch. 'Who'd have guessed?'

Harry struggled. 'Ged'off.' Mary straddled the other end of the figure and together they held him down. 'I'm drowning,' came a strangled voice.

Mary snatched back the torch. 'No you're not. Stay still you son of a bitch.' She pushed him back into the mud.

Tim pulled his mobile phone from his belt. She saw him grin broadly in the moonlight, 'At least I've taught you to swear. Police,' he turned to the telephone when the emergency service answered. Then a moment later, 'We've just caught a peeping tom – one that might be able to explain a recent arson attack.' Mary looked at him in amazement. Harry struggled again and they pinned him down harder. 'Mary, where are we?'

'In a ditch.'

'Darling, I think the police will need a little more information.'

'I'm not sure exactly where we are.' She swivelled around on Harry's back. 'Harry, where are we?'

A reply was muffled, 'Field on the Croftbury Lane opposite my place.' Tim relayed the details and hung up.

'Looks like we have 10 minutes or so to wait. There's a car in Croftbury. Are you comfortable Mary?'

'What about me?' A mumble came from below.

'I wasn't talking to you.'

'My feet are wet and I'm cold; I've a cut on my hand on some brambles, I'm stung with nettles and I've reinstated most of my bruises, but other than that, I'm quite happy sitting in a ditch in the dark. How about you?'

'Oh fine – do this all the time. But perhaps not as often as old Harry here? Eh Harry?'

Harry grunted. 'Come on Harry; tell Mary what you've been up to.'

Mary slid around on Harry's back again. 'What do you mean, what has he been up to?'

'Talk Harry.' But there were only grunts. 'Let me help. Many rats on your place are there Harry? A couple of decomposing ones that might end up under the floorboards of Mary's cottage perhaps?'

'Tim?' Mary was shocked.

'Well Harry?' Tim bounced up and down a couple of times.

'Yeah, yeah, OK so they was mine.'

'But how did he get them up there?'

'I expect that Harry had a good look around when he was blasting flies. Didn't you Harry?' There was a grunt.

'But how did he get in?'

'Come on Harry. Better explain. Was it the same way you got the bees in?'

'Slipped open a window.'

Mary couldn't speak. Tim wiggled some more. 'Sorry Harry, just trying to get comfortable.'

Mary's teeth were beginning to chatter. 'But you said arson, Tim.'

'How about it Harry?'

'Dropped some rags down the chimney. Paraffin. Then when the fire was lit...' he groaned.

They heard a distant siren.

'Why Harry?'

Tim interrupted. 'Harry has some distant relations, haven't you Harry? Name of, what was it again, Harry? Roberts?'

The figure underneath them wobbled. It was nodding its head.

Mary coughed up her voice again. 'They were right.'

'Come on Harry,' Tim continued as if he hadn't heard her. 'What about the two young women who spoke to Mary in the middle of the night? How did you arrange that?'

'Nothin to do wi' me.'

'Come on Harry.'

'Honest – I don' know what yer talkin' about.'

A blue flashing light approached and Mary shone the torch in its direction. When two men ran up the bank they released Harry from the mud.

'The gov'nr isn't goin' to be too happy about the state of the car when we get through with this one,' one of them observed, and they drove away with a very wet, cold and muddy Harry when they'd heard the story. 'Come into Leominster in the morning. Sort out a statement then.'

Declining a lift back to the cottage with a soggy Harry between them Tim and Mary walked. They hugged each other to keep warm. Mary took her squelching slippers off and Tim left wet footprints behind on the tarmac.

'There are a lot of things I want to do with you during the rest of my life, but will you note somewhere that I've had enough running around the countryside in the dark and falling into wet places.'

'Noted.' The warm chuckle came up from his chest again.

'What on earth made you suspect Harry? And why didn't you say something?'

'The night of the fire – as they were rolling you into the ambulance Harry was at the gate and a policeman told me that Harry'd been the one to call 999. But I dashed off after you rather than stay and talk to him. It didn't seem quite right somehow, that he should be there without a vehicle so far as I could see – so he hadn't just been driving by. And even you weren't likely to climb up on the roof before you'd called for help. So I checked at the fire station in the morning and they confirmed that the call had come from a woman – you of course. So I wondered what he was doing there.'

'But how were you able to find out that Harry was related to the Roberts?'

'Well, the police said there had been some sort of feud between the Freemans who you bought Rosemary from, and Harry in the past. Then I checked the electoral roll and found out that Harry's surname is Dobbs – I had a chum at school whose name was Roberts and we always called him Dobbin. So it started to add up. Then the estate agent confirmed that the Freemans had left instructions that the Cottage was not to be sold to Harry – no matter what he offered for it. Then it made sense.'

'But why didn't you say anything about it?'

He opened the gate for her. 'Well, there was always the possibility that I might have been wrong and I didn't want you to think I was a total idiot.'

They stopped and looked at the cottage. 'Do you suppose Rose and Mary are satisfied now?'

'They sound like formidable women.' They looked at the silver orchard and dove grey cottage. 'I seem to have an attraction to formidable women.' He sighed. 'I hope neither of them takes up piano playing.'